SLAMMER

SLAMMER

Allan Guthrie

HOUGHTON MIFFLIN HARCOURT
BOSTON   NEW YORK
2009

First U.S. edition

Copyright © 2009 by Allan Guthrie

www.hmhbooks.com

First published in Great Britain in 2008
by Polygon, an imprint of Birlinn Ltd

Library of Congress Cataloging-in-Publication Data
Guthrie, Allan.
    Slammer / by Allan Guthrie.— 1st U.S. ed.
      p. cm.
    ISBN 978-0-15-101295-4
    1. Prisons—Officials and employees—
Fiction. 2. Prisoners—Fiction. I. Title.
    PR6107.U84S53 2009
    823'.92 — dc22   2009013273

PRINTED IN THE UNITED STATES OF AMERICA

DOC 10 9 8 7 6 5 4 3 2 1

FOR RAY BANKS

PART ONE

Narrative Exposure Therapy

Nick Glass lifted his elbows off the desk and leaned backwards a few inches. The prison shrink's breath was sweet, like hot milk. Not unpleasant, exactly. But it made Glass feel ill. He'd have asked if he could open a window, but the pokey little office didn't have one.

John Riddell visited once a week, usually on Mondays, and the smell was stronger each time. 'How are you settling in?' he asked.

Glass said, 'Okay,' thankful that, when he breathed in now, all he could smell was furniture polish.

Riddell opened the file in front of him. 'Hmmm,' he said, nodding. He slid his specs down his nose and peered at Glass. It was a look he'd clearly practised. 'You sure about that?'

Glass gave Riddell a look back. Glass could do looks. He'd learned over the past few weeks. That wasn't all he'd learned.

Riddell said, 'Everything you say in this room is confidential.'

'Right,' Glass said. As if that mattered.

'You understand that, Nick?'

'I'm not a child.'

Riddell leaned forward. 'I didn't mean to be patronising. I'm sorry.'

The smell again. Glass saw a lime-green plastic tumbler, milk spilling out as it fell to the floor. Then the image vanished and Glass only saw what was in front of him. 'Right.'

'It's just . . .' Riddell took his specs off.

'Just what?'

'This is a chance for you to get it off your chest.'

'Get what off my chest?'

Riddell put his specs back on. 'Whatever's on it.'

'My chest's fine.' But Glass could tell Riddell didn't believe him. He wondered who'd been speaking out of turn. Shouldn't matter, he knew, but the idea that he was being spoken about made him feel as if someone had poured cement down his throat and it was hardening in his stomach. People could be telling Riddell anything at all and he'd believe it too. He looked the sort.

Riddell fiddled with his pen, eyes straight ahead.

Glass tried to guess what they might have been saying about him. He should ask. No, he didn't want to go there. You never knew where it might lead.

Maybe they'd been talking about him and Mafia. Saying they were too close. Making homosexual references. Puerile shite like that.

Glass wished they'd grow up. He was only twenty-two but he was a damn sight more mature than the rest of them. He'd lived. Seen things, done things, felt real pain, the sort that crushed your bones and scooped all the flesh out of your body.

Riddell said, 'How are the officers treating you? You okay with the nickname?'

He might as well have picked Glass up and slammed him headfirst against the wall. What the hell was wrong with Riddell that he had to be such a provocative bastard? Maybe his wife had left him. Packed a suitcase, stormed off to her mother's. It had to be something like that.

'Can I go now?' he asked.

Riddell looked at his watch. 'This is supposed to be a thirty-minute session.'

Glass glanced at the clock on the wall behind Riddell's head. Twenty minutes to go. No way could he endure that.

'So how about we just pretend?' Glass said. 'Nobody needs to know we cut it short.'

Riddell sat back in his chair and smiled. 'This session could benefit you. It's not about making you uncomfortable. It's about helping you adapt.'

Glass said nothing. He was fine. Didn't need any help. He could adapt by himself, thank you very much.

'Your wife,' Riddell said. 'And daughter.'

Glass dug his nails into his palms. Yeah, so it could be difficult for families, he knew that. But there was no need to bring Lorna and Caitlin into it. He didn't want to talk about them here. They were part of a different world and none of Riddell's business.

He'd be curt, maybe Riddell would get the hint. 'Caitlin's settled into school,' he said. 'Lorna's fine. None of us miss Dunfermline.' Glad to be rid of it. Well, glad to be rid of Lorna's mother.

'Must be tough for Caitlin, though. Difficult age. Remind me. Five, six?' Riddell waited, then filled the silence himself. 'You became a father very young.'

Glass sat it out, stared at the empty photo frame turned sideways on the desk. Tin. Pewter, maybe. Glass wasn't sure of the difference. He felt sorry for Riddell, not having a photo to put in it. Maybe his wife hadn't left him after all. Maybe he didn't have a wife. Maybe he had no one. Glass was angry at himself for feeling sorry for the poor sod.

'Okay,' Riddell said. 'Sign this.' He turned a sheet towards Glass, handed over his pen.

A list of names. Dates. Times.

Glass was surprised by how many he recognised. He scrawled his name. Then he levered himself to his feet, turned to go.

'Thanks, Nick,' Riddell said. 'Any time you feel like talking, let me know. It'll do you good.'

Prison Officer Nick Glass didn't think so. But he nodded, for show.

'WE HAVE TO take Mafia to the Digger,' Fox said, half an hour later.

Glass had been working here long enough to know that Officer Fox was talking about the segregation unit. God alone knew why it was called the Digger. Prison was so full of slang you hardly knew where to begin. And if you asked how one thing got its name, you had to ask about another, and before long you didn't care any more, so you stopped asking.

The Digger it was.

Glass looked at his colleague. 'Why us?'

Fox was at least fifty, fat and proud of it. He was the kind of man who'd walk around all day with his hand down his trousers if he could get away with it. 'Our job, Crystal, isn't it?'

Glass ignored the nickname. It had stuck. Nothing he could do about it now. At least it was better than what he'd been called at school. Nicholarse Glarse. Arse for short. 'What's he done?'

'Been at it with Caesar again.' Fox started moving, heels clicking on the polished floor.

'Is he okay?'

'He'll live. Caesar just toys with him.'

'So,' Glass said, finding it hard to believe he was struggling to keep up with the much older, much bigger man, and thinking, not for the first time given all the muscles on show here, that he should start working out, 'how come nothing happens to Caesar?'

'How do you know what's going to happen to him?'

'Just guessing.'

'Well, fucking don't,' Fox said. 'Just do what you're fucking told like a good little boy.'

It wasn't just that Glass was young. He *looked* young. Always had done. Glass wondered if Fox had always looked like a fat bastard. One of these days, he'd ask.

A cat hissed at them as they moved down C-Hall. Fox kicked out at it, missed. The cat hissed again and turned tail. Disappeared back into the guts of the building.

The cats were one of the many surprises that had confronted Nick Glass when he'd first arrived here six weeks ago. The Hilton, as they all called it, was a modern prison. When it was being built, a small feral cat population had decided that the building would make a good home. So they moved in and despite repeated attempts – humane and otherwise – to remove them, years later they were still here.

Couple of days ago, Glass had spotted a kitten. Terrified little black thing in the corner of the locker room. Glass wanted to pick it up, take it home, give it to Caitlin. She'd love it. It fled, spitting, before he could get near enough, though.

He was hopeful he'd catch it another time, and was looking out for it as he and Fox approached the cells on the left. Three levels, called flats, both sides of the Hall. Mafia's peter – his cell – was on the second flat, or, as Fox said, 'on the twos.'

Up the stairs, past the ginger-bearded Officer McDee who was too busy chatting to one of the few female guards, Officer Ross, to notice Glass. Then past a group of cons. Nods, grunts, shuffling of feet. Glass wondered if Darko was with Mafia, wondered what the hell they'd been up to. Glass might have found out from Fox, but the expression on his fat face wasn't one to inspire conversation. Fox didn't like any of the other officers paying too much attention to Ross.

Glass wasn't in a hurry. He'd get told soon enough.

Fox rattled his keys in time to the music filtering through the cell door. He shoved his key in the lock and twisted it, all in one movement, and walked inside. The radio was blasting out the chorus of a pop tune even Glass recognised: 'Ebeneezer Goode', a song the cons loved cause it was full of drug references.

Mafia was sitting on his bunk, the lower one, Darko patting his face with a cloth.

The stink crept up on Glass like it always did when he walked into one of the cells. Damn, he should use the slang. The *peters*. Fags, sweat, a faint whiff of shit. And an industrial chemical that pervaded the whole place.

Made him shake. Made him wonder what he was doing here.

'What you been up to now, you blind fuck?' Fox said to Mafia, snapping off the radio and creating the kind of sudden silence that got him the attention he was so desperate for.

The reason Mafia got his nickname: he wore dark glasses. Reason he wore dark glasses: eye problems. He had a medical condition that meant he couldn't see further than a couple of inches in front of his nose.

Mafia was one of the few cons Glass could speak to. Most of them didn't want to be seen talking to the officers. Mafia didn't care what anyone thought, though. They'd struck up a rapport right away, Glass and Mafia. Glass had been wary, having been warned that certain prisoners would try to take advantage if he got too close to them, revealed too much of himself. But Mafia wasn't playing a game. They just liked each other. Glass couldn't see Mafia as a double murderer. Not that

Mafia would talk about it, but that in itself was unusual and a sign that he might be innocent. Glass hoped so. On the outside, they'd be drinking buddies. Or at least that's what Glass liked to think.

He didn't know, though, since he didn't have any drinking buddies.

Anyhow, Fox was right: Mafia was virtually blind. Claimed he'd been run over nine times crossing the road on account of his terrible eyesight, worst injury being a broken hip. Glass wasn't sure if that made him lucky or unlucky.

Mind you, everybody lied in prison. Glass believed him, though. It was too imaginative a story to be anything but the truth.

Glass nodded towards him.

Mafia tilted his head in response. 'Who's that? McDee? Agnew? Not that fucker, Sutherland. Is it the lovely Officer Ross? I can usually smell her.'

'It's me,' Glass said.

'Don't fucking answer him, Crystal. He's a rude fuck.' Fox stepped closer, pushed Darko out of the way. It wasn't hard. Darko was only just over five foot tall and rail-thin. Caitlin could probably knock him over with a shove of her little hand.

'Hey,' Darko said.

'Hey, what?' Fox stuck his chest out, looked like he was trying to poke Darko's eyes out with his nipples. 'Eh? Want to join your cellie in the Digger?'

Darko said nothing.

'Fucking right, you don't. Now fuck off or I'll have you deported back to Yugo-fucking-slavia.'

'The Digger?' Mafia said. 'You're joking.'

'Nope.' Fox turned his attention back to Mafia. 'Although it is pretty fucking funny, now you mention it.'

'You can't put me in there.'

'Orders,' Fox said.

'Who from?'

'Your granny.' Fox stabbed a finger at him. 'Now get on your feet and start moving. And try not to fall down the fucking stairs this time.'

Mafia didn't budge.

'You want to do this the hard way?'

Mafia sighed. Stood. And Glass got a good look at his face. His cheek was puffed up, lip swollen.

'I'll lead the way,' Glass said.

'Thanks,' Mafia replied.

'You pair should just be done with it and fuck each other,' Fox said. 'Spare us all the bloody foreplay.'

A BARE CELL. No windows. At night, they'd toss in a mattress, maybe a blanket. No need to ask why they used to be called punishment cells. Glass found it hard to believe he was used to it now.

Mafia was naked, hands cupped over his groin. He looked even more naked without his shades.

Fox had taken them away along with Mafia's clothes. Not normal practice, just Fox being a bastard.

Glass had tried to persuade him not to. Got the response he'd expected.

'Don't you want to see your boyfriend's tackle out, then?' Fox's double chin was like an extra smile.

'At least leave him his shades,' Glass said. 'He can't see without them.'

'Can't fucking see *with* them. And why the tinted lenses anyway?' He looked at Mafia, who didn't respond. 'Huh?' He swatted Mafia with his arm.

'It's complicated,' Mafia said. 'Just leave me the glasses, eh?'

Fox folded them, popped them in his breast pocket. 'No fucking chance.'

'What's the point of taking them?' Glass asked.

'Man might be a danger to himself,' Fox said. 'Break them. Cut his wrists.'

'You feeling suicidal?' Glass asked Mafia.

'More murderous, I'd say.' Mafia looked at Fox, eyeballs wiggling from side to side like they were searching for a way to escape from their sockets.

'Think I'll bin them,' Fox said. 'Just to make sure they don't injure anyone.'

'Don't be a cunt,' Glass said.

Fox stiffened. 'You calling me a cunt?'

'Just don't,' Glass said.

Fox said, 'How much?'

Glass scratched his finger. 'What?'

'How much will you pay me for not stepping on them?'

'Me?' Glass said.

'Yeah, you.'

'Why should I pay you anything?'

'You shouldn't. But I bet you will.'

Well, no, he wouldn't. He wasn't going to be bullied like this. 'Go ahead,' Glass said. 'Do what you want.'

Fox said to Mafia, 'Sorry, petal. Your boyfriend doesn't love you any more.'

GLASS WAS GLAD to be rid of Fox, but he wasn't so keen on supervising the machine shop. The smell of aluminium shavings, the noise of grinding metal. Raised voices. And a sense of danger. He felt the latter all the time, throughout the Hilton. But here it was heightened. And it was soaring today.

He was standing right by the gate, leaning against the bars, trying to look relaxed. He had a key, but, still, he was locked in. Suppose something happened and he needed to get out. It would take him time to react. Maybe he wouldn't have time. He'd be stuck here with this lot.

He watched a group of inmates huddled around the big lathe. Glass knew they gave all the machines names, but he wasn't sure if she was Lydia or Linda. A head rose, looked right at him, gave a smile. Another head, another smile.

They were talking about him.

He didn't know whether to smile back or ignore them. His thoughts alternated:

Don't get too close.

Don't blank them.

Don't provoke them.

Don't let them get off with it.

Then: *Open the fucking gate and run while you can.*

Course, he didn't. He tried to look calm and in control, the bars of the gate pressing into his back. Probably just as well he was locked in. Otherwise, he might not have trusted himself to stay.

The group round the big lathe was sniggering like schoolkids. Maybe they were planning on taking him hostage.

He shivered, like he'd sucked a lemon. He had to get that crap out of his head. Ever since he'd started the job, that'd been his main worry, nagging at him constantly. His imagination took over sometimes, no question, but hostage situations were a real threat in the Hilton.

Maximum security prison. Three hostage crises in the last ten years. Four officers stabbed. One had lost an eye. One had died.

And how much training did Glass get in what to do in a hostage situation?

None. Not so much as a single word of advice.

In fact, officers had to sign a disclaimer saying that they worked here at their own risk and that no one was under any obligation to try to rescue them should they be taken hostage. Fucking great. You're on your own, pal.

If you couldn't do the time, you shouldn't be a screw. He knew that. Shitty pay, too. Scottish officers were on a much lower salary than their counterparts in England.

Glass would give it up right now if it weren't for the fact Lorna's mother would see him as a quitter. He had to stick it out, prove her wrong. And, anyway, what else was he going to do? He wasn't qualified to do a damn thing. He could strum a few chords on a guitar, but who couldn't? Couldn't make a living busking, which was all he was good for. Not that he played any more, hadn't picked up a guitar in years. He was smart enough. His teachers had had high expectations, but he'd never finished his studies. Caitlin came along and changed everything. He and Lorna had barely scratched a living for five years. But he was a prison officer now, and he had to see it through. It'd get better. He'd get used to it. He just wished he could stop shaking. He did his best to disguise it, but at some point, somebody was going to notice.

And any sign of weakness and these predators would rip him apart.

'JESUS, PEELER, YOU fucking nutter.'

Peeler was a big guy, muscled, tattoos, shaved head. A lifer, with no hope of an early liberation date. He'd killed his wife and her boyfriend. Really killed them. With an axe.

He was called Peeler because his party piece was shoving bananas up his rectum and squeezing them till they split. Apparently they came out peeled down the middle, held together only at both ends. Right now, it looked like somebody'd been feeding him, and not bananas. Peeler was out of his head. Which wouldn't have been quite so worrying if he wasn't holding a machete in his hand.

Shit, shit, *shit.* Glass should have been paying attention. Who in their right mind gave cons the means and opportunity to make their own machetes? The metalwork shop was an accident waiting to happen. This whole fucking place was insane.

Glass's legs were vibrating. He knew he should be doing something here, but he wasn't sure what. He rubbed his palms on his trousers, hoped somebody would offer a suggestion.

'Fucking mess, man,' somebody said. Sounded like Horse.

The work group had backed off, formed a distant half-circle around Peeler.

Horse was there, right enough, his huge frame shielding Caesar. Making sure Caesar didn't get hurt. Which is what he'd failed to do earlier by the looks of things. Caesar's right eye was puffy, so Mafia must have got in at least one decent shot when they'd had their scrap.

'Gross as fuck,' somebody said.

Glass silently agreed when he saw what was being referenced. Blood. Dripping onto the floor at Peeler's feet, gouts of it, like red paint from a tin.

Then he saw where it was coming from.

And heaved.

'Oh, you dirty bastard.'

'You fucking poof.'

Voices directed at him, not at Peeler.

Glass gagged again, stood up, eyes watering, stomach muscles burning.

Felt a right prick, but Christ Almighty, who wouldn't throw up?

Peeler was still standing there, his machete in one hand, his other hand by his side, blood dripping from his fingers. He had a bemused look on his face, like he was asking himself: *How did this happen?*

He made eye contact with Glass, and Glass felt his balls shrink. But it was okay. Peeler wasn't about to rush him. Quite the opposite.

Peeler dropped the machete. The hole he'd sliced in the underside of his left arm ran from the crook of his elbow down to his wrist. He inserted the fingers of his right hand into the hole. Pushed them inside. Slid in his thumb.

Oh, Jesus.

He spread his fingers, pulling the skin apart, and stared inside his arm.

'Christ you doing, you mad fuck?' Horse again.

'Would you look at that?' Peeler said. He'd grabbed hold of a bunch of veins and tendons and was showing them off, grinning.

Someone else spewed and Glass felt slightly less like a lightweight.

Then Peeler's face changed. It was as if he realised what he was doing, what he was holding in his hand. Abruptly, he let go and screamed. He ran on the spot, screaming. Jumped up and down, screaming. Threw his head from side to side, screaming.

Glass wanted to join him. But he had a job to do. He needed to restrain the crazy bastard before he hurt himself. Okay. Before he hurt himself further.

The noise, though, that screaming. Grating worse than the machines. And the cons, now staring at Glass. Expecting him to do something. Knowing he had to do something. No doubt hoping he got hurt trying to do it.

Bastards.

Couldn't think, though. Couldn't fucking think.

Maybe if he moved, he'd think of what he was supposed to do.

He stepped forward, feeling the shake in his knees. There was a sharp tang of bile in his mouth.

Peeler was still screaming, dancing. He slipped in his blood. Fell.

Now. Now was Glass's chance. He ran forward, dived on top of Peeler. *Got the fucker.* 'Help me,' Glass shouted.

Nobody moved.

Peeler was ten times stronger than him under normal circumstances and crazy men were supposed to have the power of ten men, making Peeler the serious odds-on favourite to come out victorious. Glass scrambled for Peeler's arm to get a restraining hold on him, but Peeler was wriggling and shaking all over as if he was being electrocuted and Glass's hand kept slipping in the con's blood. If nobody came to help, Glass was dead. 'Help, you bastards!'

'Fuck off,' Wireman said. 'Cunt's probably got AIDS.'

Ah, Jesus. Wireman had a point.

Glass rolled off Peeler, and Peeler lay there, staring at him, gasping. After a moment, he slapped a bloody hand on the floor, wiped it. Glass remembered the machete. Hoped to Christ Peeler wasn't going to pick it up and lunge at him now.

But that wasn't possible. The machete was gone.

Jesus Christ, this was becoming increasingly fucked up.

Perfect time for a riot. And Glass would be the perfect hostage.

Shit, shit, shit.

Peeler got to his feet. Licked his lips. Eyeballed Glass. Then his head turned towards the gate as it clanged open.

'The fuck is this crap?'

Thank Christ. Glass hated himself, but that was a welcome voice. He looked up.

Fox said, 'Move, fuckwits.'

The relief was almost sexual. Glass felt it in his balls.

Muir and Ross had arrived with Fox, all three taking in the scene.

Ross stepped forward. 'What's the matter with you, then, Peeler?' Her voice was steady, no sign that his sliced open arm and exposed veins were affecting her.

Peeler stared at her.

'Very pretty.' She nodded towards his arm. 'You should have been a surgeon.'

Peeler looked at his arm as if he'd just noticed it. Then he keeled over onto the floor.

Ross looked at Glass. 'Wasn't so hard, was it?'

'YOU SHOULDN'T BE here,' Mafia said. He was still in the Digger, sitting on the cold floor, knees hugged to his chest.

'You want me to go?' Glass asked him.

'What do you want, Glass?'

'*Officer* Glass.'

'Don't play the officer card with me. Doesn't suit you.'

Glass thought about leaving, but his curiosity had the better of him. He asked, 'What's with you and Caesar?'

'Don't like him.' Mafia pulled his knees tighter against his chest. 'And he doesn't like me.'

There was more than that. They'd fought before.

'That stoat's protected,' Mafia said.

A stoat: a nonce, a sex offender. Caesar wasn't a stoat. Mafia was just using it as an insult. In the Hilton, it was the worst thing you could call someone. Even worse than 'screw'.

'Tell me more,' Glass said.

'Why should I?'

Glass had no idea. But the dynamics of Mafia and Caesar's relationship had fascinated him from the outset. 'Never mind,' he said. Maybe he just liked Mafia and wanted to know what Caesar had against him. Maybe that's all it was.

'Hey,' Mafia squinted up at him, 'think you can persuade Fox to give me back my shades any time soon?'

DARKO PUT THE kitten down on the floor. Looked like the one Glass had seen in the locker room. It may have been feral, but Darko had it purring.

Glass wondered if Darko could teach him to do that so he could take the kitten home to Caitlin. Mind you, the thing probably had mites and God knew what else. He'd have to get it cleaned up first. But it wasn't going to be today.

The kitten bolted out of the room. Off to join the rest of the inmates for free association.

'Why d'you want to know?' Darko's English was excellent. A slight accent but you would hardly notice if you weren't listening for it.

'It'd help me do my job,' Glass said.

'Nothing will help you do that.'

Glass wasn't sure whether Darko was insulting him or the job. 'Tell me their history. As a favour, Darko.'

Darko smiled. 'Why should I do you a favour?'

'I'll owe you one.' Darko thought about that.

Glass could tell he was tempted. Always good to have a screw in your debt.

'Okay.' Darko leaned in close, whispered, 'Mafia used to be in Caesar's gang. That's their history.' He looked around as though someone might be eavesdropping. 'Until things got fucked up.' Again he scanned the cell. 'Couple of dead bodies.'

A flash. Peeler with his veins in his hand. Blood dripping onto the floor of the machine shop.

Glass rested his hand on the top bunk to stop himself falling and just about maintained his balance. He managed to speak without sounding weak. 'And Mafia took the rap?'

Darko shrugged. 'Caught at the scene.'

Glass was okay now. The feeling had passed. He moved his hand from the bed. 'I can't see him as a killer.' He waited, but Darko wasn't going to say any more. Glass prompted him: 'Must have been Caesar.'

'He had nothing to do with it.'

'How do you know?'

'Mafia confessed.'

'So Mafia did kill these people?'

'That's what he says.'

'You believe him?'

'Why would he lie?'

'I don't know,' Glass said. 'To protect someone, maybe.'

'That's possible, I suppose.'

Glass nodded. 'I wonder who.'

'Not Caesar.'

'Why do they hate each other?'

Darko looked towards the door again, then said, 'You should ask Watt.'

'Watt?'

'Mafia's little brother.'

Glass hadn't heard of him before but he didn't want to let Darko know the extent of his ignorance. 'What did Caesar do to him?'

Darko shook his head, folded his arms. 'Look, if you want to know more, speak to Mafia. I've said enough.'

'Come on. I just want to understand.'

'Sorry, but there has to be a reason Mafia doesn't want you to know.'

Glass heard footsteps and then Horse appeared in the doorway holding a mop and the chance to persuade Darko was gone.

'Not interrupting anything, am I?' Horse asked.

'Officer Glass was just leaving.'

'What do you want?' Glass asked, forcing himself to make eye contact.

Horse was huge. Every time Glass saw him, he kept expecting to get knocked to the floor and trampled on. That's what had happened to some poor bastard four years ago. Rumour had it that Horse had broken off in the middle as the guy lay dying, gone to the shops for a packet of cigarettes and a can of Coke, then returned to finish the job of stomping the guy to death.

Horse said. 'Something I want to speak to you about in private.'

Glass didn't want to speak to Horse. He particularly didn't want to speak to him in private. But maybe Horse had something legitimate to say to him, something that would help him do his job, whatever Darko thought about that. He turned and left the cell, Horse by his side.

Horse put his mop in a bucket by the door. 'I'll keep this quick,' he said out of the side of his mouth. He picked up the bucket, nodded at a passing inmate. There was lots of nodding in the Hilton. Not greeting someone you passed on the landing could be enough of a slight to get you slashed. If the cons were dogs, they'd eat their own tails to relieve the boredom. Not saying hello could be seen as a nice big juicy bone.

Horse said, 'Need a favour.'

Glass didn't like the sound of that. Even though he'd just asked Darko for one. Or maybe *because* he'd just asked Darko for one.

Horse carried on, side-mouthing: 'We're having trouble getting gear in at the minute.'

'Jesus.' Glass whispered back. 'I don't want to know about that.'

Horse steered him by the elbow. They were on the bottom flat now, heading for Horse's peter. 'Too late,' he said. 'You know now. So either you're in or we have to kill you.'

Glass stopped to look at Horse. He wasn't smiling. 'I'm serious,' Glass said.

'Me, too,' Horse told him and started walking again.

'Look,' Glass said, 'this is crazy, talking to me like this. I don't want to know about your –' he looked around, but nobody was near '– drug deals. I'm a fucking –'

'Get in.'

They'd stopped two doors short of Horse's peter. This was Caesar's cell, the one he shared with Jasmine.

'I don't think so,' Glass said.

'Come on in, Officer Glass.' Caesar stood in the doorway. Behind him, Jasmine sat on the bed, legs crossed, foot dangling.

She waved her long-fingernailed hand at him and said, 'Hiya.'

'I don't think you're listening to me,' Glass said.

'Please,' Caesar said, stepping to the side, gesturing in the direction Glass should take. 'How are Lorna and Caitlin?'

Glass felt sharp pains in his chest, as if a thorn bush were growing inside him. He turned, headed back to the office. Didn't look behind him.

Every con he passed on the way was his enemy. He could have jumped any one of them, ripped their throats out with his teeth. They were animals. But so what? He was an animal too.

He had to think like that. He had to. By the time he reached the office, he'd just about convinced himself.

He knocked. Entered when he was invited to do so.

'You okay?' Senior Officer Neil Shaw asked him.

'You mind if I use your phone?'

'Feel free,' Shaw said. 'You sure you're okay?'

'Just want to call home.' Glass dialled, hands shaking. He could feel the bones shaking under his skin. Surprised he couldn't hear them rattle.

Ring.

Ring.

Ring.

He muttered, 'Come on.'

Ring.

'Hello?'

Thank Christ. 'Caitlin, babygirl. It's Daddy.'

'Daddy!'

'You okay?'

'Fine.'

'Is Mummy okay?'

'She's baking. We're making a cake. Want to speak to her? Mummy!'

Glass sank into a chair. 'No, sweetheart. Just tell her Daddy called to say he loved her.'

'Me, too. *Me.*'

'You, too, of course. I love you too.'

She giggled.

He blew her a noisy kiss, hung up, ran his hand across his brow. When he looked up, Shaw was staring at him.

'Problem?' Shaw said.

Glass shook his head and got to his feet. 'Everything's fine,' he said.

'Just how you want it to be.'

Seemed like an odd thing to say, but Shaw smiled, and Glass smiled back and nodded.

'It was freaky,' Lorna said, taking a sip of her gin, propping her foot on the coffee table and flexing her toes. Apple-green nail polish. Glass had never seen anyone else wear that shade. 'He knew me.'

She'd been telling Glass about her visit to the supermarket that morning, the guy outside, sitting on the wall, accosting her when she came out.

'What did he say?'

'Asked me how I was.'

'Maybe he fancied you.' Highly likely. Lorna had a pretty face, long blonde hair, athletic body, those sexy toes. She was eight years older than Glass, but thirty wasn't past it, however much she said she felt old. Hardly.

Everybody'd said their relationship wouldn't work. Well, they hadn't. Just her mother. But Glass knew what the rest of them were thinking.

She's pregnant. He won't stick around. He's too young.

Right. Fuck the lot of them. He'd stuck around long enough to get married and he'd keep sticking around. Even if things weren't always perfect. Nobody had a perfect marriage. Maybe Lorna wasn't the same person who'd once climbed naked onto the windowsill of her flat above the bakery to wave to the pedestrians below. Just because he dared her to. 'You'll be safe,' he'd said. 'Nobody looks up.' And he was right. He joined her on the ledge and they stood there, arms around one another's waist. And nobody looked up.

She'd call him a twat if he suggested doing that now. She'd changed. But then so had he.

Anyway, they were settled in Edinburgh and he had a steady job. What he didn't need right now was some arsehole messing everything up.

'He used my name,' Lorna said. 'He said, "Nice day, Lorna. How are you?" Knew Caitlin's name, too.' When she said 'Caitlin', Lorna looked up.

Glass did too, half expecting Caitlin to bounce downstairs, tell them she couldn't sleep and was ready for Daddy to read her another bedtime story, the one about the dragon who got angrier and angrier till he breathed all the fire out of himself.

Glass caught himself smiling. He liked that one too. That was one lucky fucking dragon. But Caitlin didn't appear. It was just him and Lorna, and her tale about the creepy guy outside the supermarket.

'Weird,' Glass said. He had an inkling who the guy was – or at least who'd sent him – but didn't want to tell Lorna in case he was wrong. He didn't want to worry her.

'You think so?' she said. 'You think it's "weird"? Really?'

He winced like she'd cut him with a razor blade. Her sarcasm was one of the changes he'd never adjusted to, didn't think he ever would.

'I said to him, "Do I know you?"' She paused. 'Know what he said?' She waited for Glass to respond. He gave a slight shake of his head.

'"Not yet."' She sipped her drink, her hand unsteady enough that her teeth clinked against the edge. 'Freaked me out.'

'I bet,' Glass said. 'I can imagine.'

She took a breath, switched her glass from one hand to the other, wriggled her toes again. 'So I wondered if he was someone you knew. I asked him. He said, "We have mutual acquaintances."'

The topic was moving into dangerous territory.

Glass said, 'What did he look like?'

Her eyes narrowed, mouth opened slightly, tongue pressed against her teeth. 'Short brown hair. Unshaven. Sort of charity-shop look. Army surplus.'

'Doesn't ring any bells.'

'If you know, Nick, tell me. I don't want to be protected. I'm a big girl.'

'Sorry,' Glass said. 'I've no idea who he is.'

He walked round the side of the coffee table, got down on his knees, reached across and cupped both hands round her foot. Something to take their minds off the supermarket guy. She leaned back, closed her eyes. He prodded the ball of her foot with his thumbs. 'Early night?' he said.

She opened her eyes, slid her foot out of his grasp. 'No,' she said, 'I'm not in the mood.'

WEDNESDAY

Glass slotted in the key, unlocked the door to Caesar's peter. He still found it hard to resist the urge to knock. You see a door that isn't yours, you knock before you enter. That's how we're all brought up. But he couldn't do that here.

He pushed the door open and stepped inside. 'We need to talk,' he said, his voice tapering off on the last word.

Caesar's eyes were closed, his trousers around his ankles. Jasmine was on her knees. Her eyes widened when she saw Glass but she didn't stop what she was doing. If anything, she seemed to set to it with more enthusiasm.

'I ought to put you on report,' Glass said.

Caesar grinned, his eyes still closed. 'Officer Glass, give me a couple of minutes and I'll be right with you.'

Jasmine waved her fingers at Glass, carried on.

Glass turned and walked out.

IN THE SHOP, the work party was stationed round the room at the lathes, milling machines, bandsaws. All quiet.

S.O. Neil Shaw was addressing the prisoners.

Officers Fox and Ross hovered by the gate next to Glass, Fox stifling a yawn.

'...close supervision.' Shaw said. 'Any more blades discovered and this workshop gets closed down permanently.'

Groans from the cons. If they didn't get out to work, they'd be spending twenty-three hours a day locked in their cells and none of them wanted that.

'Not fucking likely,' Fox said, under his breath.

Glass looked at him.

'Prison's got a contract to manufacture road signs, Dumbo,' Fox explained in a whisper. 'Nice little earner. No way the governor's going to let that go.'

Shaw clapped his hands twice, held them together. 'So get back to work,' he said, 'and play nice.' He walked out, giving a curt nod to the officers as he passed.

'Can't believe he wants three of us here,' Ross said.

Fox said, 'All on account of one person's incompetence. You'd think, after six weeks' training at Polmont, Officer Glass would have learned how to set off the alarm.'

'Maybe we can work it out between the three of us,' Ross said. 'How much training does it take to press a button?'

It had been like this since day one. Some of Glass's colleagues had taken an instant dislike to him. And he didn't understand it. Wasn't as if he'd done them any harm. They treated him like a fucking con. Worse, in some ways. They respected a lot of the cons.

It had to be the fact that he was so much younger than them. He couldn't think of anything else.

'Hey, Crystal, your boyfriend's out of the Digger today,' Ross said.

Glass couldn't help himself. He said, 'He's not my boyfriend. I'm married. I have a kid. Go fuck yourself.'

'Ooo,' Ross said. 'Touched a nerve, Fox.'

'You believe him?' Fox said to Ross.

'Too young to have a kid. Doesn't look like he shaves yet. If he is married, I bet the wife's just for show.'

'Yeah,' Fox said. 'I bet the kid's not even his.'

Glass could have cried. Or he could have kicked several shades of crap out of them, even if Ross was a woman. She wasn't the type to hide behind her tits. He did neither, though. He just stood there and tried to look like it wasn't bothering him.

After a bit, they turned, walked away, Ross saying to Fox, 'Bet you a tenner he doesn't last the week.'

HALF AN HOUR later, the noise in the machine shop making his skull rattle, Glass bent his head for a minute, and that's all it took.

Thwack.

Bing.

Rattle.

He heard it. Didn't know what it was.

Cold broke out on his forehead. No sweat, just cold.

He looked down to the side. And there it was, rolling in a slow arc on the floor.

A fucking metal spike.

Laughter rose above the whine of the machines.

He dared to look up and Caesar was baying at him, fixed grin like some cartoon character. Horse was bent double, acting like he'd just witnessed the greatest comedy show on earth, the prick. The other cons were all laughing too.

Funny. Yeah. Fucking side-splittingly fucking funny.

Fox and Ross had followed the gaze of the cons and were looking Glass's way now. Side by side, they moved to a position where they could see the spike on the floor.

And they laughed too. Course they did.

Glass picked up the spike. 'Turn those fucking machines off,' he shouted.

Nobody paid him any attention. Well, he'd see who could press a button.

He walked over to the wall, switched off all the power. The machines died, and the laughter crashed around him, loud. He had their attention. Problem was, he didn't know what to do next.

Hit the alarm.

Like he should have done when Peeler went berserk with the machete.

Throw the spike back at them.

But at who?

Try to find the culprit.

He scanned the room.

Catch his eyes, he'll look away.

Not these fuckers. They weren't normal. They'd hold his gaze. Guilt didn't register.

It was pointless. There was nothing he could do.

They were still staring at him. Waiting, quiet now, for him to speak. The weight of the spike in his hand was dragging him down. That fucking thing had narrowly missed his head. Jesus fucking Christ.

He had to say something. He said, 'Somebody lose this?'

Silence expanded like a balloon until it was about to pop.

Then, a chuckle. And another. And another.

He tried to hold his smile but his lips quivered, so he placed the spike on the nearest bench to show them he wasn't scared. He bowed his head, turned the power back on. As the machines coughed back into life, he returned to his post at the gate and folded his arms.

No big deal.

When he looked up, Fox was staring at him, shaking his head. Fox gestured with his wrist and mouthed the word, 'Wanker.'

'I KNOW IT was you,' Glass said.

Free association once again, and there they were in Caesar's peter, the radio blasting yet another forgettable pop song. No blow-job to embarrass Glass this time, Jasmine having taken the opportunity to strut her stuff in front of a bigger audience.

Caesar and Horse were both on their feet, arms folded across their bare chests. Advertisements for muscles. Glass tried not to stare at the tattoos that wound around Caesar's torso and arms but it was hard to drag his eyes away. The centrepiece was a beautiful green-eyed Medusa with snakes for hair.

'Officer Glass,' Caesar said. 'Nick. If I wanted you hurt, you'd *be* hurt.'

Jesus Christ. Was that a threat, or just a statement of fact?

'Listen, mate,' Caesar carried on, 'if you want to find out who threw that piece of metal at you, why don't you check the surveillance tapes?'

Talking at cross-purposes. But that was Caesar being deliberately obtuse.

As it happened, Glass *had* checked the tapes. Five minutes after leaving the machine shop. Went to the tiny room known grandiosely as the Control Booth. The surveillance cameras operated only in select areas of the prison. The machine shop was one of them. He'd checked the tape only to discover that it wasn't set to record on Mondays, Wednesdays or Fridays.

Typical. No, not typical. The fuckers knew that. Knew they could get away with it on a Wednesday.

'That wasn't what I wanted to see you about.' Glass didn't need to explain further, but he did. 'Wasn't to talk about what happened in the machine shop.'

'No?' Caesar said. 'Then what?'

'Yeah, how can we help?' Horse tilted his head back, pushing his chin forward. As if he was daring Glass to punch it.

'The other thing.' Glass didn't want to say it aloud. The music was thumping, but the peter door was open. 'You know.'

Caesar shook his head.

Glass said, quietly, 'With my wife?'

Caesar went all wide-eyed, palms raised in cluelessness. Life was just one big mystery to him. 'You know what he's talking about?' he asked Horse.

Horse shook his head. 'Fucked if I do.'

Glass felt the tension in his shoulders, in his neck. Now that he was forced to describe how they'd threatened him, it was as if he was threatening them by doing so. It was all arse backwards. He said, 'The guy at the supermarket.' Left it at that.

Caesar frowned. Shrugged. Looked at Horse. 'Some guy fuck his wife when she was shopping?'

'Wasn't me,' Horse said. 'I've got a pretty fucking concrete alibi.' He laughed, a strangely gentle sound.

'Just lay off,' Glass said. 'Fucking lay off. That's all I wanted to say.'

Caesar took a step forward, arms by his side, flexing his triceps. 'You threatening me?'

'I –' Glass said. Fuck it. 'Yeah.'

Caesar breathed out. 'Well, I'm duly intimidated. Listen, Nick.' He lowered his voice. 'We need your help. We really need you to bring in this gear for us. It'll be easy. No risk.'

'I told you, no.'

'You're our only hope.'

'What's wrong with your regular mule?' He hadn't wanted to get drawn into a conversation about this. Just wanted to say his piece and leave. But he didn't feel he could leave till everything was sorted out.

'Lying low,' Caesar said.

'What does that mean?'

'Why? You trying to work out who it is?'

He was curious, certainly. And it wouldn't hurt to have

some information he could use against Caesar. But there was no chance of that now.

'Oh, yeah,' Caesar said. 'I can see through you, Glass.'

Horse laughed. 'See through him. Nice one.'

'Never heard that one before,' Glass said.

'Lighten the fuck up,' Caesar said. 'Point is, I'm not in the business of fingering anyone. Very trustworthy, me. That right, Horse?'

'Fuck, aye. Trust you with my liver.'

Caesar squinted at him.

'You know,' Horse said, 'if my liver ever fell out or something and you found it, I'd trust you with it.'

'You wouldn't trust anyone else?'

'Nah,' Horse said. 'Most of the cunts round here would fry it up and eat it.'

'I'm touched,' Caesar said.

Glass didn't want to listen to these arseholes any longer. Sometimes he forgot what they'd done, why they were in the Hilton. Caesar liked to brag about his crime, introduced himself to Glass on his first day as someone who liked to play games with people. And when Glass thought about what that meant, the literal nature of it, it made his balls leap for his stomach. He shouldn't forget. It was dangerous to forget. He said, 'I won't do it. I can't.' He'd be risking his job, jeopardising his family's future, facing the possibility of some jail time himself. P.O.s who committed crimes got dealt with much more severely than ordinary citizens. Made an example of. Rightly so.

'Then we have a problem,' Caesar said. 'If we don't get this piece of business through soon, we're going to lose the whole deal.'

'Tough.'

'I can't be responsible for what happens then.'

Glass clenched his fists. 'What does that mean?'

'What I said,' Caesar said. 'Anything that might happen to . . . your loved ones, for instance.' He shrugged.

So the guy at the supermarket *had* been sent by him.

Glass said, 'I thought my family had nothing to do with you.'

'Even more reason Caesar can't be responsible,' Horse said.

'We'll pay you, of course,' Caesar said. 'Make it well worth your while. You could use the extra cash, I'm sure. Starting salary for a P.O. sucks, doesn't it? And I hear you have a nice house and no doubt a hefty mortgage to go along with it. Wife doesn't work. Kids ain't cheap.'

'You have that guy spying on me?'

'Keeping an eye out. In case you get hurt. Come on. Name your price.'

'What makes you think smuggling drugs for you could ever be worth my while?' Glass asked him.

'Everybody has a price.'

'I'm not doing it,' Glass said. 'I don't have a price.'

'How old's your daughter? I hear she's pretty. Like your wife.'

Glass imagined drawing his baton. Launching himself at them. Beating the pair of them till their tattoos ran red. Instead, he said, 'No.'

'Think it over,' Caesar said.

'I don't need to.'

'I insist. Twenty-four hours.'

'I'll still say no.'

'That's a shame,' Caesar said. 'Cause I promise you, something very bad will happen.'

'I'll report you.' The threat sounded pitiful as soon as he'd said it.

'You're not taking me seriously,' Caesar said, 'and that's a really big fucking mistake. You're not as headless as you look, now, are you?'

'DID HE HURT her?' Glass said.

Lorna was better now than she'd been when he was on the phone with her earlier. He'd hurried home from work, told her not to call the police till they'd spoken.

This is what she told him.

About half an hour before she was due to pick up Caitlin from school, the man she'd seen at the supermarket had come to the house.

Lorna had answered the door, not expecting him, certainly not expecting him to barge in. Well, you didn't, did you? She insisted they get a chain on the door. Glass agreed, didn't have the heart to tell her a chain wouldn't stop him next time and wouldn't have stopped him earlier today.

The supermarket guy had clamped his hand over her mouth to stop her screaming, dragged her through to the sitting room.

She was fucking terrified.

When she was telling him this, Glass's skin felt like it had been out too long in the sun. All prickly, hypersensitive.

'I'm going to be nice today,' the supermarket guy had said to her, 'so there's no need to get upset.'

She'd tried to wriggle out of his grasp, but he'd squeezed her till she hurt. He was strong. She thought he was going to break her ribs.

She stamped on his toes, raked her heels down his shins.

He laughed at her, switched her hands behind her back, locked his grip on them. Like wearing a pair of handcuffs, she said.

'Keep struggling,' he'd said. 'I like it.'

At which point Lorna feared the worst.

He forced her into an armchair. She sat up again as soon as he let go, ran at him, screaming. She wasn't going to let him touch her without a fight. She managed to hit him with her elbow. He absorbed the blow without so much as a grunt.

'Shut up.' He wrapped his arms around her again.

She kept screaming.

'You want me to gag you?'

Looked like he meant it. She quietened. Her breathing was rapid, though, heart beating like crazy, echoing in her ears. She asked him what he was going to do. Was he going to kill her?

'Just sit down,' he said. 'Relax.'

She sat down. Her arms trembled. Couldn't keep them still.

'Mind if I put the TV on?' he asked her.

She couldn't believe this. She was dreaming. A nightmare. She didn't respond.

'No?' he said. 'Okay, now which is the remote?'

She made a run for it. Didn't make it to the door. For a moment she hung in mid-air, legs kicking.

He'd caught her round the waist, lifted her, turned her round.

He threw her towards the chair.

She fell over the arm, sprawled into the seat.

'Try that again,' he said, 'and I will get nasty. Now sit still and watch some TV with me.'

She sat still, as best she could, and watched *Take the High Road*, the supermarket guy having first asked if that was all right. After five minutes, she said, mouth dry, 'Why are you here?'

'Can't I come round to visit?' He didn't take his eyes off the screen.

'I don't know you.'

'I'm trying to remedy that.' He gave her a quick look, flashed his teeth at her.

'Why?' she said. 'What do you want?'

'It's not about what I want, Lorna. Ask your husband. He'll tell you.'

'What do you want with Nick? What's he done to you?'

'You should speak to him yourself. Not my place to tell tales.'

'Okay,' she said. 'I will. Would you please go now?'

'I'm watching this,' he said.

'Please,' she said.

He looked at her. Sighed. Turned off the TV. 'You want me to pick up Caitlin for you?'

She yelled at him: 'I don't fucking know you and I don't want you in my house and I don't want you within a hundred miles of my daughter. Now get the fuck out.'

'Hey,' he said, 'that's not a nice tone of voice.'

'Get the fuck out. Get out. Get out.'

'Just offering to help,' he said. She didn't think he'd go, but he got to his feet and said, 'I'll see myself to the door then.'

First thing she did once he'd gone, she phoned the school. Got them to check that Caitlin was okay, told them on no account to let her get in a car with anyone other than her mother.

Then Lorna went to pick her up.

Only once Caitlin was safe did Lorna phone Nick. He told his S.O. that Caitlin was ill and came right home.

Caitlin was safe in her room now, playing, while Mummy and Daddy talked downstairs.

'So who is he?' Lorna asked. 'And don't lie to me this time.'

'I don't know his name,' Glass told her. And then he told her about Caesar. About what Caesar wanted Glass to do.

'You think he's behind this?' she asked once he'd finished.

'I'm sure of it.'

'We have to call the police. Put a stop to it.'

'The police can't do anything.'

'They can arrest the bastard who put his hands on me.'

'I don't know.' Glass shook his head. 'Lorna, these guys are heavy-duty.'

'Even more reason to involve the police.'

'Let me tell you what Caesar's like. How he ended up in jail.' He looked at her and she nodded slowly. 'Caesar was caught red-handed. Out of his gourd on a cocktail of drugs. Playing football in the street.'

'Doesn't sound so terrible.' Her lips tried to hold a smile.

'The football,' he said. He swallowed. 'It was somebody's head.' He swallowed again. 'They found the body in Caesar's house. In his bath.'

'Jesus.' She sat down. 'Sweet Jesus.' Looked at him, her fingers plucking at each other. 'So this guy, Caesar, he can fuck us up. Even though he's in prison. That's what you're telling me?'

'He doesn't have boundaries.'

'Good for him. I'm calling the police.'

Catch him when he's vulnerable.

Caesar was taking a dump, couldn't *be* much more vulnerable.

Glass couldn't sneak up on him without being seen, though. The cubicle doors were cut away at the top and bottom, leaving only the middle of the body covered.

Glass could see Caesar's head and feet, but Caesar could see all of Glass.

And Glass couldn't see Caesar's hand, didn't know if the rummaging around was him scrunching up toilet paper or pulling out a hidden shiv.

Earlier today, an inmate had attacked another with a piece of sharpened pork chop bone. Luckily, Glass had been in the library at the time. The attack wasn't that serious but it had resulted in a lockdown till ten minutes ago.

Which was why Caesar had been holding on to go to the toilet. Didn't want to go potty in his peter unless he absolutely had to. Would have had to live with the smell, which was something nobody enjoyed. Some of the cons regularly wrapped their excrement in paper and lobbed it through the bars of their peters and out the window. It lessened the stink, but if they got caught they'd get reported, could get sent to the Digger or lose remission.

Glass heard a plopping sound as he got closer to Caesar.

'Been thinking about what we discussed?' Caesar said, over the top of the mini-door, casual as anything.

'Oh, yeah,' Glass said. 'Just a bit.'

'And you've decided you still won't do it, haven't you?'

He could tell from Glass's face?

'That's a shame,' Caesar said. 'Cause Watt really likes your wife.'

Ripped flesh, blood on the floor.

Peeler.

His machete. Which had gone missing.

The fingers dripping blood belonged to Caesar, though. Joined his wrists, his tattooed arms.

Peeler had tattoos too.

Their names weren't that different. Peeler. Caesar.

Did Caesar have the machete now?

It still hadn't been found. There'd been a cell search for it but that'd been a waste of time.

It couldn't have been taken into the general population. The only way back inside from the machine shop was through the metal detectors and although there were ways of sneaking smaller objects through, a machete would have been a bit of a challenge.

Nah, some bastard had hidden it, somehow, in the workshop. Either that, or it had been disguised as a large shoehorn.

Why was he thinking about the machete now?

Caesar was staring at him. Had he said something?

God, yes. About Lorna. About Watt really liking her.

Watt?

Watt was Mafia's brother. According to Darko, Watt was somehow the reason Mafia and Caesar hated each other. Watt worked for Caesar?

Well, that information might have made a difference when he and Lorna had spoken to the police. They'd been no help at all. Lorna had opened the door to the supermarket guy, she didn't have any serious injuries, and all the cops had to act on was a description. The police might as well have said, 'Don't waste our time.'

Glass didn't want to think about this. He wasn't going to think about it. He'd think about something else, anything else.

Shit, though, they had a name now. He could hand Watt to the police gift-wrapped.

Caesar said, 'Watt *really* likes her. I think he's in love.'

Glass could have kicked the door, whacked the bastard on the face. Would have been oh so very rewarding. But Lorna was right. The answer was to let the police deal with it.

'Saturday,' Caesar said.

Glass opened his mouth but didn't get a word out.

'No, you're not working. I checked your shift rota.' Caesar leaned forward, placed his hand on the top of the door. 'Four o'clock. Castle Esplanade. Don't be late.'

'Which castle?' The words were out before Glass could stop himself.

'Edinburgh, you tit. And don't worry about recognising him,' Caesar said. 'He knows what you look like.'

ON THE WAY home from work Glass popped into the local police station, spoke to the desk sergeant, gave him Watt's name. The policeman scribbled in the file, ignoring the constant barking that had been coming from a room along the corridor ever since Glass had set foot in the building.

The desk sergeant looked up. 'Not mine,' he said. 'Collie. Running amok on the golf course. Had to bring him in cause he was stealing folks' golf balls.'

'What do you think'll happen?' Glass asked.

'His owner'll be in touch, probably. If not, there's this woman, Mrs Carrick –'

'Not the dog. What'll happen with Watt?'

'Of course.' The policeman nodded. 'We'll be in touch about that.'

'Maybe I can help. Find out his address for you.'

The policeman frowned. 'Best stay out of it. Let us deal with it.'

'Will you?'

The policeman's lips tightened.

'Be honest with me,' Glass said. 'I'm a prison officer. I deal with these types all the time.'

'Truth is, I can't say for sure, sir.' The cop looked at the notes. 'If he's done something, then we'll have a word with him.'

'He's threatened my family, scared my wife.'

'I understand that. But, you know, the law . . . It's difficult, and I understand your concern. Problem is, he hasn't actually committed a crime, you see.'

'In my book he has. He attacked my wife.'

'Technically, yes, pushing her might be an assault. But was she injured?'

'She was bruised. Her wrist.'

'But not badly enough that we could photograph it.'

'Jesus. She was scared to fuck.'

'I don't doubt it. But it's his word against hers. Bottom line, it won't go to court.'

'So you're saying you can't do anything until he really hurts somebody?'

'Have a word with him, maybe. But, yeah, that's about it. Sorry.'

'Right,' Glass said. 'But if he'd stolen a golf ball, you'd lock him up with the dog.'

'SO HOW DO we get them to back off?' Lorna said, later, once Caitlin had gone to bed.

They were sitting on the floor, backs to the settee, two-thirds of the way through a bottle of cheap wine. Glass had only opened it ten minutes ago. 'I could do what Caesar wants.'

'Be serious.'

He was being serious, but he didn't push it. 'I just want to make sure you and Caitlin are safe.' He'd put chains on the front and back doors, and had spoken to a security company about getting an alarm fitted. But that didn't seem like enough.

'Maybe we should leave.' She crossed her ankles. 'Go back home.'

'To Dunfermline?' Now it was Glass's turn to wonder if *she* was serious. 'To your parents'?'

'Yeah,' she said. 'I know what you're going to say.'

'We've worked hard for what we have,' Glass said. 'Might not be much but we can't let these bastards ruin everything.'

'My mum would be happy to have us.'

'She'd be ecstatic. Finally, proof that she's been right all along. You married me because you had to. We're not good for each other. It'll never last. Great.'

'What's that got to do with it?'

'She thinks I'm a crap husband and father. I can't provide. Can't look after you.'

'It wasn't my fault I got sacked.'

'I didn't mean that.' Shit, he really hadn't meant to bring that up. 'I *want* to look after you.' An old-fashioned attitude, maybe, but there wasn't much choice. Lorna had been sacked from her last job, part-time admin assistant for an insurance company. Caitlin had caught a bad case of chickenpox, and Lorna took the week off to look after her. When she returned, her boss, childless and in her mid-fifties, was entirely unsympathetic. Said some pretty harsh things to Lorna, in private, about how much it pissed her off that mothers expected to be treated differently. It was Lorna's choice to have a kid, she'd said, and if it was going to interfere with her job, she wasn't much good to the company. Lorna had kept her mouth shut that time. Her boss continued to make her viewpoint clear, though, and, a few weeks later, when she told Lorna she was 'interfering with productivity' by showing her colleagues photographs of Caitlin's fourth birthday party, Lorna dropped the photos on her desk, spun round and slapped the bitch. And while she stood there, shocked, Lorna calmly unplugged her computer keyboard and smacked the cow over the head with it.

Lorna was very lucky she wasn't charged with assault. But, yeah, hard to get another job after getting sacked for violent conduct. So they'd agreed that Lorna would stay at home and look after Caitlin while Glass brought in the money. Had to be practical.

'I just meant that going back home would be admitting defeat,' Glass said.

'Doesn't matter what Mum thinks. We'll get through this.'

'Not by running away.' Glass pressed his thumbs hard against his temples. 'I'd have to give up the job. We'd have to take Caitlin out of school. Sell the house.'

'We can start again.'

'By taking a massive step back? Is that what you want? We've built a life here. It's not ideal, but it's ours. You really want to live with your mother again? A weekend in her company and you're ready to strangle her.'

There was something else. Lorna's dad had never recovered from losing the bakery in Dunfermline where he'd worked most of his life. He'd had one breakdown after another. He was so fragile, he cried at the slightest thing. Like seeing Lorna or Caitlin, or the postponement of a football match, or poor TV reception. Glass had never known a more miserable bastard. For Lorna, seeing her old man in such a pitiful state was unbearable. Glass knew that and he knew he'd hate to hear himself say, 'And what about your dad?' But he said it anyway.

He thought she might cry too. But her voice stayed firm. She said, 'Do we have a choice?'

'Give me a few days.' He looked at her. 'I'll sort things.'

'What are you going to do?'

'I'm going to stop him.'

'How the hell are you going to do that?'

'That's my problem. Let me deal with it. I'll make sure you're safe.'

'And what about you?' Lorna asked.

'I can look after myself.'

'You think so?'

He was going to reply but she wasn't even looking at him.

She gulped down her wine, filled her glass. 'Another bottle, please.' She smiled at him, lips purple. 'I need to get rat-arsed.'

FRIDAY

'But just supposing,' Glass said to Mafia.

They were in his peter, whispering. When Glass had first come in, he'd asked if he could speak to Mafia in private and Darko had shrugged, put on his headphones and turned up the volume on the radio. Prison privacy. Hardly ideal, but Glass had decided to take the chance. He'd lain awake all last night wondering what Watt was going to do next. And then he'd spent all morning hoping for a call from the cops to let him know they'd visited Watt. He checked with Lorna to see if they'd called her. But they hadn't, of course. It was pretty clear after speaking to the police yesterday that they weren't going to do a damn thing.

There was only one person who could help him now and that was Mafia. Problem was that Mafia wouldn't be likely to put his own brother in danger, so Glass couldn't tell him the truth. And Glass had to hope that Mafia wasn't in the loop. Caesar certainly wouldn't have told him what was going on. Glass crossed his fingers that Watt hadn't either. Because if Mafia did know about it, that meant he hadn't done a thing to persuade his brother to stop harassing Glass's family. And Glass wouldn't be able to deal with that.

Mafia whispered, 'This is called entrapment.'

'I promise you,' Glass whispered back, catching the odd tinny thump from Darko's headphones. 'It's personal. I just want a name.'

'Why should I believe you?'

'Haven't I always been honest with you?'

'Yeah, but that's no reason to suspect it to continue.'

'Come on, Mafia. I just want to know where I can buy a fucking gun.' Glass had made up a story. Told Mafia a version of the truth, leaving out the fact that his wife's stalker was Watt and that Caesar wanted him to smuggle drugs into the prison. Okay, it didn't bear that much relation to the truth. But it was a story. And Mafia seemed to believe it.

'You've been to the police?'

'They won't do anything. Not till it's too late.'

'So,' Mafia said, 'you get a gun. What then?'

'I find this bastard.'

'Aha,' Mafia said. Indicated with a circular motion of his hand that he wanted more.

'And I threaten him.'

'Okay,' Mafia said. 'And then?'

'And then my family's safe.'

Mafia scratched his chin with a thumbnail. 'You think this stalker will scare when you show him your gun?'

'Why not?'

''Cause you won't use it.'

'He won't know that.'

'Yes he will.'

'How?'

'It's written all over your face. Even I can tell you're soft and I'm a blind bastard.'

'I swear,' Glass said, 'I'll use it if I have to.'

'I don't think so.'

'I will. I'll prove it. I'll prove it to . . . to him.'

'How?'

'Kneecap him or something.'

Mafia chuckled. 'That'll certainly stop him. But only for a while. Till he's better. Then he'll come after you. Limp or not.'

'So what would you suggest?'

'If it was me,' Mafia said, 'I'd kill him.'

Glass stared at the toes of his shoes. His face was in there, small and distorted. He wished he saw Mafia's face instead.

Wished he had that kind of bottle, that kind of resolve, that kind of… bravery. Cause it *was* brave. Must be, since however nice it might be to believe that the reason Glass wasn't prepared to kill Watt was a moral choice, the reason Glass was copping out was because he was terrified of the consequences. Prison officers were treated like stoats on the other side of the bars.

Glass said, 'I can't do that. I can't kill someone.'

'Then forget about the gun.'

'I need it. I'd feel safer. Lorna would feel safer. Tell me, for fuck's sake. You want me to get down on my knees?'

'I really don't –'

'Tell me.'

Mafia folded his arms. 'If I do, you'll owe me.'

'Big time,' Glass agreed.

SATURDAY

Mad Will was a chubby guy with an unfashionable hair parting. Glass could see how he'd got his nickname: his teeth and eyes were way too big for the rest of his face, giving him a sort of crazed look.

Before they'd spoken on the phone earlier, Glass hadn't thought about the fact he would have to avoid using his real name. But when Mad Will introduced himself it became obvious Glass would have to make up a name for himself too. So he gave the first one that came into his head.

'Jesse,' Glass said. 'I'm Jesse James.' Well, he was buying a gun.

No reaction from Mad Will.

'Mafia vouched for me,' Glass continued. He'd given Mafia fifty quid and bought him a phone card, asked him to say a few nice words on Glass's behalf. Get things moving. Quickly. *I have an appointment at the Castle Esplanade at four o'clock. With your brother. I'm in a fucking hurry.*

'Mafia vouched for some guy called Glass,' Mad Will said. 'Not for some Jesse James arsehole. You can fuck right off.'

Wasn't the best way to start off, but they'd sorted it out after an awkward minute or so and here they were now, face to face, all nice and friendly, in the sitting room of a flat in a highrise in Niddrie, midday sun streaming through the window, a handgun and a thermos flask of coffee angled on the slightly lop-sided glass table between them, and Mad Will lighting a half-smoked joint.

The room was as sparsely furnished as a prison cell. The whole block of flats was abandoned, most of the windows boarded up. Presumably squatters had moved in at some point, but it didn't look as if anyone lived here now. Glass expected it was used only for conducting illegal transactions. Not just guns either, by the looks of things. Glass could see various pills and powder in bags and packets and bottles and blister packs in the open shoulder bag at Mad Will's feet.

'Regular pharmacy,' Glass said.

'Guns're a sideline,' Mad Will said. 'Drugs are the mainstay. Need anything?'

Glass hesitated. 'I'm fine, thanks.'

'You don't dabble?'

'No.' He used to smoke a fair amount of blow. Everybody did. And he'd done the odd line of coke, and smacked out with some pills at parties. Speaking of smack, he'd even tried that once or twice. Three times, to be precise. Well, if he was being precise, it wasn't smack, but moonrock: a mixture of smack and coke. Only dabbled, though, as Mad Will would put it. Glass was fifteen the first time and his curiosity got the better of his good sense. Second and third times were on consecutive days, a year later, with a ginger-haired girl from Moffat. He left on the third day when she brought out her needle and invited him to feel God caress his insides.

But since he knew he was going to be a dad, he hadn't touched a thing. Mad Will didn't need to know any of that, though.

'Fair enough,' Mad Will said. 'If you change your mind, you know who to call.'

'Thanks,' Glass said again.

In the bedroom, someone was having sex, loudly. Whether it was a couple, or just a guy on his own, was hard to tell. But either way he sounded as if he was enjoying it. If Glass hadn't had an illegal arms deal to negotiate, he might not have been able to focus.

'Nice piece,' Mad Will said.

Glass wondered how to respond but when Mad Will blew out a plume of smoke and picked up the gun Glass realised

Mad Will wasn't referring to what was happening in the bedroom.

'Semi-automatic,' Mad Will said. 'Single action. Full chamber.' He pulled back the slide. 'And there's one racked for you.' He ran his pudgy fingers over the grip. 'Made in Poland, you know. Don't see many of those. What do you want to use it for?'

Something else Glass hadn't expected to answer. Thought he'd been through all that crap with Mafia. What business was it of Mad Will's what the gun was for? Nosy fuckers, these criminals.

Mad Will stared at him, smoke curling from his spliff. 'What's it for, eh?'

What the hell was Glass going to say? Shooting grouse? 'Defence,' he settled on. 'Personal defence.'

'For yourself?' Mad Will asked.

'My wife.'

'Someone giving her a hard time?'

He wasn't going to repeat his conversation with Mafia. Fuck that. Glass had said too much already. He didn't seem to be much of a liar. Who'd have thought lying was so hard? 'No,' he said. 'It's just that there are a lot of nutters out there these days and my work takes me away from home a lot.' He shrugged. 'We'd feel safer if she had a gun in the house.' He shrugged again, wondering how artificial all this shrugging looked. 'In case.'

'Get a dog.'

Glass didn't have to stop and think. He said, 'My daughter's allergic.' That much was true. Any contact with dogs and Caitlin's eyes swelled up and started weeping. Cats were no problem, which is why he kept asking Lorna if they couldn't get Caitlin a kitten. Thing was, Caitlin preferred dogs, in spite of the allergy. Lorna preferred dogs too. Glass was the one who liked cats.

The moans from the bedroom were growing more urgent.

Mad Will said, 'You have a kid?'

Glass swore under his breath. *Done it again.* He said, 'Yeah. What's that got to do with anything?'

'Don't look old enough.'

Glass said nothing.

'You don't want a gun in the house,' Mad Will said. 'Not with a kid around.'

Just Glass's luck. A gun dealer with a conscience. 'I appreciate your concern,' Glass said, 'but it's my responsibility.'

'And it's for your wife, huh?'

Glass nodded. Good God. The guy in the bedroom sounded close to death.

Mad Will wasn't paying the noise any attention. 'If she fires this at someone,' he said, 'she'll probably go to prison.'

'Maybe,' Glass said. 'Depends on the circumstances.'

'Reasonable force, the law states.'

'I know.'

Mad Will topped up his coffee. Silence from the bedroom now. 'Guns aren't reasonable,' Mad Will said. 'By any stretch of the imagination.'

'And even if they were, this baby's illegal.' Glass paused. 'I know.'

'Worth thinking about.'

'Okay.' Glass waited a few seconds. Then: 'I've thought about it. I want to buy the gun. Do you want to sell it to me or not?'

'Absolutely,' Mad Will said. 'But I want to make it abundantly clear that it's not a toy. Owning this baby can change your life.'

'Fine.'

'Well, if you're sure.' Mad Will made a sound with his lips, ran a hand through his straggly hair. 'Gun's yours.'

Finally. Glass laid a pile of notes on the table. 'That's what we discussed on the phone, right?'

Mad Will nodded.

Glass waited.

Mad Will looked at him, pointed towards the door. 'You can see yourself out, eh?'

IN THE CORRIDOR, Glass closed the sitting room door behind him and, as he passed the bedroom where the moaning and grunting had come from, he couldn't help notice that the door was ajar.

Just a slit. But enough of an opening to see the girl's face.

She was gagged. Black mascara-bruised eyes. Tears rolling down her cheeks. She looked into Glass's eyes. If she hadn't, he might have been able to sneak past. But not now. She'd seen him.

His breath quickened as he leaned closer to the door and peered through the crack. Her hands were clamped together behind the bedpost. He couldn't tell if they were tied or cuffed.

A grunt, and then the back of a man's head came into view, a dark shutter falling down over the girl's face. Now was Glass's chance. He could no longer see her eyes pleading with him. Maybe he could get away. Escape.

There was the sound again, though. Grunting. Moaning. But it was different. Slightly higher pitched. As if . . . yeah, a different man. Two of the fuckers? At least.

As if to confirm it, someone said, quietly, 'That's it. Fuck the bitch, Jocky.'

Behind Glass, the sitting room door was closed. Mad Will couldn't see Glass in the corridor. Mad Will thought Glass had left the flat. And the men in the room didn't know he was there. Only the girl knew.

Glass could do this. He should do this. He had to do this. He couldn't do anything else. He backed away from the door until he felt the wall press against his shoulder blades. His mouth was dry. *Do it.* He couldn't just walk in there, hold them at gunpoint while the girl escaped. But if he didn't, she'd continue to get raped by Jocky and whoever else was in the room. He couldn't leave her to be gang-banged. Maybe killed afterwards. Humped and dumped, as the cons would say. Glass couldn't stand here thinking. He thought too much. He had to act.

One step across the corridor, kick the door open, step into the room.

Easy.

Do it.

Done.

Just the two men, thank Christ. The girl was spread-eagled on the bed.

'Get off her,' Glass said to Jocky, gun arm stretched out, shaking. Felt like he might drop the weapon. Didn't trust his grip. He'd seen cops on TV. They used two hands. He did the same, his left hand supporting his right. Felt better.

'What the fuck is this?' the other guy said. He was standing up, naked, making no attempt at modesty.

Jocky's hips only stopped thrusting now. He raised himself and turned his head to the side. He had a moustache, thick and brown. Looked like a walrus. He said, 'Who are you?'

Glass was tempted to say, 'Jesse James.' He licked his upper lip. Tasted salt. 'Get off her,' he said again.

'Christ's sake,' Jocky said. 'Are you for real?'

Glass stepped closer. Thrust his arm out. 'Last chance.'

When he'd stepped into the room Glass hadn't had any idea if he'd be able to pull the trigger if called upon. Now he knew.

He couldn't. No way he could take a human life, no matter how despicable that human was. He just wasn't a killer.

Luckily, Jocky didn't call his bluff. 'Okay,' he said, and moved backwards, slowly, palms raised. Slid away from Glass, off the girl.

Glass caught a flash of her breasts, small and flattened, nipples puffy and wet. He tore his eyes away, watched Jocky, still hard, back off the bed. A big guy. Ridiculously big.

'Take off the gag,' Glass told him and wiped his forehead. It was hot in here. Stank of sweat and seafood. He kept his eyes off the girl. Away from her body.

Jocky bent over, muttered something to the girl and untied the gag.

The girl shook her head hard, spat. 'The fuck's going on?' she said to Glass. 'You can't just fucking waltz in here like you own the place.'

'I . . .' Glass said, staring at her breasts.

'You fucking arsehole,' she said. 'Untie me so I can shove that fucking gun up your stupid fucking arse.'

This was hardly the reaction Glass had expected. She didn't seem upset. Well, she *was* upset. But with Glass, not with the guys who'd been raping her. And she didn't appear to be hurt.

Something was wrong here.

Glass didn't get it. It was as if he'd walked into another world, one where nothing made sense.

She didn't sound like she'd been crying, but he could see from her face that she had been. Those were tear streaks. Weren't they? What else could they be? Trickles of sweat?

'Thank fuck, Will,' the girl said.

Glass felt a tap on his shoulder and turned to see Mad Will right behind him.

'You said you were leaving,' Mad Will said.

'I thought . . .' Glass said. 'I thought she was . . .' And then he saw the tripod in the corner of the room, the camera perched on top. Oh, fuck.

He'd stepped onto the set of a fucking porno shoot.

He lowered his arm. 'I'm sorry,' he said. 'Shit, I'm really sorry.'

Jocky said, 'Can we use this?'

'Dunno,' the other guy said. 'I doubt it.'

'Fuck you,' the girl shouted at Glass. 'Now I have to do all that again.' She swivelled on the bed, arms still stretched behind her, and swung her foot at him. She missed by a distance. 'You think I like this? You want to get fucked for a living?'

Glass stepped back. He had no answer for her.

Mad Will said, 'You're lucky she's still tied up. Cause even with the gun, I wouldn't fancy your chances.'

'I'm sorry,' Glass said again. 'I'm really –'

'Yeah, yeah,' the girl said. 'Fucking twat.'

'You better go,' Mad Will said. 'I'll see you out.'

THE GIRL CALLS him a twat and Mad Will says, 'You better give me that.' He looks at the gun in Glass's hand.

Glass says, 'I paid for it.'

'Here,' Mad Will says, sticking his hand into his pocket, pulling out a wad of notes. 'A full refund.'

'But I need it,' Glass says. 'You can't take it back.'

'Give,' Mad Will says.

Glass looks around, at the girl, at her breasts, at the two naked men, back at Mad Will. 'No,' he says.

Mad Will says, 'I asked nicely once. I won't ask nicely twice.' He raises his eyebrows.

Glass doesn't know what to do.

Mad Will says, 'I warned you.' He grabs the barrel of the gun.

Glass stares at him, amazed at what Mad Will has just done. Why isn't he scared? Is it really so obvious Glass won't shoot him?

'I'll pull the trigger,' Glass says.

'Go on then.'

Glass really wants to, but knows he can't. Damn, though, it would be something to surprise Mad Will. Wipe that buck-toothed smile right off his face.

But Glass isn't a killer.

Fuck it. We all change, all the time.

Glass pulls the trigger.

The joint drops from Mad Will's mouth and he falls back onto the bed.

The girl screams.

Jocky says, 'Shit.'

Glass lets his grip on the gun loosen. Drops the gun.

The girl's still screaming.

GLASS TELLS MAD Will he'll pull the trigger.

'Go on then.'

Glass really wants to, but knows he can't. Damn, though, it would be something to surprise Mad Will. Wipe that buck-toothed smile right off his face.

But Glass isn't a killer.

Mad Will takes the gun away. 'Thanks,' he says.

'How did you know?' Glass says. 'I could have shot you. You couldn't have known.'

Mad Will says, 'You ain't going to shoot anybody unless you turn off the safety first.' He thumbs a lever on the side of the gun. 'Like that.' Points the gun at Glass. 'See?'

Glass swallows, nods.

'Right,' Mad Will says. 'What are we going to do with you?' He looks around. 'Any suggestions, guys?'

THEY MAKE GLASS strip. He stands in his underwear.

He feels how the inmates must feel when an officer searches them. He hears Fox saying, 'Lift your balls up. Good. Bend over. Spread your cheeks.'

At least they haven't made him do that. But they don't know he's a prison officer. Mafia wouldn't have told Mad Will. Glass hopes not, anyway.

Jocky has moved over to the camera. He's recording this.

'The rest,' Mad Will says to Glass.

Glass shakes his head. His knees are trembling.

'Need a hand?' The girl approaches him. Presses her face right up to his. Presses her chest against his.

He feels her warmth. Smells her. She smells like Ross.

She presses her hand against his crotch. Rubs. 'Not much happening down there,' she says.

'Not going to either,' Glass says, sure of himself.

'We'll see.' She slides her fingers down the front of his Y's.

He stares at her. Wills himself not to feel anything. A twitch, though. Something stirring. He places his hands on her shoulders, fingers instantly oily. He pushes her away.

She thumps onto the bed, legs splayed. He gets an eyeful.

'Hey,' Mad Will says to him. 'That's not nice. Think we'll have to tie you up.'

'Come on,' Glass says. 'This is crazy.'

Doesn't get much further cause the girl springs off the bed and slaps him. 'That's for fucking pushing me.' She faces Mad

Will. 'Do what you want with him. I don't want to touch him again. He makes my skin crawl.'

She leaves the room, grabbing a dressing gown off a hook on the back of the door, bare feet slapping on the floor.

Jocky says, 'You up for some boy-on-boy, Brad?'

The other guy, Brad, looks at Glass, gaze dwelling on his underpants. 'Fuck, no,' he says, scratching his stubble.

'Will?'

Mad Will looks at Glass, takes a toke on his joint. 'Fuck, no.'

'Me neither.'

Mad Will says, 'Well, Glass. Looks like none of us fancy you.'

Will they let him go? Can it be that simple? 'That mean I can get dressed now?' he asks.

'Suppose so.'

'Can I have the gun?'

Mad Will chuckles.

'I need it,' Glass says.

'Suck my fat dick,' Mad Will says.

'YEAH, YEAH,' THE girl said. 'Fucking twat.'

'You better go,' Mad Will said. 'I'll see you out.'

Glass knew he was lucky to be getting away so easily. He turned, half expecting Mad Will to hit him over the head with a hidden cosh. But he behaved like a gentleman. Showed Glass to the door, opened it for him, said goodbye.

Sometimes Glass's imagination got the better of him. He'd run through all those possibilities and they'd all seemed equally real. Not real in his head, but as if they were actually happening.

He was okay now, though. Facts were, he'd interrupted a porn shoot, pulled a gun on them, and he was getting away with nothing more than being called a fucking twat.

Which he was.

He looked at the gun in his hand. *That* was real enough.

IN THE CAR, Glass turned on the radio, tuned into the weirdest shit he could find. Some atonal classical piece with cellos and violins that sounded like they were crying together. Did a pretty good job of summing up how he felt.

He wouldn't need to fire the gun when he met Watt a couple of hours from now. Just point it at him, show the fucker he was serious.

Like with the porn stars back at Mad Will's?

Shut up.

What he'd said to Mad Will was close to the truth. He wanted the gun to protect Lorna. But he didn't want her to have it. Protecting his family was *his* job.

The girl back at Mad Will's was different. She wasn't family. If she was, he wouldn't have hesitated to pull the trigger.

Yeah, you would.

Shut up. Stop interrupting.

Probably just as well under the circumstances.

Watt had picked a public venue for their meeting. Deliberate, no doubt. But if he was intent on handing over drugs, they'd have to go somewhere else. Wasn't something that could be done in the open. Right?

Some time later, Glass pulled into his driveway. Caitlin was at the window, waving.

'WHAT'S MY BABYGIRL been up to?' he asked Caitlin once he was inside.

The table was littered with colouring books and the TV was on. There was no sign of Lorna.

'Drawing,' Caitlin said. 'Stickering.'

'And watching your video?'

'*Beauty and the Beast.*' She clapped her hands. A blue crayon flew out. 'Oops-a-daisy.'

'You're so lazy.'

'I'm so lazy!'

Glass bent down to pick it up. Handed it to her.

'Thank you, Daddy.'

'My pleasure, sweetheart. Do I get a kiss?'

'Yes!' She walked over to him, book in hand. 'Look.'

'Very pretty,' he said. 'You did that all by yourself?'

'Aha,' she said. 'And look.' She turned the page.

'That's lovely,' he said. 'Really beautiful. Where's my kiss?'

He lifted her into his arms and she smacked her lips against his and said, 'Mwa.'

He tasted Ribena. His lips were sticky.

'Where's Mummy?' he said.

'In the kitchen,' Caitlin said. 'She was thirsty.'

LORNA WAS STARING at the wall, fingers curled round a wine glass, an empty bottle on the table in front of her. She didn't look up.

'Daddy's home,' Caitlin said, wriggling in Glass's arms.

'That's nice.' Lorna didn't even smile.

Glass put Caitlin down. 'You go back and watch TV,' he said.

'Want to stay here,' Caitlin said.

'You're going to miss the best bit.' He put on his actor's voice, said, '*He's no monster, Gaston.*'

'*You are,*' Caitlin shrieked.

'No, you are,' he said.

'*You,* Daddy. Mummy, tell him!'

Lorna said, voice flat, 'You're right. Daddy's a monster.'

'See?' Caitlin said. 'You're the monster.'

'Off you go,' Lorna said to Caitlin. She smiled this time.

'Watch it too,' Caitlin said.

'We'll be through in a minute,' Glass said.

She pulled a face. 'Promise?'

'Promise.'

Once she'd gone, Lorna's smile vanished.

Glass took a seat opposite her.

'You okay?' he said.

She shrugged. She didn't look okay. She got up, went to the wine rack, pulled out another bottle. Grabbed the corkscrew off the work surface where it lay next to a slab of meat and a cleaver on the chopping board, and returned to the table.

'Want a glass, Glass?' she said.

Another old joke. And one that wasn't funny the first time.

'Well, do you?'

He'd have shaken his head but she wasn't looking at him, focusing instead on opening the bottle. 'No, thanks.'

She burped. 'So where the fuck were you?'

'When?'

'For fuck's sake,' she said. '"When?" he asks. Just now.'

She was drunk. And pissed off. Bad combination.

'When I was out?' he asked. 'I told you. Doing a spot of shopping.'

The cork popped. 'A spot.' She filled her glass. 'Of shopping.' Turned to look at him. 'For what?'

'Just . . . things.'

'And where are those "things"?'

'Lorna, what's wrong?'

'Did I say something was wrong?'

'Don't be like this.'

She stared at him. 'What am I being like?'

'You're drinking,' he said. 'Too much.'

'You're lying to me,' she said. 'That's a fucking good reason to drink too much.'

'I can't tell you where I was,' he said.

'Oh,' she said, 'that's a fucking shame.'

'I'm sorry.'

'I bet. I have to trust you, is that right?'

'Yes.'

'And why should I do that?'

'Because I have your welfare at heart. Yours and Caitlin's.'

'Our welfare? Jesus, you're something else.' She pinged a fingernail off her wineglass. 'So you're not seeing someone?'

Where the fuck had that come from? 'Why would I do that?'

'I don't know,' she said. 'I was hoping you'd tell me.'

'What's going on?'

'You're a bastard.'

'I don't know what the fuck you're talking about.' He placed his hand on hers.

She pulled away. 'So you don't know anything about some bondage session? A naked girl, tied to a bed, gagged? Sound familiar?'

Jesus Christ! How the hell had she found out about that?

'Fun, was it? You've never asked to do that with me. I never knew it was your thing. Is that what you like, then?'

'No, it's not,' he said. 'I don't want to do that.'

'Good,' she said. She burped again. 'Wouldn't let you anyway. You're a fuck. A fucking fuck. Fucker.'

'Keep your voice down.'

'Don't tell me to keep my fucking voice down. I'm not the one who's been fucking around.' She took a breath. 'Only David and you can't hold that against me for ever.'

'I don't.' He didn't.

'David was a mistake.'

'I know.'

'So why are you fucking around?'

'It wasn't like that.'

'Ah,' she said, 'not denying it any more?' She poured herself another glass. 'It's just me you don't want to do it with. She pretty, is she? Young? Slim? Big tits? Nice tight fanny, not like the bucket Caitlin left me with?'

'Don't be gross.'

'Jesus shit, you're so fucking prissy.'

'You're so fucking drunk.'

'Fucking right I am. But I'm not drunk enough.'

'I went to visit someone,' he told her.

'Who?'

'Doesn't matter. Point is, the girl was already there.'

'Like shite.'

'She was, Lorna. Listen to me.'

'You'll just lie. Lie, lie, lie.'

'Hear me out. Just for a second.'

She ran her tongue over her teeth. 'Go on then.'

He explained about finding the bedroom door open, the girl looking like she was being raped. 'I thought I was helping.'

'You didn't touch her?'

'No.'

'Expect me to believe that?'

'What do you think happened? Really?'

She was quiet. 'I don't know.'

He tried placing his hand on hers again. This time she didn't pull away. 'Who told you?' he asked.

She gulped more wine down. '*He* did.'

'Who?'

'Him.' She screamed. '*Him.*'

Glass looked at the wine bottle. It was tempting to knock back a glass or two. Really tempting. 'Watt?'

She nodded. Repeated his name.

How did Watt know where he'd been? And even if the bastard had been following him, how would he know about the girl?

Glass asked, 'What did he say?'

'Said you were busy . . . fucking some little tart. Said he thought I should know what my husband was like.'

What a bastard.

'I told him he was talking shit,' she said. 'You wouldn't do that, I said. He asked me if I knew where you were. I said I did, but I didn't. And I think he knew.'

She knocked her glass over. Might have been deliberate. It hit the table and rolled in an arc. Didn't break. No spillage. She'd already emptied it. She left it there.

Glass set it upright.

Lorna continued: 'He said it was on video, you and the slut. Said he'd send me proof. In a brown jiffy bag.'

Glass kept his voice even. 'It's a lie.'

'Why would he lie?'

Glass wasn't sure, but he could guess. 'He's messing with us.'

'Is he?'

'Believe it. There's no video. There's nothing for him to send.' He paused. 'It's a lie,' he said again. 'You'll see.'

She dragged her glass towards her. 'I don't know what to believe.'

'I don't understand,' he said. 'Why don't you believe me? I've never given you any reason to think I'd be unfaithful to you.'

'Blame me, that's right.'

'I'm not.'

'Well, it sounds like it. I'm the one who was unfaithful. Just keep reminding me of it, why don't you?' She refilled her glass. 'What were you doing there?'

He looked at his hand. Rubbed his thumb over his knuckles. 'Okay,' he said. 'If you must know.' He took the gun out of his pocket, laid it in front of him.

She moved back in her seat. 'Is that real?' she asked.

'Yeah,' he said. 'That's my shopping. That's what I was buying.'

'Get it out of here.'

'It won't bite.'

'Get it the fuck out of here.'

'Okay.' He picked it up, put it back in his pocket. 'Better?'

'No,' she said, on her feet. 'I want that out of here. Out of the fucking house.'

'It's for our protection.'

'I don't give a shit,' she said. 'Get it out of here.'

'You believe me about the girl?'

'Get that away from here or I'll call the police.'

He laughed. 'Come on, you're drunk.'

'You think that'll make me *less* likely to do it?'

'Okay,' he said. 'I have to go out anyway. I'm meeting Watt.'

'With that?' she said, indicating his pocket.

'Yeah,' he said. 'I don't think he'll be bothering us any longer.'

'Don't,' she said.

'It's just to scare him,' he said.

'Don't go.'

'I work with criminals every day,' Glass said. 'Watt's just another one. I'll be fine.'

'What about me?' she asked. 'And Caitlin?'

'I won't be long,' he told her. 'You'll be fine too. I'm making sure of that.' He really wanted to believe it. He leaned towards her. Kissed her cheek. Stepped back.

She looked at him, eyes shiny. 'I can't live like this.'

That was just the drink talking.

'Nick,' she said. 'I'm sorry about David.'

'I know you are,' he said. David. Some guy she'd slept with twice about six months ago. Glass didn't even know his last name. It was over, she said. But clearly she'd never managed to get him out of her mind. Another good reason for them to stay in Edinburgh. Go back to Dunfermline and there was every chance it would all start up again. Glass didn't think he'd recover a second time.

He walked over to the worktop, dropped the cleaver into the sink, put the meat on a plate and wrapped cling film over it.

'I was going to make stew,' Lorna said, 'but then he phoned.'

'Don't worry about it,' Glass said. 'I'll bring some pizza back with me.'

WHEN FOUR O'CLOCK came, Glass was waiting by the north wall of the Castle Esplanade looking out across the Firth of Forth.

Tourists spilled out from the Castle in regular spurts. They milled about, gibbering in languages Glass didn't understand, pointing, exclaiming, crossing from one side of the Esplanade to the other, taking in the scenery, snapping photos.

A solitary fat cloud squatted in the sky. Hardly a breath of wind. Stunning views. In fact it was fucking beautiful.

But it wasn't what Glass wanted. The weather was wrong. It ought to be stormy. Thunder and lightning. Lashing rain. Zero visibility. An atonal kind of weather, dissonant clouds, clashing light and dark.

Wasn't like that, though. The sun was lower in the sky but still strong. He felt his forehead prickle and knew he'd burned a little. Fair skin. Never tanned. Pain in the arse that he'd had to wear a jacket.

'Good to see you again,' a voice behind him said.

Sounded familiar.

Hand in his pocket, Glass touched the warmed-up gun, traced along the ribbed grip till he touched the base of the magazine, smooth as Caitlin's elbow.

Could he go through with it? He had to. No choice. With a family of Japanese tourists right next to him? Course not. Lead the bastard to a secluded spot. Show him the gun. Freak him out. Job done.

Glass turned. Immediately he had his explanation as to how Watt knew what had happened at Mad Will's flat.

'If that's a gun in your pocket,' Watt said, 'I hope you'll use it. Don't want you fannying about like earlier.'

Watt looked different with his clothes on and, somehow, Glass doubted that his real first name was Brad. Maybe that wasn't even his porn name. But here he was. From bedroom to Castle. Having seen Glass make a fool of himself just a short time ago.

What the hell had Mafia's brother been doing at Mad Will's? Well, Glass knew the answer to that. He was making a porno. And, actually, it wasn't all that surprising that Watt and Mafia would know the same people. They'd both run with Caesar. Watt still did. And Mad Will was probably one of Caesar's suppliers. The signs were all there. Glass was a fucking idiot. He had to learn to pay attention, not let his mind drift all over the place.

'Take your hand out of your pocket,' Watt said.

'I'll use the gun,' Glass said, looking at the ground.

'Wasted your money on it. You've got no balls.'

'This is different.' Glass wanted to take the gun out, show him just how big his balls were. He noticed Watt was dressed for colder weather too. Brown suede jacket, not unlike one Glass had at home. Didn't match the combat trousers and boots. 'Why did you tell Lorna I'd slept with that girl?'

Watt laughed. 'Just wanted to see how things were between you. I don't think she loves you, you know. Too quick to believe you'd cheat on her.'

'She didn't believe you for a minute.'

'That what she said?' Watt grinned. 'She's lying to you.'

'I should kill you.'

'Why don't you?' Watt planted his feet firmly, folded his arms. 'Go on. Shoot me. See if you can.'

'What do you mean? I can't shoot you here.'

'So where then? Tell me and we'll go there. I'll make it easy for you.'

Glass didn't know what he could say to be taken seriously. 'I will shoot you.' He hoped he sounded convincing. 'You better believe it.'

'Oh, my.' Watt unfolded his arms. 'Look, let's stop fucking about. Forget about your new toy. Just take the gear into the Hilton like Caesar wants. Piss easy.'

Glass shook his head. 'I can't do that.'

'But you can shoot me? You're all messed up, Nick.'

'You think?'

'Officers don't get searched, so I'm told. There's no risk for you.'

'Course there's a risk,' Glass said. 'We can get searched any time. Your information's wrong.'

Watt stared at him.

Glass squeezed the gun tighter. There *was* a fucking risk. What did this prick know? Rub-downs of officers were rare, but they did happen. It was well within the prison authorities' rights.

Anyway, Glass wasn't shoving anything up his arse.

'All right,' Watt said. 'Maybe there is a risk. But it's hardly one that bears comparison with what'll happen to you if you shoot me. And if you shoot me, you'll get caught. No doubt about it. You had those nice policemen pay me a visit. To be honest, I'm pissed off at you for that.'

'Great,' Glass said. That was good to know. Felt like a small victory and any kind of victory was welcome at the moment.

'Not really. Pretty stupid of you, in fact. Who are they going to suspect now if I turn up dead?'

Glass said, 'How do I know you won't keep this up? How do I know that if I smuggle the dope in, that'll be an end to it?'

'You don't. But I'm just doing what Caesar asked me to do. Once the job's done, I'm out of your face. You'll never see me again.'

'Why should I believe that?'

''Cause I don't work for free,' Watt said. 'Got my standards. No matter how pleasant the work.'

Glass hesitated. It was possible Watt was telling the truth. 'If I do this, you'll leave Lorna and Caitlin alone?'

'You have my word,' Watt said. 'Scout's honour.'

Right. 'Swear on your brother's life.'

Watt's face tightened. 'What does he have to do with this?'

'Swear on Mafia's life.'

Watt shrugged. Then he laughed. 'Okay,' he said. 'If that makes a difference to you.'

'Say it.'

'I swear.'

'If you're lying,' Glass said, 'I'll kill you. I promise. And I'll walk right into the police station afterwards and hand myself in.'

'Fine,' Watt said. 'Now, if the melodrama's over, can I give you the merchandise?'

And contrary to Glass's expectations, Watt took a package out of his jacket pocket and handed it to him. Simple as that. In broad daylight and in full view of dozens of people.

Glass took it. The package was wrapped in gold paper like a box of chocolates. There was an envelope sellotaped to the outside. 'This is it?' he said.

'That's it,' Watt said.

'Bit bulky.'

Watt sighed. 'Open it when you get home.' He turned, said, 'And be careful with that gun, now. Don't want to have an accident.'

Glass winced as a sharp pain struck him from behind. Felt like something sharp had slammed into his shoulder. But there was nothing there.

Watt winked.

Glass took his hand out of his pocket, rubbed his shoulder. Just a nerve playing up, muscle spasm, something like that.

HALF ELEVEN, GLASS was watching television alone.

'Hope curry's okay,' he had said to Lorna when he returned. 'Got a *korma* for Caitlin. Didn't fancy pizza.'

'Anything to soak up the booze. How did it go?'

Glass told her the cops had visited Watt. 'He got the message.'

'That's it? No need for us to worry?'

'None at all. He won't bother us again.'

'And you got rid of that gun?'

'Dropped it down a drain.' He was getting better at lying. He'd hidden the gun inside an old chocolate biscuit tin at the bottom of a tea chest in the garage.

'Give me a hug.' She leaned towards him.

He smelled her. Sour wine mixed with something sweeter. He put his arms round her. She was warm.

She said, 'I'm sorry about earlier.'

'That's okay,' he said.

Caitlin appeared in the doorway.

'Hi, baby,' Lorna said. 'Come and join us.'

Caitlin padded across the room, her favourite teddy, Mo, in her hand. She stretched her arms wide, flung herself at Glass and Lorna hard enough to make Lorna take a side step.

'Hey,' Lorna said. 'You're knocking me off my feet.'

'It was Mo,' Caitlin said and giggled. She pressed her cheek against Glass's thigh. 'Are you happy now?' she said.

'Yes, babygirl,' Glass said. 'We're happy now.'

A few hours later, Glass wasn't sure about being happy, though. He got up, switched off the TV. Had to get ready for work in the morning.

In the kitchen he made himself a couple of cheese sandwiches. Wrapped them in foil. Put them in a Tupperware container.

Then he popped into the garage. Got Watt's package out of the boot of the car. He unstuck the envelope from the outside and opened it. A bunch of twenty-pound notes. He counted them. Three hundred quid. Paying him was Caesar's idea of a joke. Fuck him.

He put the money in his wallet for now. Opened the box.

It was full of bags of brown powder. A couple of dozen of them.

He started to salivate. It was like he was starving and the

bags contained food. His belly ached with a hollowness that needed filling and the solution was right in front of him.

'*Take some. It'll stop the ache.*'

He shook his head, swallowed.

'*Take some. It'll stop all aches.*'

'I don't think so,' he said aloud, hands shaking.

'*Don't you want to?*'

'Why would I?' he said, and bundled the bags into two piles of six. Wrapped them in foil. Added them to his lunchbox. 'Why would I?' he asked again.

'*When you smoke it, it takes seven seconds to hit your brain. Then God caresses you from the inside.*'

'I don't want to touch it.'

'*Takes away your troubles, your anxieties. Makes you feel safe, protected.*'

'I'd rather feel like this.'

'*A warm intense glow in the pit of your stomach. Pleasure radiating throughout your body.*'

'Not me. No.'

'*You feel it?*'

He felt it.

Maybe a little toke now wouldn't hurt. He could use all the help he could get.

SUNDAY

He hated having to work on Sundays. Only done one so far, but the time had passed even more slowly than usual. All he could think of was how much he'd rather be at home. Even with the new alarm installed and locks on the windows and chains on the doors, he didn't like leaving Lorna and Caitlin alone. But he consoled himself with the thought that Watt no longer had a reason to go anywhere near them.

No reason at all, now that Glass was taking the stash of heroin into the Hilton.

When he arrived at reception, he said hi to the guys.

Crogan, one of the older and friendlier officers, said, 'You're early. Don't want to be too keen, you know.'

Glass said, 'Didn't realise how empty the roads would be.'

Crogan grunted. 'Sunday traffic.'

A trustee, Donald Moore, was on duty, bringing cups of tea for Crogan and another officer, Aitken. 'Want one?' he asked Glass.

Glass shook his head. He didn't want to hang around here. Certainly didn't want to talk to the trustee. Some of them could be bigger sticklers than the officers. Wanted to do their jobs *right*. Not that there was much to be a stickler about.

'Go on,' Crogan said. 'Have a cup of tea. Not as if you don't have time.' He offered Glass his mug.

'Milk and sugar?' Glass said.

'Your lucky day.'

Glass took the mug, nodded his thanks to Crogan and Moore. The trustee looked at Crogan and the look Crogan returned was enough to send Moore off to get another mug.

This was just what Glass did not need. He wanted to get through the metal detector and get con-side as soon as he could. Get it over with.

Normally, he just walked through and headed for the locker room. Nothing to it. He looked guilty, though. He knew he did. He expected Crogan and Aitken could see him sweating. The tea was piping hot, making it worse. His armpits were drenched. He could feel the rough, cold fabric of his shirt rubbing against him. Felt a dampness at his hairline. He clutched his bag tight. Same bag he always took in. Same bag they could check if they wanted but they never did. Not yet, anyway.

Another sip. Spilled some on his chin. Pretended it wasn't there. Let it itch until it evaporated.

All they'd find would be sandwiches.

It'd be fine.

'You okay?' Crogan asked.

'Fine,' Glass said. *Shit. Crogan knew.*

'Got a drop of tea there.' Crogan pointed at his face.

'Thanks.' Glass wiped his chin with the back of his hand. 'Yeah, I'm fine. Couldn't be better.'

'The thought of working with some of those fucks,' Aitken said. 'It's enough to make anyone feel like shite.'

Glass wasn't sure who Aitken was referring to: the officers or the cons. But he appreciated the sentiment. 'I feel fine,' he said again.

'Fox'll get his comeuppance,' Crogan said.

Nobody liked Fox. Well, nobody apart from Ross. 'Not a fan of his?' Glass said.

Crogan lowered his voice. 'Between you and me. And Aitken.' The trustee returned, handed Crogan a steaming mug. 'And Moore here. Between us, what Fox needs is a fucking good hiding.'

'Aye,' Moore said. 'That cunt needs to get his cunt kicked in.'

'Exactly,' Crogan said. 'Almost as bad as Caesar.'

Glass went cold in the forehead. Why was Crogan talking about Caesar? Was it just a coincidence? Or did he know something? 'You had a run-in with Caesar?'

Crogan laughed. 'One or two. Work here long enough, you'll have a run-in with him.' He sighed. 'All in the past now, though. Stuck here in the gatehouse till I retire. Never have to see the fucker again. And that makes me very fucking happy.'

He sounded genuine. Maybe he was just letting off steam. Didn't look like he was going to push the topic anyway.

'I really better go,' Glass said, and handed his mug to Moore.

'You've only had a couple of sips,' Crogan said.

Glass looked at his watch. 'Got to take a few minutes to psyche myself up.'

'Right,' Crogan said. 'No problem. Stop by any time for a chat, though, you hear?'

Glass stood, stepped forward, and cleared the metal detector, legs shaking.

Just like any other day.

They didn't suspect him. He was too normal, too boring, far too unadventurous to be a drugs mule. Too fucking *scared* to be a drugs mule.

It was only once he was in the locker room that he breathed normally again.

He'd thought Crogan had known something was up there for a minute, thought he'd been set up. That Caesar had arranged all this just to get Glass sacked. But, no, Caesar had better things to do. And he wanted his drugs.

No one else was in the locker room yet. Still early for the next shift.

Glass changed quickly, put on his uniform. Distributed the foil-wrapped heroin bundles among his various pockets. Felt bulky, but he doubted anyone would notice. He took the wad of notes out of his wallet, crammed it in his pocket.

He was ready. There was no way back now.

GLASS DIDN'T WANT to walk straight into Caesar's cell. He might be doing something indecent with Jasmine again. But Glass couldn't knock. So he looked through the Judas window. Saw Caesar on his bed. Alone. Jasmine was in the upper bunk. Both of them were staring right at him as if they knew he was on the other side of the door.

Glass put his key in the lock, opened the cell door.

Found Caesar on his feet. 'Well?'

Glass emptied his pockets and tossed the foil parcels onto the desk.

Caesar picked one up, grinned as he unwrapped it.

'Hiya!' Jasmine leaned over the edge of her bunk. 'Oh, honey, Officer Glass, I'm so happy I could suck you off.'

'Don't let his new reputation get to you, bitch,' Caesar said.

Glass looked at him.

'Heard you fucked Mafia in the Digger,' Caesar explained.

'Oh, Officer,' Jasmine said, pouting.

Glass took the notes out of his pocket. Tossed them at Caesar. 'I don't want your fucking money.'

Caesar said, 'Up to you. But I suppose you should pay for what you took.'

Glass had redistributed the bags. No way Caesar could have noticed, not without weighing the contents. 'I didn't take anything.'

'It's light.'

'That's all I got.'

'That so?' Caesar said. 'You want a little for yourself, I don't mind. Especially if you don't want paid. But don't think you can steal from me. If I hear of you dealing –'

'I'd never –'

'That's right. Never. And one more thing,' Caesar said. 'Next pick-up will be a week on Tuesday. Same place. Same time.'

'No way,' Glass said. 'I can't.'

'You're on nights that week. Course you can. Should be even easier.'

LATER, DURING THE hour of free association after dinner, Mafia walked towards Glass outside the TV room.

'That you, Officer Glass?' he said.

Sometimes Glass thought Mafia had to be putting it on. Wasn't possible that somebody could be so blind, especially with glasses on. But someone must have seen Mafia's medical records before he was authorised to wear shades 24/7.

'It's me, yeah,' Glass said.

Mafia muttered, 'Can you spare a few minutes?'

'What is it?'

'Just want to talk,' he said.

'Okay,' Glass said. 'Your peter?'

'Nah, folk'll see us. They'll gossip. They gossip enough. Where can we go for a bit of privacy?'

'This is a prison,' Glass said. 'It's not designed for privacy.'

'Thanks for pointing that out,' Mafia said. 'An expert already and you've only been here . . . six weeks?'

'Seven.'

'Forgive me. Extra week makes all the difference.'

'I know where we can go.' Glass started to walk away and

Mafia followed, standing on Glass's heel. He apologised but Glass had the feeling it was deliberate.

THE EDUCATION BLOCK consisted of four classrooms. Today, only one was occupied.

Glass led Mafia along to the room at the end. He swung his key chain. Fiddled around for the right key. Unlocked it.

Inside, a cold breeze was blowing into the room. The windows were open but barred, like all the windows in the prison.

Glass went over, closed one window, then the other.

On the whiteboard, someone had scribbled some mathematical equations that meant nothing to Glass. He'd always preferred English. He'd been good at English. Enjoyed words. He'd been planning on studying English at university. Or maybe music. If he'd practised his guitar a bit more.

Mafia took off his shades.

Glass said, 'What's this about?'

Mafia said, 'Come over here, I can't see you.' Glass walked towards him. Stopped a couple of feet in front of him.

Mafia said, 'You mind?' He reached out a hand, touched Glass's chin.

It felt odd, this man's fingers touching his face, but Glass stood where he was, watching Mafia's eyes dart about in their sockets.

Mafia traced his jawline, then moved his hand over Glass's cheek.

Then:

WHAM.

Out of nowhere.

Glass reeled backwards, the taste of blood in his mouth. He spun off the edge of a desk, almost went down. Felt like he'd bitten his tongue, but the blood was coming from his lower lip. It was swelling already, tasted raw. He braced himself for another whack, but Mafia hadn't moved.

'I can't let that pass,' Glass said. Mafia was a stupid fuck. Why the hell had he done that? Glass really couldn't let it pass. Letting an inmate hit him without reporting it wasn't possible. Not even if that inmate was Mafia. And even if it was, after what Mafia had just done, Glass didn't care. Mafia deserved whatever was coming to him. What the fuck was wrong with him?

Mafia said, 'You can let it pass if you want.'

'You're going on report,' Glass said. 'They'll ghost you out of here.'

'Gosh,' Mafia said. 'Got all the slang now, haven't you?' He paused to shake his head. 'Maybe the governor will be interested to know you're bringing drugs in for Caesar.'

Cold crept out of the air and into Glass's body. The backs of his legs first, behind his knees, then up his legs and into his spine until he could feel it in the back of his neck. 'I can't believe Caesar told you,' he said. He spat out a mouthful of blood. A string of it stuck to his upper lip. He wiped it with the back of his hand.

'He didn't.'

'Who, then?'

Mafia rubbed his knuckles. 'My fuck-up of a little brother. Called me up, special.'

Watt was a total bastard. Why couldn't the fucker leave him alone?

Glass said, 'Well maybe he explained what *he's* been doing.'

'I don't care.'

'Your brother's been threatening me.'

'I don't care. He's not my responsibility.'

'Threatening my family.'

Mafia shouted, 'I don't fucking care.'

'Well, I fucking do,' Glass shouted back.

'You can't do it,' Mafia said.

'It's done.'

'Then don't do it again.'

'What choice do I have? Your brother will hurt my wife. Or, God forbid, Caitlin.'

Mafia said nothing.

'He will, won't he?' Glass said. 'He's not bluffing.'

Mafia shrugged.

'He's your brother,' Glass said. 'Tell me I'm right. I won't put my family at risk.'

Mafia still didn't speak.

'Why's it so hard? Tell me the truth.'

'That's why you got the gun?'

Glass didn't answer.

Mafia said, 'Let's go.'

'I thought so.' Glass nodded. 'Just one last thing.'

'Yeah?' Mafia turned and Glass caught him a beauty on the jaw.

PART TWO
Confabulation
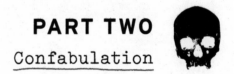

MONDAY, 16 November 1992

'Nothing you'd like to talk about?'

John Riddell still had that strange milky smell about him. And it was a little sour. Glass reminded himself that Riddell was the sort of man who didn't have a single photo to put on his desk. Just that empty frame.

Glass said, 'I've no more to say now than I did last time I was here.'

'Tell me about your job.'

'What do you mean?'

Riddell scratched his goatee. 'You happier with it?'

'It's fine.'

'But are you happy doing it?'

Glass leaned back in his chair. 'If I wasn't, what difference would it make?'

Riddell bent forward. 'I don't follow you.'

'I have to work here, happy or unhappy.'

Riddell tapped the rubber end of his pencil on his notepad. No pen today. Maybe he was making too many mistakes. 'If you spoke to me about what was making you unhappy, maybe it'd help.'

'I didn't say I was unhappy.'

'You asked —'

'— what difference it would make,' Glass said. 'I was speculating.'

Riddell drummed his pencil on the desk. 'So you like the job?'

'I've had better.'

Glint of interest in Riddell's eye. 'Like what?'

'Worked in a cinema once. Didn't enjoy having to push the food and drink, but that's where they make all the money. Free films, though. That was good. I like films.'

'So why did you leave?'

And psychiatrists were supposed to be bright. 'Money,' Glass said. 'We don't get paid that much here, but it's a damn sight more than retail.'

'Apart from the cinema, you ever worked anywhere else?'

Of course he had. But for a moment, he couldn't remember where. He felt hot all of a sudden and was sure it was connected. Trying to remember was making him feel sick. And then just as suddenly, he was okay. The bakery. Where he met Lorna. But he didn't want to share that with Riddell.

'No,' Glass said. 'I haven't had any other jobs.'

Riddell seemed pleased he'd got a response, though. Pushed for more. 'Would you say you've settled in now?'

Glass shrugged. 'I know the ropes.'

'And your colleagues?'

'Most of them seem to know the ropes too.'

'No, I meant, how are you getting on with them?'

'Look,' Glass said, 'the majority of them are arseholes. I know that. You know that. They know that. But there's no point me sitting here talking to you about it.'

'Why not?'

'Because it won't stop them being arseholes.'

Riddell let that hang for a while. Then he said, 'What have they done?'

'What do you mean?'

'What is it they've done to you? Why are they arseholes?'

'They're just arseholes. You must know. You speak to them too.'

Another pause. 'You don't want to talk about it?'

'You got that right.' For a shrink, Riddell wasn't exactly perceptive.

Riddell smiled. 'You may think that.'

'I may.'

'But that doesn't mean you're right.'

'Shouldn't I be the judge of that?'

'Of course,' Riddell said. 'I was merely –'

'Time to go,' Glass said. 'I have something more important to do.'

'We have plenty more time, Nick.'

'You're not listening, *John*,' Glass said. 'Try it sometime. You might be surprised what you learn.'

TUESDAY

One day about ten years ago, Sandy 'Headcase' Harris had been drinking alone in a bar in Falkirk. He liked to drink alone in bars. He was the last customer and the barman was on his own, it being a typically quiet Monday night.

The barman asked Harris, politely, if he'd drink up.

Harris didn't want to. He didn't say that, though. Instead, he grabbed his bottle of beer by the neck, smashed it against the edge of the counter and shoved it deep into the barman's throat.

The astonished barman didn't know what to do. He made a mistake and pulled the glass out. Blood gushed onto the bar counter, splattered all over the newly cleaned glasses and onto the floor. As the barman fought for breath, Harris leaped over the counter, got behind the barman, and put him in a half nelson.

Harris levered the barman onto the counter. Then he raped him.

By the time Harris had finished, the barman was dead.

Harris helped himself to another bottle of beer, returned to his seat, and drank it. After that, he had two more.

Then, calm as you like, and apparently not sounding the least intoxicated, he dialled 999 and explained what he'd done.

When the police arrived, he was finishing off a bag of salted peanuts.

Everybody in the Hilton knew the story. Headcase Harris was happy to talk about it, and smile as he did so.

Which is why, when Glass was told he was wanted in the Digger, he hoped it wasn't anything to do with Harris.

'HE NEEDS EXERCISED,' McDee said. 'It's his legal right. We can't deny him his time in the exercise yard.'

'I don't dispute that,' Glass said. 'But why do *I* have to walk him?'

'You're the only officer available,' Fox said.

Glass stared at him. 'That can't be true.'

'Sorry, Crystal,' Fox said. 'Wouldn't call on you to do this if it wasn't necessary.'

So they thought he was scared. No doubt they'd spent ages deciding who was the most dangerous prisoner in the Hilton and guessed that Headcase Harris's reputation alone would turn Glass into a snivelling coward.

Well, Glass would show them. 'Okay,' he said. 'No problem.'

'Good,' McDee said. 'He has to be cuffed to you. That okay?'

'Fine,' Glass said. 'Why wouldn't it be?'

Course, the last thing he wanted was to be handcuffed to Harris. Bad enough being in the proximity of a psycho like Headcase, but it was even worse when you knew you wouldn't be able to escape in a hurry if the psycho went psycho. Still, somebody had to have been walking Harris on previous occasions and as far as Glass knew, nobody'd been hurt.

'Where is he, then?' Glass asked.

Fox stayed where he was while McDee led Glass down the block to the cell second from the end. 'Here we are,' McDee said.

Fox was talking on his radio, although Glass couldn't hear what he was saying. Seemed to be having a laugh, though. Probably telling Ross a dirty joke. She was every bit as bad as him. Glass wouldn't have been surprised to discover they were screwing each other, that their families meant nothing to them. Yeah, both of them were married with kids.

McDee opened the cell door.

The stink hit Glass first. Not the usual pong. No, this was a stench that overwhelmed the senses. He flinched just as surely as if someone had thrown a punch at him.

But there was nothing moving, nothing throwing punches. Just the thing crouched in the corner of the room. Covered in feathers. Feathers in its hair, on its face, all over its body. Feathers all over the floor, and a few feet away what must have been a pillow before it had been gutted.

The thing was human. It had eyes, limbs. But it was the strangest-looking human Glass had ever seen.

He put his hand over his nose. The stench crawled through his fingers and up his nostrils. And then he realised why the feathers were adhering to Harris's body.

Glass gagged. It couldn't be.

But it was. The smell was undeniable, no matter how much Glass had wanted to think it was just a full chamber pot.

The crazy bastard was covered, head to toe, in shit.

Tears welled in Glass's eyes. He blinked them back. He said to McDee, 'This isn't funny.'

Glass heard Fox scurrying down the corridor towards them.

'Not supposed to be,' McDee said. He was standing well outside the door, hand cupped over his nose and mouth.

'Fuck's sake,' Fox said. 'That's one heady aroma.'

Glass said, 'This is beyond a joke.'

'Who's laughing?' Fox said. 'The prisoner needs to be exercised.'

'Not like that,' Glass said. 'I'm not taking him anywhere in that state.'

Fox looked at McDee. 'Better tell the S.O.,' he said. Then, to Glass, 'Shaw's not going to be too pleased with you.'

'What's it got to do with Shaw?'

'He's the one who suggested you for the job.'

Glass doubted it. 'Why pick on me?'

'Nobody's picking on you,' McDee said. 'I took Harris out yesterday. Fox took him out the day before. We've all had a turn. Show you the paperwork if you want.'

Fox said, 'Part of the job, Glass. You don't want to do it, hand in your notice.'

Glass wished that were possible. 'Hose him down first,' he suggested.

'Nope,' McDee said. 'Wish we could, but that's against the rules too. Prisoner's got rights, you know.'

Glass stepped into the cell, the stink growing all the time.

Headcase Harris looked up at him, eyes seriously white against his D.I.Y. suntan.

Glass wanted to call him names. *Reeking bastard, stinking fucker.* All he could think of to do. But he couldn't say anything. This shit-encrusted, feathered nutjob wasn't the sort of person who'd stand for it. As soon as he got the opportunity, he'd kill Glass. Maybe fuck him afterwards. And he'd have the opportunity very soon.

'Exercise time,' Glass said to him.

'Is it raining?' Harris wanted to know.

His teeth looked too white, like his eyes. He had shit on his lips. He'd done a hell of a thorough job.

'Dry as a bone,' Glass said. He gagged again. Swallowed. Kept swallowing. He was producing a lot of saliva. 'Why did you do this to yourself?'

'Oh,' Harris said, tilting his head. 'I didn't think anyone cared.'

Glass shrugged. 'I'm full of surprises.'

Harris eyed him, then grinned. 'Fuckers wouldn't empty my bucket,' he said. 'Been stinking the place up for a week. So I emptied it myself. You get used to the smell, by the way.'

He held out his arm. 'Put on the bracelets. Can't wait to get all cosy with you.'

Glass wanted to check he wasn't being lied to. He asked Harris, 'Did you get exercised yesterday?'

'Always get exercised. Have to,' Harris said. 'I've got rights.'

Course. He had rights. Glass nodded. Fox and McDee weren't conning him.

THE EXERCISE YARD measured about ten feet by ten. It was completely enclosed.

McDee and Fox stood by the entrance, watching Glass walk round in circles practically hand in hand with Harris.

So Glass was the only officer available, was he? He'd known that was a lie. The fuckers had come to gloat. They seemed to be finding it pretty funny. Well, let them.

Truth was, Glass was more concerned about Harris than about his dickhead colleagues. Harris was behaving himself so far, though. Humming a little song, something Glass didn't recognise, a few feathers on his shoulder fluttering in the breeze.

But with each circuit of the yard, Glass was finding it increasingly difficult to avoid bumping into him. It wasn't just that Glass didn't want to get crap on his uniform. There was also the fact that Harris was barefoot and something as simple as Glass standing on his toes might drive him into a murderous frenzy. He'd already killed a man for less.

Glass just wanted to get this over with. The smell was tolerable because they were outside, but he could feel it clinging to his clothes, seeping into his skin, his hair.

More officers joined Fox and McDee. First Ross, then MacPherson, then, before he'd completed another couple of circuits, Hynd, Lambe, White, Carson, and a couple of faces Glass recognised but whose names he didn't know.

So many of them that they'd spilled out into the exercise yard.

Half of them were smoking. And each time Glass and Harris completed a circuit, they'd cheer.

'Did they do this yesterday?' Glass asked Harris when they were furthest away.

'Nope.'

'So why am I so fucking special?'

'You're walking around a psycho who's covered in shite and feathers.'

Glass paused. Made Harris pause too. 'But so were McDee and Fox.'

'Nope,' Harris said. 'I only started my dirty protest last night.'

GLASS STUFFED HIS uniform in a large carrier. Even once he'd changed into his civilian clothes, he could still smell Harris's shit.

On the way home in the car, he felt sick. He pulled over, opened the glove box, took out a couple of pills he'd stuffed inside the fingers of one of his gloves. Extra-strength beta-blockers. Slowed you right the fuck down.

After sneaking the heroin for himself, he'd started to siphon off a bit of everything. Kept the stuff in the biscuit tin in the garage, along with his gun. The deliveries were varied. The last few weeks he'd muled smack, coke, speed, acid, poppers, Es, tranx, anti-psychotics, anti-convulsants, painkillers. Each time, he put a little aside for himself. He wasn't a regular user, but why not have options? His job was stressful – his *life* was stressful. Lorna felt free to get out of her head all the time. Why shouldn't he sample a little of what was right in front of him? He'd built up a tidy supply. It'd come in handy of late, mind you. The tin was starting to empty.

He could go a line right now. Get some Charlie up his nose, let that rubber-in-the-sun smell obliterate the reek of Harris, let the drip wash down his throat, cool and clean.

When he arrived home, he rolled up the driveway, waving to Caitlin at the window, and nosed the car into the garage. But the minute he turned off the engine, Caitlin bounced into the garage to welcome him home. He couldn't get to his stash. But, worse, he found he couldn't let Caitlin near him. Couldn't let her give him a kiss.

Lorna stood in the doorway in her dressing gown and slippers, arms folded, watching him get out of the car.

He said, 'Daddy's not feeling well, babygirl,' walked past Lorna, stuck his uniform in the washing machine, then went upstairs and ran a shower.

Lorna came into the bathroom after a few minutes, asked him what was wrong.

'It's nowhere near bedtime,' he said. He was naked, testing the temperature of the water.

'So?'

'Why aren't you dressed?'

'What's it matter?'

'Did you take Caitlin to school today?'

'Course I did. What the fuck's wrong with you?'

'Can't tell you,' he said.

'What did I do? You want me to get changed?'

'It's work.' The room was steaming up. The hairs on his arms were glistening. 'Nothing to do with you.'

'Well, no need to take it out on Caitlin.'

'I didn't,' he said.

'She wanted to kiss you.'

'Well, she can't.'

'And why not?'

'Lorna,' he said. 'Please leave me alone.'

'You want to be alone? I can arrange that.'

'Don't start, please.'

'What am I starting?'

'For Christ's sake.' He felt his stomach tighten. She'd been drinking again. He couldn't smell it, could only smell shit, but he could tell. 'I stink,' he said. 'I fucking stink.'

'Yeah,' she said. 'You do.' She stormed out of the bathroom, slamming the door behind her.

He stepped into the shower. The curtain was on a rail that looped right round the edge of the bath. He stretched it all the way, so he was completely hidden. Then he stuck his head under the spray and let the water run over him. He washed his hair. He soaped himself all over. Then he washed his hair again. Soaped himself again.

He stood there, the water drumming against his scalp.

Still felt dirty, though.

So he washed his hair once again. And used a different soap on his body. It helped. A stronger smell. Masked the smell of Harris.

Then he crouched down. So much noisier down here. The noise was good. He sat for a while, letting the water dribble into his mouth.

He felt better. He felt okay. He felt safe. His mouth was dry, though. Despite the water running into it.

He didn't hear the door open. Just saw Lorna pull back the shower curtain. Saw her lips move.

He couldn't hear her. He moved his head from under the spray.

His legs felt stiff.

'Your daughter's wondering if you can spare five minutes,' she said.

Glass nodded.

'Before she goes to bed.'

Glass said, 'What time is it?'

She told him. He'd been in the shower an hour and a half. He could have stayed in it for another hour and a half. Easy.

'Okay,' he said. 'I'll be out in a minute.'

Lorna pulled the shower curtain back in place. Glass washed his hair a final time, and gave himself one last good scrub. Then he yanked the curtain to one side and stepped out.

When he was drying himself, he caught sight of himself in the mirror. Noticed a patch of red skin on the front of his right shoulder. Sunburst.

First thought: too long under the shower.

He touched it. Felt smooth. Too smooth. Moved closer to the mirror. And there was another patch on the back of his shoulder. Just as red and angry as the one at the front. Different shape though. This one looked like a large beetle. Elongated body, tiny legs sprouting in random directions.

But that was just his mind playing tricks.

It wasn't a beetle. It was just a scar. Scars both sides of his shoulder. He wondered how the hell he'd never noticed those before.

'Are you sure you saw them?' Riddell asked.

'Definitely,' Glass said.

'Okay. Carry on.'

Horse had grabbed him after dinner, told him they needed to speak privately.

'You said we were done.' Glass had struggled to keep his voice down. 'Finished, you said. Caesar fucking promised me. Last one, he said. He fucking promised.'

Horse pointed his finger at him. 'Don't swear at me. It's not nice. Just be at school in five.'

Glass hadn't had reason to be back in the education block since his run-in with Mafia a couple of months ago. If he was honest with himself, he'd made sure he'd stayed away.

It wasn't just Horse who was waiting for him outside the classroom, of course. Caesar had turned up too. With Jasmine.

Glass didn't like this, but they weren't going to take no for an answer. So he unlocked the door, let them in, and followed. Same classroom as last time. Different scribbles on the whiteboard.

Jasmine closed the door behind her. She had tits, Glass couldn't help noticing. Well, she had something stuffed under her jumper. Or she was wearing a padded bra.

Glass said, 'I've done more than enough runs for you, Caesar.' And it wasn't just the number of runs either. The amount he'd been taking in had increased too. He'd had to use a much bigger sandwich box. 'I can't do it any more. I won't. I fucking refuse.'

'All right,' Caesar said.

Horse didn't give Glass time to reply. 'This is about something else,' the big bastard said. 'Something much more fun.'

'You did a good job, by the way,' Caesar said. 'Don't even mind too much that you were dipping into the goods. Got enough to keep you going?'

Glass thought about denying it. 'I'm okay,' he said. 'I'm fucking okay.'

'You're fucking okay. I'm glad you're fucking okay. It's important that you're fucking okay, because we need your help elsewhere.'

Glass felt a tremble in his knees, tried to cover it up by saying, 'What the fuck do you want this time?'

'Can the attitude,' Horse said. 'It doesn't suit a soft prick like you.'

Glass worked his hands into fists. If he had his gun, he'd kill them. He'd kill them all. They couldn't do this to him.

Jasmine pulled out a seat, plonked her skinny arse down in it.

'Here,' Caesar said, handing Glass a couple of tube-shaped objects.

'What are they?'

'Stesolid. Valium suppositories. Swedish or something. Shove them up your arse, they'll calm you the fuck down.'

'I don't want them. I'm calm.'

'Well, have them, anyway. For later.'

'Fuck off.' Glass sat down. His legs were shaking and he was sure everybody could tell. Sitting disguised it. He hadn't had the shakes for at least two weeks. From the minute Caesar had told him it was over. Said that their original mule was back and ready to work again.

Glass was off the fucking hook and he'd never felt so relieved.

He'd gone home, intent on giving Lorna a night to remember. But she was drunk again and had fallen asleep on the settee. He thought about giving her a night to remember anyway, but he kicked a plate of gnawed-at sandwiches she'd left lying on the floor, and then got disgusted with her and then got disgusted with himself for having such thoughts in the first place. He took a swig from an open bottle of wine. Three-quarters full, but there were other bottles, empty, in the fireplace. He took the wine into the garage and drank it as if it was water while he plucked the biscuit tin out of the tea chest and rooted around in his stash. Found some Temazepam gel caps. Took a couple of the jellies to help him sleep, finished off the wine, then went to the bathroom and jerked off and got even more disgusted with himself.

He'd woken up in the bathroom next to a pile of vomit. His head pounded, but he felt good nonetheless. He felt very good. It was over. His family was safe. Sitting up, Glass realised his gun was perched on the edge of the bath, no idea how it had got there. Must have brought it back with him from the garage. He wondered if he should get rid of it now. But he'd paid good money for it, and he'd got used to having it around.

Just had to keep it out of Lorna's sight. Out of the fucking bathroom. The fuck was he thinking? Well, he didn't know what he'd been thinking because he couldn't remember.

He'd cleaned up the mess, stored the gun, popped another couple of jellies and gone to bed. The bed was empty and he thought it was strange but couldn't work out why. He was still awake when Lorna crawled under the covers a couple of hours later. He said, 'You weren't here.'

'Fell asleep on the settee,' she told him. 'You should have woken me up.'

'You're cold,' he said.

'You want to warm me up?'

IN THE CLASSROOM, Horse coughed and Glass looked up from his seat. Horse and Caesar had remained standing. Glass realised sitting might have been a mistake.

'Asked if you'd seen Watt recently,' Horse said.

Glass pictured Watt sitting in the chair in Glass's lounge watching TV with Lorna. She was still scared. Middle of last week, Glass had walked into the kitchen when Lorna was making dinner. When he spoke to ask if he could help, she'd screamed, dropped her glass and said, 'Jesus. Don't sneak up on me like that. Christ, Nick.' Glass swept up the broken fragments, mopped up the spilled wine. Lorna fetched another glass and filled it. He blamed Watt. Blamed Caesar. It was their fault she'd started drinking again.

'Course he hasn't,' Caesar said. 'No reason for him to.'

Caesar was right. Now that Glass wasn't running drugs, he didn't have to meet with Watt every few days. They'd become professional, scarcely exchanging a word, just the gear. Most of the time. They usually met at public spots, but on a few occasions they'd met at Mad Will's flat, and Mad Will always poured Glass some coffee from his thermos which Glass took a sip of before leaving. Once, Watt was busy in the bedroom and Glass had to hang around till he was finished.

'Couldn't he have given you the package?' Glass had asked Mad Will.

'Got a thing about the handover being personal,' Mad Will had said.

'He just likes to fuck with me.'

'He likes to fuck with everyone.' Mad Will took a wrap out of his shirt pocket. 'Bump of Charlie?'

'Bump?'

'I'd offer you a rail but it's uncut. Your head might explode.'

'I'll take my chances.'

When Watt appeared in his dressing gown ten minutes later, Glass was on his feet with his hand out before he even thought about it. Or maybe he did think about it but his thoughts were blurting out, instant and rapid, and he felt fast and confident and the back of his throat was melting ice and Watt was no danger and everything was okay, course it was, never better.

'The fuck've you been feeding him?' Watt asked Mad Will.

'He's just being friendly,' Mad Will said.

Watt faced Glass. 'Put your hand away.' He shook his head. 'You don't want to be friends with me. You don't want to be part of this gang.'

'I HEAR THAT boy's *weird.*' Jasmine's voice screeched in the classroom. She clutched Caesar's arm. 'In a good way.'

'You know why,' Caesar said. 'Mafia ever tell you what happened, Nick?'

Glass couldn't concentrate. His thoughts kept jumping from one thing to another.

'Well?'

'No,' Glass said.

'I'm glad to hear he can keep his mouth shut.'

'You're forgetting,' Horse said. 'Crystal and Mafia had a lover's tiff. Not speaking to each other any more, are they?'

'What happened?'

'None of your concern.' Caesar turned to look at Jasmine. 'We've had one or two barneys, haven't we?'

'Making up, though,' Jasmine said. 'That's sweet.'

'Will that be sweet for you?' Caesar asked Glass. 'When you and Mafia make up?'

'We won't.'

'Caesar was just guessing about the fight, you know,' Horse said. 'But it's nice of you to confirm it.'

He and Caesar laughed. They thought they were so fucking

smart. But Glass didn't give a shit. He said, 'Makes no difference to me what you know.'

'It should,' Caesar said. 'Cause I know enough to put you away for a long, long time.'

A bluff. Sounded bad, but there was no way Caesar could prove a thing.

'You think I can't prove anything?'

'It's like you're psychic,' Glass said.

'Well, that's where you're wrong.'

Caesar was enjoying the moment. Glass could tell he wanted to draw it out for as long as possible.

'How?' Glass said.

'Got one of the baggies stashed in a safe place,' Caesar said.

Glass didn't see how that affected him.

'Dear me,' Caesar said. 'I used to think it was because you were young. But now I realise you're just fucking slow. You need some speed to perk you up.' He looked at Jasmine. 'Tell him.'

Jasmine raised her hand, waggled her fingers. 'Prints,' she said.

'That's a joke,' Glass said. 'You could have got my prints on an empty bag. Put the gear in it afterwards. Nobody's going to believe you.'

'But we didn't put those prints there, did we?'

'The only people who know that are us and Watt.'

Horse took his hand out of his pocket. He had something in it. 'Thanks, Officer Glass,' he said. Pressed a button and the tape recorder stopped.

'Beautiful,' Caesar said. 'You're a real fucking dim-witted twat, Crystal.'

'Jesus,' Glass said. The fuckers were going to blackmail him now.

'Actually,' Caesar said, 'it's not Jesus. It's Julius.'

High fives all round.

'I can't pay you,' Glass said. 'I've no money.'

'I don't want your money, you tit.'

'What do you want?' Glass asked.

'Wait and see,' Caesar said. 'You'll find out soon enough.' He moved towards the door, his cronies following. He turned, asked Glass, 'You sure you don't want a nice relaxing rectal tube to slip up your arse?'

'Crystal doesn't need one,' Horse said. 'He's already fucked.'

Caesar said, 'Glad you could make it.'

They were in his peter. Jasmine and Horse were there too. The radio was off, so it had to be serious.

'So?' Glass said. 'What is it?'

'Fuck, he's impatient,' Horse said.

'Teach him some manners,' Jasmine said.

Glass stared at her. If she wanted to try it on with him, she was more than welcome. He wasn't scared of a transvestite. Not any more. He'd dropped some Temgesic before coming to work. Wished he'd kept more of those, but he was down to his last four. 'You lot still think you can intimidate me?' he said. 'You're wrong.'

'Oh,' Caesar said. 'That's a –' he lunged forward, punching the air right where Glass's nose would have been if he hadn't snapped his head back and out of the way in time – 'fucking shame.' He stared at Glass, mouth puckered as he sucked his front teeth.

'You know,' Horse said. 'I'd swear you seem just a bit intimidated to me, Glass.'

Caesar cocked his head.

'What the fuck do you want?' Glass said, taking a step back, wiping his nose with the back of his hand. Then he realised what he was doing, and that there was no need cause Caesar hadn't hit his nose and it wasn't bleeding, and he put his hands by his sides. 'I'm fucking fed up of this.'

'Ooooh,' Jasmine said. 'Balls like those, you make me want to reach out and polish them.'

'That's enough,' Glass said.

'No, it isn't.' Caesar nodded to Horse, and Horse slammed the cell door shut. The noise was the sound of the end of the world. 'You'll stay here and you'll fucking listen to what you're fucking told.'

He poked Glass hard in the chest with his finger.

Glass said nothing, stood there as if Caesar's finger punch didn't hurt.

Caesar jabbed him again. 'Okay?'

His fucking fingers were like rocks. 'What is it you want from me?' Glass said.

'Apart from your gorgeous body?' Jasmine said.

'Shut your fanny,' Caesar told her.

Glass flinched as Caesar's hand found his shoulder.

'Look,' Caesar said, his voice all friendly, 'we just need that bit of help we mentioned.' Glass was about to speak, but Caesar continued: 'No risk in it for you.'

'I've heard that before,' Glass said.

'And it was true, wasn't it?' Caesar squeezed Glass's shoulder.

Glass felt the scars on his shoulder burn beneath Caesar's fingers.

'Not exactly.'

'Well, you didn't get caught. And this is even less risky.'

Glass didn't want to know. He didn't want to have to say he wouldn't do it, cause then everything would start up all over again. And whatever it was, there was no way he could go through with it. He wouldn't be able to pull it off. He couldn't. Not without getting out of his head.

'What it is,' Caesar said, removing his hand from Glass's shoulder, 'is, we're a bit fed up of this place, the three of us.'

'Don't blame you,' Glass said.

'Yes,' Caesar said. 'But you get to go home to your lovely wife and kid at night.'

Glass stiffened.

'I'm being sincere,' Caesar said. 'You get to see your family. Whilst I have to bunk up with Jasmine here. Who's lovely too, but she's got a dick. Think you'd like that?'

'Course not,' Glass said.

'I didn't think so,' Caesar said. 'So you understand how we all might want to be somewhere else?'

'I can understand it, yeah.' Glass resisted stating the obvious.

'Good,' Caesar said. 'That's very good.'

There was a pause. Glass couldn't hold it back any longer. 'But you're all lifers,' he said. Even Jasmine. Only two years into a minimum ten-spot. She looked like skin and bones held together with lipstick but she was an accessory to a double killing. Her accomplice had torched a flat they'd robbed, killing the young couple they'd left tied up in the bedroom. Maybe he ought to be afraid of her after all.

Caesar lowered his voice. 'That's why we're breaking out.'

'I don't want to hear this,' Glass said.

'But you've no choice,' Caesar said. 'Our escape plan won't work without you.'

THEIR PLAN WAS simple and it might even have worked.

In C-Hall, once the prisoners were locked up, there was very little to do, so staffing was at a minimum. The officer on night duty was the lone guard and he'd spend most of the night sitting in the office or the staff room with his feet up and his slippers on, reading a book and drinking coffee.

Cushy number. Glass didn't mind night shift at all, not since he'd been muling for Caesar and Lorna and Caitlin were safe.

All the duty officer had to do was patrol at set intervals, check the cons were okay, and peg in at the appropriate station – 'pegging' being a simple matter of slotting a key in a wall panel and turning it clockwise or anti-clockwise, depending on what instructions you received at the gate. It was just a way to make sure you didn't spend the night asleep.

He'd be given his code for the night too. A phrase to say if everything was okay, and another to say if there was trouble. In other words, if he'd been taken hostage. But that was unlikely. The only risk arose if an inmate needed to leave his cell. And that'd only happen in a medical emergency. In which case, the duty officer would call down to the gate for assistance before unlocking the prisoner's cell.

Follow procedure and you're fine.

Caesar's plan was to create a hostage situation with Glass next time he was on nights. Jasmine would pretend to be sick. Glass would screw up, and fail to get back-up from the gate before opening Caesar and Jasmine's peter. Once Glass was inside, they'd take him hostage. And after opening Horse's peter, they'd all leave with Glass in tow. Then they'd get into Glass's car, and he'd drive them to safety.

They'd let him go afterwards. Nobody need know he was in on the break.

There was silence for a moment after Caesar finished outlining the plan.

'So, you'll do it?' Horse said.

'And get my arse handed to me? They'll cut me loose.'

'Nah,' Caesar said. 'You'll be all traumatised. Imagine how it'd look if they sacked an officer who'd been taken hostage.'

'Nobody's going to believe I'm not in on it.'

'Why not?' Caesar asked.

'Cause it would take a fucking idiot to open your peter when he's the only officer on duty.'

'That's why you're the perfect choice,' Horse said.

Glass needed to talk to Mafia. It was time to make up.

FRIDAY

During free association, some of the cons who might be nervous of interaction with the others preferred to stay in their peters. So did some of the cons who were just plain anti-social. And sometimes, there wasn't an obvious reason. Glass didn't know why Darko and Mafia were in their peter this afternoon, but that's where he found them.

Darko held a tortoiseshell kitten.

When Glass walked towards Darko, the kitten spat at him.

'Hey, precious,' Darko said. 'Officer Glass won't hurt you. He's one of the good guys.'

Hard to tell if there was a trace of sarcasm there or not.

The kitten wriggled a little, then settled down again and let Darko stroke it. After a bit, it started to purr.

Glass wanted to pet it too. It annoyed him that it trusted Darko and not him.

Mafia said, 'They only like Darko.'

Glass nodded.

'It isn't that they don't like you.'

'I didn't think it was.'

'Whatever,' Mafia said. 'What do you want?'

Painful though it was, Glass said, 'I need to talk.'

'Last time we talked, it didn't go so well.'

'I know.'

'And you're sorry?'

Glass knew he should say yes. But he was glad he'd whacked Mafia in the jaw and he'd do it again if the same situation arose. 'Can't say I am,' he said.

'Oh,' Mafia said, 'that's encouraging.'

'It is?'

'Absolutely.' He looked towards Darko. 'We might make a man of him yet.'

'Don't talk about me like that,' Glass said.

'Like what?'

'Like I'm not here.'

'Even better,' Mafia said. 'I'm impressed.' He moved within a foot of Glass. Close enough for his breath to touch Glass's cheek when he spoke. 'What do you want?'

'In private.'

'Okay. Darko won't mind leaving us alone for a –'

'No, let Darko stay. We should be the ones to leave.'

'It's okay,' Darko said. 'I don't mind.'

'You don't need to do that,' Glass said.

'Yes,' Darko said. 'I think I do.'

He walked out, the kitten in his arms still purring.

GLASS TOLD MAFIA about Caesar's escape plan.

Mafia said, 'You can't.'

Glass said, 'I know. But they'll get Watt to threaten my family again or blackmail me about the drugs.' He explained about the tape recording.

Mafia said, 'You've stopped taking in gear for them?'

Glass nodded.

'That's something.' Mafia paused. 'You're a stupid fuck, though. What do you want me to do?'

'Help me,' Glass said.

'How can I do that?'

'Have a word with Watt. Tell him to back off.'

'What's he done?'

'Nothing yet. But if I don't agree to help Caesar escape –'

'He won't listen to me,' Mafia said.

'He's your brother.'

'I'm sorry. Believe me, Nick, I'm the last person he'd listen to.'

'But he talks to you. He told you about me bringing in drugs for Caesar, didn't he?'

Mafia said, 'You don't understand.'

'Right,' Glass said. 'Right, I get it. Well, I suppose I still have that gun.'

'Now there's an empty threat.'

'Is it?' Glass asked him. 'I can't do what they want. And I can't let your brother harm my family. So it leaves me with very little choice.'

Mafia took off his shades. 'I almost believe you.'

SATURDAY

'You ready?' Lorna asked.

Glass turned off the TV. 'Just get my keys,' he said, and went to pick them up from the kitchen, yawning.

He hadn't slept much again last night. Kept waking up shaking, unable to remember what he'd been dreaming about but knowing that it was horrible enough that he didn't want to go back to sleep.

Lorna had snored through it all, occasionally kicking him with her heel as she stretched out.

He'd got up about six. Tidied the sitting room, washed the dishes. Caitlin appeared as he was finishing, and told him she'd wet herself. He washed her, stripped the bed, slung the wet pyjamas and bedding into the washing machine. Then he hoovered while she had breakfast. Afterwards, when he asked her if she would put the toys away in her room, she replied, 'I can't be bothered.'

He stared at her. 'How about if I give you a hand? We can do it together.'

'I just can't be bothered.' She stared back at him. 'I need a drink.'

Thank you, Lorna.

Glass understood that his wife had been through a traumatic experience with Watt, but she'd behaved exactly this way when she broke up with David. Became self-destructive, started picking fights. Drank to cope and then started to act as though she couldn't give a shit about anything. Glass knew Watt was to blame this time, but sometimes he still couldn't be sure she wasn't thinking about her ex-lover. Didn't really matter. Either way, she was telling Glass he was inadequate. And it was all starting to have an effect on Caitlin.

They'd gone to see an animated movie last week and Lorna'd talked most of the way through it. Laughing at inappropriate moments, criticising the 'stupid' story aloud. Pissed off the family in front of them. The father kept turning round, asking her to please be quiet.

Even Caitlin had got sick of her mum's snide comments and told her to shut up. Not in those words, exactly. But that's what she meant.

About halfway through, Lorna had walked out in a huff.

Today, when she got up, Glass told her about Caitlin wetting herself and about what their daughter had said.

'Promise I'll stay sober from now on,' Lorna said. 'Turn over a new leaf. Starting right now. No more drink. I've been indulging too much.'

Sounded too good to be true.

'Why didn't you say something before?' she asked. 'I've hardly been a fit mother the past few weeks.'

So now it was Glass's fault she was drinking? He knew she was goading him. He said, 'It's not exactly the first time.'

She looked at him, didn't argue.

Another day, she might have thought he was goading her back. But really he was just stating a fact.

She was responding already to being off the booze, though. More laidback. Less emotional. At least he hoped that's what it was. Alcohol was such a shit drug, but she refused to try anything else.

He could tell her about Caesar's escape plan. He wanted to. But he wouldn't. She didn't trust him to cope. She'd get upset, and that'd probably be enough to start her drinking again. Anyway, it wasn't necessary that she knew. Glass had everything he needed to deal with the situation in his biscuit tin in the tea chest in his garage.

God, though, he was tired. And his right index finger hurt, like he'd stubbed the tip of it against something during the night, and his shoulder nagged like an old injury in bad weather.

He picked up his keys, stepped out into the hall as Caitlin was stomping down the stairs. She grinned at him and he realised he was grinning too.

'Waiting on you, Daddy,' she said.

Lorna was standing by the door, ready to go. 'Get your coat on, cheeky,' she said.

'You get your coat on, cheeky,' Caitlin said back.

'Don't talk to your mum like that, babygirl,' Glass said.

'Leave her alone,' Lorna said. 'She's not doing any harm.'

'She shouldn't –'

'Nick, please.'

'I'm sorry, Daddy,' Caitlin said. 'Don't fight with Mummy.'

'That's okay,' Glass said. 'We're not fighting.'

Lorna shook her head. 'I'll wait outside.'

THE AIR WAS cool. The sky was grey and a pleasant November drizzle sprayed Glass's cheeks.

He was about to comment on how nice it was when Lorna said, 'Foul weather. I hate this country.'

Caitlin said, 'I like rain.'

'Me, too,' Glass said. 'Mummy just likes to moan.'

Course, that wasn't the smartest thing he could have said, and he regretted it immediately. He wished she didn't piss him off so easily, but the constant negativity wasn't something he could cope with on so little sleep. Not surprising he needed some chemical help now and then.

She stopped, said, 'You think that? I like to moan?'

'I –'

'You do. You think I have nothing better to do than complain.' Her eyes grew small, her lips thinned. 'Well, you don't know what it's like to bring up a kid virtually single-handed.'

'That's not fair. One of us has to work.' He saw the hostility in her eyes and carried on before she could respond, 'I'm not criticising, Lorna. Just telling it how it is.'

'You think I don't want to work? I miss people.'

'I know.'

'You do? Do you know the kind of strain it can put on a person, being Mum all the time?'

'Not now,' Glass said. He grabbed Caitlin's hand. She squeezed his fingers.

'Surprise, surprise,' Lorna said. 'It's never the right time to talk about this farce we call a relationship.'

'It's not a farce,' he said.

'What's a farce, Daddy?'

'Oh, yes it is,' Lorna said.

And he almost said, 'Oh, no it's not.' He laughed. Maybe he shouldn't have. He'd been provocative enough already. But what did a little extra provocation matter? Lorna was being completely unreasonable. He laughed again.

'Grow up,' Lorna said. 'You're incapable of taking anything seriously. Worse than a bloody child.'

'Get in the car, Caitlin,' Glass said. 'I want to have a quiet word with Mummy.'

Caitlin looked like she didn't like the sound of that. 'You won't argue?'

He shook his head.

'What's a farce?'

'Something that's fun,' he said. 'Honest.'

'Okay,' she said.

Once Caitlin had closed the car door, Lorna placed her hands on her hips and said, 'So let's hear your quiet word.'

'Don't.' Glass placed his hands on her shoulders. 'You're the mother of my child. You're my wife.'

'Jesus, that's depressing.'

'We have to try.'

'I'm trying,' she said. 'Believe me. I'm always trying. Very fucking hard.'

He let his hands drop, took hold of his wedding ring between his middle finger and thumb. Turned it. Turned it again.

'And it gets harder all the time,' she said.

She was telling him she didn't love him. Well, he knew that. You didn't sleep with someone else if you were in love with your partner. He'd forgiven her. Tried to make it work. But it seemed that neither of them could forget.

There were times when it didn't hurt, when he felt numb. Like now. And those were the best times.

'Let's go,' she said. 'The rain's getting heavy.'

THEY LISTENED TO one of Caitlin's CDs in the car. By the time they got to Kinnaird Terminal, the rain had stopped and the sky had cleared.

'I've changed my mind,' Lorna said when they got out of the car. 'I'm not in the mood to watch a film.'

'Oh, Mummy,' Caitlin said.

'You two go on,' Lorna said. 'I'll wander round the shops.'

'I already booked the tickets,' Glass said.

She opened her handbag, took out her wallet, snapped it open. Thrust a fiver at him.

He looked at her. Then he took the money.

INSIDE THE SHOPPING mall, hand in hand with Caitlin going up the escalator. He had to stand sideways, but she wouldn't let go and he didn't blame her.

He looked up to the top of the escalator. And there he was. Waving.

A gun shot. Blood. Glass looking down at his hand, the gun in it, dropping it.

Would have been nice, but Glass didn't have the gun with him so he glowered at Watt instead.

'HELLO, CAITLIN,' WATT said when they got to the top of the elevator. He looked at Glass. 'Where's the lovely Lorna?'

Glass said, 'Why are you here?'

'Why do you think?'

'Never mind.' Glass tugged Caitlin's hand. 'We're going.'

Watt said loudly, 'I said hello, Caitlin. Very rude not to answer. Doesn't your daddy teach you any manners?'

Glass turned, said, 'I'm not in a mood to play games.' He leaned in close to Watt and whispered, 'So fuck off.'

'Ooooh,' Watt said, 'that's scary.' Looked at Caitlin. 'Scary man, your dad, eh?'

'No, he's not. You're a scary man. Daddy's right. Fuck off.'

'Caitlin!' Watt grinned. 'Smart kid. Bigger balls than you. I like her.'

'Let it rest, Watt.'

'Okay,' Watt said. 'Just tell me where I can find Lorna.'

Glass squeezed Caitlin's hand, hoped she realised he meant that she should say nothing. She did. Smart kid. Watt was right about that.

Watt said, 'Guess I'll go have a look for her, then. No tips as to where I should start?'

'Daddy, let's go.' Caitlin pulled his sleeve with her free hand. 'Daddy. The film's going to start.'

'Sorry, babygirl,' he said. 'I don't think we can watch a film today.'

'But, Daddy.'

'Another time.'

'Not on account of me, I hope?' Watt said. 'I'd hate to spoil your day out.'

Glass started to lead Caitlin round to the opposite end of the mall where the down escalator was situated.

Watt followed. He said, 'Hey, you'll never guess who I got a call from.'

Glass stopped.

Watt said, 'Yeah, I thought you'd know about it. My brother seems to like you. I don't know why that is. Do you, Caitlin? You like your dad, babygirl?'

Glass gripped her hand more tightly.

She said, 'Ow.'

'Careful,' Watt said. 'You're hurting her. You okay, babygirl?'

'Leave us alone,' Glass said.

'I can't see anything to like,' Watt said. 'Apart from your family. Those two girls are the most attractive thing about you.'

Images of Watt's wide open mouth, the sound of him screaming, flashed in front of Glass's eyes and roared in his ears.

Glass said, 'Whatever Caesar wants, I won't be part of it.'

'I believe you,' Watt said. 'If you don't want to do what Caesar asks, that's fine by me. Generates a little bit of extra work, but that's no problem. I don't mind the work at all. Looking forward to it, in fact.'

'Right,' Glass said.

'Right,' Watt said. 'Exactly. Better leave you now. I'll go find Lorna. You should help her to stop drinking, you know. Bit of a problem there if you ask me. Got to watch out for people with addictive personalities. It can be catching.'

'I'm watching out for her,' Glass said. Didn't convince himself, let alone Watt.

'Who's watching out for you?' Watt asked.

SUNDAY

Glass had checked that Lorna was okay, and settled in for the night shift. Put on his slippers. Yeah, sounds daft, but it wasn't just that it was far more comfortable: if you wore shoes, the noise woke up the inmates.

You wouldn't have thought that anybody would care about waking up the poor souls. But if they didn't sleep, they didn't behave too well the next day. So it was in everybody's interest for them to get a good night's sleep. And if you woke one of them up, he'd start shouting and banging on his cell door, and then someone else would join in, and then another and so on until the place was a deafening racket.

And they could keep that up all night if they wanted to.

The duty officer had to do a circuit every half an hour, so it wasn't as if taking a walk was avoidable. Some of the officers wore trainers, but Glass had never liked them. For him, it was shoes or slippers.

First night shift he'd done, he'd had bouts of tiredness, got heavy-lidded a few times towards the end of it. Never quite hit the point where he found himself jolting awake, but he didn't want to take any chances. Got to peg in. Miss a round and you got your arse handed to you. No second chances.

He'd learned, though, and now he took some speed before the shift started and got through it no problem.

He walked over to the kettle. Filled it, humming to himself. The nightshift was a rare respite. It was good being alone. Nobody to hassle him. If it weren't for Watt being back on the scene, he'd be content. But Glass wasn't too concerned. After the incident at the cinema, he'd bought himself some time. Told Caesar he'd think about it.

He'd get some strong coffee down him to top up the speed, then he'd be set.

He grabbed his mug out of the cupboard. Crossed to the fridge. Found some milk that looked okay but he sniffed it to make sure. He teased the lid off the container of coffee. It was one of those industrial-sized tins of cheap instant crap. Just the right size.

Oh, Jesus, no.

Tears poured down his cheeks. Couldn't stop them.

He put the lid back on. Couldn't bear to look at it.

Shook the tears out of his eyes.

A joke was a joke, but these fuckers were evil. He could imagine one of the cons doing it. Peeler maybe, cause he was such a nutter. But this was one of the officers, one of Glass's colleagues, and they'd done it just to get a rise out of him.

He opened the lid again. Looked inside at the tortoiseshell kitten. Darko's kitten.

Glass put his hand inside and stroked the fur on its back. It was still warm but it wouldn't be for much longer.

The way it was lying, jaw sagging, tongue sticking out of its mouth between sharp glistening white teeth, head to the side, it was obvious some cunt had broken its neck.

Fox, most likely. He hoped somebody broke Fox's neck.

Glass would have to be the one to tell Darko. Shit, *shit, shit.* He considered wrapping up the poor thing in newspaper and putting it in the bin, but Darko might want to bury it and Glass didn't want to prevent him from doing that.

He'd take the kitten to him now. Get it over with. Get that coffee container out of his sight.

Jesus fucking Christ. These fuckers were total fucking scum.

GLASS REALISED AS he was walking along to Mafia and Darko's peter that he was doing exactly what he'd said to

Caesar that only somebody completely stupid would do. He was going to enter a cell at night without any back-up.

But, then, it wasn't as if he was being buzzed from one of the cells. No, it was his decision. Darko would be no trouble. He never was. And Glass had made up with Mafia, so he'd be fine too. But even if Mafia decided to try to escape, he wouldn't get more than five feet outside his peter because of his eyesight.

So Glass was safe.

Outside the cell, he wondered if maybe he should tap on the door. If walking into their peter unannounced during the day felt wrong, it felt infinitely worse to be doing it at night. Especially when Mafia wouldn't be able to tell who was there.

He might freak out. Start shouting. Cause a commotion.

So Glass tapped on the door.

Waited.

Nothing.

He rapped his knuckles on it, harder.

Still nothing.

So he slid open the Judas window and whispered, 'Darko. It's Officer Glass.'

Heard a moan from inside.

'Darko.' A little louder. 'Darko. It's about your kitten.'

He heard some mumbling in Serbo-Croat or whatever Darko's native language was.

'Darko. Can you hear me?'

Muffled: 'A moment.' Then the padding of bare feet and after a second or two Darko's face appeared in the Judas window. He yawned. 'What is it you wake me up for?'

First time Glass had ever heard him sound foreign. 'Your kitten.'

'My kitten, yes.'

How was Glass supposed to tell him? 'There's been an accident,' Glass said.

Darko yawned again.

Nothing for it. Glass would have to spit it out. 'The kitten's dead,' he said.

Darko yawned a third time, didn't say anything.

Glass said, 'Did you hear me?'

'The kitten's dead,' Darko said. 'And?'

'I thought you'd like to know.'

Darko raised his voice. 'You woke me up to tell me the fucking kitten was dead?'

Glass said, 'I thought, maybe, you'd want to . . .'

'Crystal,' Darko said, 'I'd appreciate it if you'd let me get back to sleep.'

'You don't want the kitten?'

'I don't want the fucking kitten.'

'You don't even want to say goodbye?'

'I don't want the fucking kitten.' He turned to go.

'Should I keep it for you?' Glass said. 'For the morning?'

Darko shouted: 'I don't want the fucking kitten now and I won't want it in the fucking morning.'

Glass slid the Judas window shut.

In the next cell Wireman shouted, 'Shut the fuck up.'

Glass tiptoed along the landing, hoping he hadn't triggered a chain reaction. But it was okay. No one else stirred.

When he got back to the staff room, he set the coffee container to the side. He'd bury the kitten on the way home.

He rummaged around in the cupboards, finally finding the clear glass jar the instant coffee had been transferred to. Somebody had written in red marker on the lid: Just Add Kitten.

By the time Glass had made his coffee it was time to peg in.

IT WAS ABOUT two o'clock when the buzzer from Caesar's cell came on the alarm panel.

Glass wanted to ignore it, but if it signalled a real medical emergency and he failed to respond, he'd be out of a job. He'd go see what the matter was, and if he needed to open the door, he'd follow procedure and call the guys at the main gate to send someone along.

If Glass was lucky, it was a genuine call. Maybe Caesar had contracted some fatal disease and was puking his guts out. You could only hope.

When he got to the peter, he opened the Judas window and Caesar's face was right on the other side of it.

Glass stepped back.

Caesar whispered, 'What kept you?'

Glass whispered back, 'What do you want?'

'Couldn't sleep. Too much going round and round in my head. Come on in. We can talk in peace.'

'I'm not opening the door.'

'You don't trust me? I'm hurt.'

'Who you talking to, baby?' Jasmine said sleepily.

'Shut your fanny,' Caesar said. 'Come on, Glass. This is stupid, talking through this fucking hole.'

'I like it,' Glass said.

'Okay,' Caesar said. 'You like talking through a hole. To be honest, that doesn't surprise me, you're such a tit. You want to know why I couldn't sleep?'

'Not particularly.' Caesar grunted and continued anyway: 'Because of you.'

Glass said nothing.

'I'm not entirely insensitive,' Caesar said. 'I was thinking how all this must seem to you. How you must feel threatened and bullied.'

Glass said, 'I'm okay.'

'You're talking pish,' Caesar said. 'You're far from okay. You're a fucking wreck and you couldn't get through a shift now without dipping into the shite you've sieved off for yourself. Must have your own pharmacy at home, right?'

'I haven't –'

'When you run out, let me know.'

'I'm fine.'

'Well, you know where to come when you're not. Anyway, that's not why I wanted to see you. I wanted to surprise you.'

Glass didn't like the sound of that. 'What do you mean?'

'You'll see tomorrow.'

'Don't touch them,' Glass said. 'If Watt goes anywhere near either of them, I swear I'll kill you.'

'That's right, think the worst of me,' Caesar said. 'I'm going to do something *nice* for you, Crystal.'

Glass tried to think of something nice that Caesar might do, and failed. 'Why would you do that?'

'Because then you might do something nice for me. I told you, I'm a decent guy really.'

'One who likes to play football with people's heads.'

'If you'd met that fucker, you'd have joined in the game.'

'I don't want any favours from you.'

'We'll see,' Caesar said. 'Ask around when you get to work tomorrow. I hope you'll like what you hear.'

He retreated into the darkness.

MONDAY

It was 9.30 by the time Glass got in the front door. He'd dawdled as long as he could after depositing the kitten in a hollowed-out tree in the local park, but he couldn't put off coming home for ever. Lorna was out and Caitlin was at school, so he showered and went to bed.

The bed was still warm, smelled of lavender.

He tried to sleep. No joy. The speed was still in his system. He lay in bed, restless, kicking the covers off cause he was too warm and they were making him itch. Then he grew cold and pulled them back up again. Kept wondering what Caesar had in mind. He couldn't think of anything Caesar could do that would be 'nice'. The crazy fuck didn't know what 'nice' was.

The curtains were closed but light blasted through them. He needed a heavier material. Something that would black everything out. He should write that down or he'd forget.

He should just get up. Admit to himself that he wasn't going to get to sleep.

But he had to try to get a few hours. Another night shift tonight. Four in a row, then three days off. Took some getting used to.

If Caesar really was planning something, Glass would find out what it was in under twelve hours.

Sleep. He needed to sleep. He had some nembies in the garage. Couple of those would knock him out in ten minutes.

HE HEARD A door close. Wasn't a bang. Someone was being quiet. Deliberately so.

Lorna was in a good mood, then. He wondered what time it was but couldn't be bothered opening his eyes to find out.

He must have been dozing. Not asleep, exactly, even with the help of the Nembutal. But not awake either. Could have sworn the kitten had been licking his finger. He could feel a tingle where the rough tongue had been on his skin.

He yawned. Wondered if Lorna was going to go straight to the booze. Her 'new leaf' hadn't lasted long. He had to stamp that out. She was right. Fuck it, Watt was right. She seemed capable enough but he wouldn't let her get behind a wheel in that condition so why would he let her look after a five-year-old?

She had to stop. She was dangerous. He'd told her that before, though. Hell, he'd tell her again.

Her footsteps approached the bedroom.

He braced himself. Could do without this right now. Maybe he'd just pretend he was asleep till he gauged what kind of mood she was in. Cause there was no point talking to her if she was drunk.

What time was it anyway?

He forced his eyes open, blinked, looked at his watch. Made out the numbers, just: 11.30.

Early. Far too early.

The bedroom door started to open.

He closed his eyes.

Heard her walk over to the bed. Felt the mattress sink as she sat down on it. Felt her hand rest on his shoulder. Felt heat in his shoulder. Throbbing.

She was okay. Wouldn't touch him like this if she was in one of her moods.

He didn't need to pretend. He could admit to being awake, talk to her. Maybe ask her if she wanted to get in bed with him for a few minutes.

He turned, opened his eyes.

Jesus fucking Christ.

Scrabbled backwards, kicking his heels against the sheet, till his back was pressed against the headboard, knees tight against his chest.

Jesus fuck.

Jesus.

Watt stared at him. He had a gun in his hand. Glass's gun. He pointed it at Glass's head. 'Give me a good reason not to, Nick.'

Glass couldn't think of anything. 'What are you doing here?' he said.

'Had to see you, pal.'

Glass shook all over. 'The fuck did you get that?' he said.

'Where you left it.'

'How did . . . how?' He couldn't believe this. Didn't know how to feel, or what to ask. Wouldn't have been surprised to find out he was still asleep.

'How? Strange question. Maybe I know what you know. Maybe I looked. And I found.'

Glass pulled at the quilt but couldn't wrap it round himself any tighter with Watt sitting on it.

'And don't worry,' Watt said. 'I didn't touch your stash.'

'Why are you doing this?'

'Most folk wouldn't care. But you, Nick, you've got a genuine interest in people. I sensed that the first time we spoke.' Watt patted the side of Glass's knee. 'So I'll tell you. It's simple.'

Glass waited.

'I'm a bit of a cunt.'

'You're sick,' Glass said.

'That's possible.'

'This isn't fair.'

'Don't piss me off.' He looked away for a second. Then back again. 'Pisses me off when people say that, you know. You moaning fuckers. Complaining about things not being fair. Who the fuck ever said things *were* fair? All you arseholes think you're born with some kind of entitlement. You know what, Nick? Look at you. Beautiful wife. Lovely daughter. Perfect family. Hardly fair on me, is it? Where's mine?'

'Your wife and kid?' Is that what he meant? Glass looked into Watt's eyes, past the gun. His expression looked genuine. Nothing but pain and anger. Glass asked, 'Did something happen to them?'

Watt leaned forward, whispered: 'You think you know everything.'

Glass said, 'No, I don't –'

'Shhh. Just listen. Do you know why Mafia's in prison?'

'For murder.'

'And do you know who he murdered?' Watt's face screwed up for a second, like he'd just been shocked.

'Mafia would never do that.' Glass couldn't believe what Watt was suggesting. Mafia killed Watt's wife and kid? 'No way.'

'Ask him. Ask him what he did.'

'You're crazy.'

'Caesar warned me,' Watt said. 'Said Mafia was going to flip. You know, Caesar's never let me down. He's the one who was there for me, the one who behaved like a real brother. I asked him not to hurt Mafia and he hasn't. Well, not much.' He patted Glass's hand and Glass pulled it away. 'I understand you. He said you really loved Mafia. Cute little prison romance, he called it. But I know what it's like. I feel like that about Caesar. Nothing gay about it. Is there?'

Glass ignored him. 'I don't believe you. Mafia's not a killer.'

'Hurt like you've no idea to think that my brother could have done that. But these days I'm more philosophical about it all. I've thought a lot about death. And you know what I've concluded, Nick? Anybody can be a killer. Circumstances, you know. Shit happens. You put your head down for a while. When you look up, somebody's dead. You know how it is.'

'No, I don't.'

'I think you do. You never dreamed of killing Lorna or Caitlin?'

'Course I haven't.'

'Funny thing,' Watt said. 'I have.'

'Get out. Get the fuck out.'

'Yeah,' Watt said. 'I will. But I want you to have this.' He turned the gun to face the other way. Offered it to Glass.

Glass made no attempt to take it.

'Go on.'

'Why would you want to give it to me?'

''Cause I'm bad and I think you should shoot me. Before I do something I regret.'

They'd been here before, the first time at the Castle. Glass wasn't going to be dragged into this again. Maybe he *should* just shoot the fucker.

'You shouldn't be here,' Glass said. 'Caesar said he'd give me time to think.'

'Am I stopping you thinking?'

Glass reached for the gun. Watt didn't pull away. Glass's fingers wrapped round the grip. Watt's hand flopped down onto the bed. Glass's finger slid inside the trigger guard. The gun felt lighter than he remembered.

'Go on.' Watt wasn't smiling. He meant it.

'Leave,' Glass said. 'Leave us alone.'

'I don't know that I can do that. I've missed you.'

'You having fun? You enjoying this?'

'It's been a long time since I've enjoyed anything.'

Glass raised his hand.

'That's it,' Watt said. 'Shoot me. It's the only way to protect Lorna and Caitlin. Trust me. I should know.'

Glass's finger pressed against the trigger. So fucking tempting. So very fucking tempting.

'Did you check the safety?' Watt said.

Glass stared at him.

'Turn it off. Won't work otherwise.'

And Glass remembered Mad Will telling him that, too. Or had he imagined it? He flicked the switch with his thumb.

'At this distance,' Watt said, 'I'm going to make a real fucking mess. Bits of brain all over the nice clean bedclothes. Can't be helped, I suppose.' He smiled. 'You going to do it, then? Or are you a ball-less cunt after all?'

Glass pulled the trigger.

There was a click. No explosion.

Watt shook his head. 'Nick,' he said. 'You're just like me.' He got off the bed and walked towards the door. As he passed the dresser, he put his hand in his pocket. Took it out, and moved it over a bowl where Lorna kept bits and bobs for her hair. Watt opened his hand, and dropped in the magazine. 'Lucky I checked the chamber, too.' He dipped into his pocket again, pulled out a single bullet and let it clink into the bowl. 'I'll see you in your dreams, if not before.'

'WHY ARE YOU dressed?' Lorna said when she got back.

'Couldn't sleep.' He'd loaded the gun again the minute Watt left. Slid the magazine back into the grip. Racked the slide to load a bullet into the chamber. Flicked the safety on. Tucked the gun in the back of his waistband.

While he waited for Lorna, he checked his stash in the garage. Watt had left it alone, like he'd said. He was full of surprises. Glass popped a couple of bennies. Needed to be awake now. Needed to think about what had happened and what he was going to do about it. He had to make them stop.

He wanted to tell Lorna everything, but he knew if he did, she'd leave with Caitlin. He couldn't go with her, give everything up, let Watt win. And he couldn't face life here on his own. She'd get back with David. Glass would be fucked. Some other bastard would bring up his child.

He'd come to a decision.

He'd tried to shoot Watt once. Next time he'd make sure the gun was loaded.

First step was to find out where the fucker lived.

'Everything okay,' Lorna asked.

'Yeah,' he said.

'Then why are you crying?'

She put her arms around him and the warmth and shape of her reminded him how good things used to be.

GLASS HAD THOUGHT about hiding the gun again before heading off to work, but where was he going to put it? Couldn't leave it in the usual place for Watt to find again. He finally decided to put it in the glove compartment of the car. For now, at least, till he could think of somewhere better. During the drive, he thought about relocating his stash too, but decided that if Watt had wanted to nick it, he'd have done so already. Glass had never seen Watt so much as take a drag of a joint at Mad Will's. Seemed totally disinterested. Maybe it interfered with the porn. Or maybe he was a recovering junkie.

After he'd parked and started the walk towards the gatehouse, Glass almost turned back to the car. He'd love to take the gun into the Hilton with him, blast the fuck out of Caesar and Horse. Problem solved. Well, partly. There would still be Watt to deal with. But the problem would be reduced, at least. Course, he'd never get the gun through the metal detector.

He walked on, unarmed.

Inside, Crogan was on duty alone, looking bored. But as Glass approached, his face grew more and more animated until he looked as if someone was standing on his toes.

Glass said, 'Something the matter?'

'Some people want to see you. Shaw's office.'

'Who?'

'You better go straight up. I'll let them know you're here.' Crogan turned and picked up the phone.

Some people wanted to see Glass? This time of night? That didn't sound good.

IN S.O. SHAW'S office, Shaw said, 'It's what they call a blanket party.'

'Never heard of it,' Glass said.

He looked at the pair of suits sitting next to Shaw, chairs pulled at an angle round the desk. One of them looked about fifty and was taking delicate little puffs on a Meerschaum pipe. The other was twenty-five years younger, continually scanning the room as if he expected a lorry to come crashing through one of the walls any minute just so he could say, 'I knew that was going to happen.'

They'd introduced themselves when Glass stepped into the office: Detective Sergeant Fitch and Detective Constable Richmond. Said they just wanted a little chat. So far, though, they hadn't said anything, let Shaw do the talking.

There was a small package on the desk. Wrapped in gold

paper. Exactly the kind of paper Watt used when handing Caesar's drugs over to Glass.

'No,' Shaw said, glancing at the detectives. 'Fortunately blanket parties don't happen too often.'

'So what happened?' Glass said. 'And' – looking at the cops – 'why do you guys need to speak to me?'

'No need to get defensive.'

'I'm not.' He wasn't. But he hadn't slept much and it was hardly surprising he'd be a little irritable. He'd have to be careful how he responded. He needed to find out what a blanket party was, and what he had to do with it.

And why these policemen wanted to speak to him. And what was in that fucking package on the desk.

Fuck it. He needed to calm down. He shrugged. Hoped he looked the picture of nonchalance. He breathed in a lungful of smoke and coughed. Hoped his sore eyes weren't going to start watering. That was all he needed.

Shaw continued: 'Fox is in hospital.'

Glass's first thought was that maybe Fox had been struck by a virus. A particularly nasty one, of course, to have hospitalised him. Or maybe he had appendicitis. Or kidney stones. Something like that. But then he realised that Shaw wouldn't be talking in quite this manner if it was something so straightforward. And the police wouldn't be here either.

Shaw said, 'He was beaten up.'

A moment of elation, Glass thinking, *just what the bastard deserves*. He had to hold a smile in check. 'When?' he asked.

'This afternoon,' Shaw said. 'By some of the inmates.'

'Who?'

Shaw shrugged. 'We don't know. A blanket party. What they do, they sneak up on the victim and cover his head with a blanket. Somebody holds it there while the rest of them – pardon my French – beat the shit out of him. The victim has no idea who his attackers are. He can't rat on them afterwards.'

'What about the cameras?'

'Fuckers picked the right day.' Shaw looked pained. 'Cameras were off.'

'Oops,' Glass said. 'So you've no idea who might have done it?'

'Course I do,' Shaw said.

'But that's speculation,' D.S. Fitch said.

Glass coughed again, cleared his throat, said, 'Is Fox very badly hurt?'

'Bad enough,' Shaw said. 'Broken ribs. Broken wrist. Lots of bruising. Lost some blood. But he'll live.'

Shaw stared Glass in the eye for so long that Glass had to look away.

'How do you feel about that?' Richmond said.

'Glad he's going to make it, of course,' Glass said.

'Of course,' Fitch said. He moved his pipe into the corner of his mouth. Placed both hands on the package on the desk.

Glass's face flushed. The temperature in the room seemed to have cranked up several notches.

Fitch turned the package to face Glass. Someone had written on the outside: *For The Atenshun Of Nick Glass.*

'This was found in Officer Fox's pocket after the attack,' Fitch said. 'We've already taken the liberty of opening it.'

Glass saw that the outside packaging was loose. He knew they'd been waiting for him to look inside. He felt uncomfortable about doing so, though.

He reached forward, picked the package up, hands shaky. He hoped they didn't notice. The gold paper came away easily enough. It had been loosely wrapped around a wadding of bubble wrap. Inside the bubble wrap was something Glass recognised right away.

But he had to carry on. He found the end of the wrap and unrolled it. Peeled the cassette tape out of the packaging. Turned it over. Pretended to examine it. Laid it on the table.

Then he tucked his hands under the desk, linked his fingers together and squeezed. Looked up at Shaw, but Shaw wasn't paying attention to what he was doing. Shaw was looking at his face, trying to fathom what he was thinking.

The cops were staring at him too.

Glass wasn't sure what to think. Or what to say.

He looked at the desk again, at the cassette tape lying there. Jesus, his face was hot. 'What's . . .' His throat was dry. He started again, 'What's on the tape?'

'The parcel's addressed to you,' Fitch said. 'So I wonder if you'd like to guess.'

Glass shook his head hard. 'Shouldn't you be having that . . . thing . . . analysed?'

'You think?' Fitch said. 'Dust it for prints and all that? I thought I'd just take it home and record over it.'

Took Glass a second to realise Fitch had made a joke. He didn't laugh. 'S.O. Shaw said he had an idea who was behind this. You should pursue that line of enquiry.'

Fitch looked at Richmond. Nodded. 'Pursue that line of enquiry. Hmmm. What do you think, Constable?'

'Hard to prove,' Richmond said.

'That's not the point,' Glass said. 'You can't let these guys away with it.'

'What guys?' Fitch said.

'Whoever it is you think did it.'

'Did what?'

'Beat up Fox.'

'What about the tape?'

'What about it?'

'Good question,' Richmond said.

And right away Fitch said, 'What if we think it was you?'

Glass stared at him. Then looked at Shaw, who looked down at his lap. What the fuck had the bastard said? What if they thought it was him on the tape? They recognised his voice? Well, they would. That was the whole point.

Shaw straightened up and nodded. 'Officer Glass, it's no secret that you and Officer Fox don't get on too well.'

'I wouldn't say that,' Glass said.

'Well, I would. And it's not hard to back up. Want me to cite incidents?'

Richmond said, 'We know about the kitten.'

Jesus Christ. Glass said, 'It wasn't mine.'

'Taking Headcase Harris out for exercise,' Fitch said. 'Him all covered in excrement. Must have made you feel terrible.'

They'd done their homework all right. Probably not that hard. Shaw wouldn't take much persuasion to blab. 'Yeah, I can see how you might think I was provoked,' Glass said. 'I don't like Fox. That's no secret. But I didn't arrange to have him beaten up. That's the truth.'

'That right?' Fitch dipped into his jacket pocket and his hand reappeared with a piece of folded paper. He made a big show of unfolding it. 'This came with the package.' He gave it to Glass. 'Take a look.'

The note read: *Job done. Fox on the run! Hope u & ur luvd ones r well, watt?*

Caesar. If there was any trace of doubt in Glass's mind, it was gone now. He swallowed. 'What's on the tape?'

'A pop song. Pro-drugs, apparently. "Ebeneezer Goode"?'

Glass breathed deeply.

'Maybe there's a message there,' Fitch said. 'For you.'

'It's a set-up,' Glass said. 'If I had arranged this blanket party, I would have told the fuckers not to contact me. And I'd specifically have said not to leave a package addressed to me with a fucking stupid note in it and a shite pop song. You can't take this seriously.'

'Can't we?' Richmond said.

'No,' Glass said. 'Only an imbecile would think I was involved.'

'Well,' Richmond said, 'lucky for us we don't.'

Now that he knew the tape wasn't the one he'd feared, Glass was all set to carry on being angry, but Richmond's comment stopped him short.

'It's transparent, as you say,' Fitch said. 'Somebody wanted to drop you in it, so they concocted this afternoon's little scenario. Just for you.'

'Looks that way,' Glass mumbled.

'What I want to know,' Fitch said, 'is why.'

Glass felt his lower jaw clench. He said nothing. Wondered if the policemen saw the veiled threat in Caesar's note. Probably not. It was hard to figure out how an outsider might read those words: *Hope u & ur luvd ones r well, watt?*

But Glass knew exactly what it meant. He supposed Caesar thought that was a clever piece of misspelling.

'Why this particular "shite pop song"?' Fitch carried on. 'Do you know something about drugs and this prison?'

Maybe he should tell the police. Here they were. He could tell them. Get it all over and done with.

But what was the penalty for bringing drugs into a prison? Illegal possession of a firearm? Jesus, no, he couldn't tell them. It was too late for that. He had to take responsibility for himself. His actions had got him to this point. His actions would have to get him out of it.

Glass shook his head.

Fitch said, 'Well, if you don't know why, then I'd settle for who.'

'Someone who can write,' Shaw said. 'Which eliminates two-thirds of the prison population.'

Glass got up. 'I've no idea.'

'And you really don't have any idea why someone would send you this?' Richmond said.

Glass stuck his hand in his pocket. 'These people, they're hard to understand. I don't know why anyone would slit someone's throat and fuck them to death. Or what motivates someone to cut a guy's head off and play football with it on the street. No, I've no idea what provoked this. Maybe I looked at someone the wrong way. Or I'm too tall. Or too small. Or my hair's too long. Or short. Or curly. Or I have a stupid name. Or –'

'I get the picture.' Fitch sighed. 'We may need to speak to you again, Officer Glass.'

'You know where to find me,' Glass said. 'Mind if I get to work?'

CROGAN WALKED INTO the locker room, in civvies. 'How'd it go?'

Glass said, 'Shouldn't you have gone home by now?'

'Wanted to catch you. Find out what happened. See if you were okay.' He grinned. 'Okay, I'm just a nosey fucker.'

Crogan was more than that. He wasn't exactly a bosom buddy, but he'd always been friendly. And that was such a rarity in the Hilton that Glass took a chance.

'I need a favour,' he said.

Crogan rubbed his chin with his thumb. 'From me?'

'It's to do with Caesar.'

'That cunt.' Crogan stopped rubbing his chin. 'Keep talking.'

DURING THE NIGHT, Glass pegged in every half hour, like he was supposed to, walking up and down the corridors, checking that everything was okay.

It was. Apart from Caesar. His cell alarm went off, again and again and again.

Glass ignored it. Caesar could make an official complaint in the morning. Glass didn't think he would, though.

All Caesar wanted was to talk to Glass, see if he was suitably scared now, scared enough to take part in the escape plan. But Glass wasn't scared at all. Not any more.

He had a plan of his own. Just the thought of it was giving him a major buzz. Felt just like a cocaine rush.

Caesar had controlled Glass's life for far too long and it was going to stop soon.

TUESDAY

When Glass woke up, it was with a shout. His finger felt as if someone had grated it down to the bone, and set it alight. It throbbed and burned like no pain he'd felt before. He lay in bed wondering what kind of hell he'd fallen into.

He threw back the quilt and raised his hand. His right index finger was gone. Well, most of it. There was a stump attached to the knuckle, a bandage over it, spotted with blood. After the shock passed, he tried to remember what had happened.

He remembered driving home from the Hilton. The last thing he remembered was pulling up outside. After that, nothing.

He called for Lorna. She didn't come so he called again. Maybe she was out. Then he remembered something. She'd been packing. He remembered seeing her suitcase. He thought maybe she said she was going to her mother's with Caitlin. She'd left him? Then what? He'd taken a bucketload of pills and had a horrible accident?

His gun was on the bedside table. Maybe Lorna'd found it, got pissed off with him for not getting rid of it like he'd promised. A couple of blister packs of pills lay on the table too. And a handwritten note. Wasn't Lorna's writing, though. It read: *OXYs. Powerful painkiller. Take one every four hours.*

Half of one pack was gone. He squeezed out another pill with his left hand until it poked through the foil, grabbed it between his teeth. Swallowed. Did the same again.

He stared at his hand, trying to will his finger back where it belonged. Maybe there was something wrong with his eyes. He looked at his other hand and all his fingers were there.

He ought to remember losing his finger, for Christ's sake. He stuck his hand back under the quilt, out of sight, tried to think who might have left the note.

When he did get up, he was none the wiser.

He kicked something on his way out of the bedroom. One of Caitlin's tumblers. He bent down to pick it up. Smelled sour milk and something meaty, saw the carpet stained red. Noticed the walls, pink patches against the magnolia. Looked like he'd cut his finger there and tried to clean up the mess.

He needed to examine his finger, see the extent of the damage.

In the bathroom, he removed the bandage, his hand shaking. He glanced at the stump, saw the charred flesh, the bone sliced through, and vomited into the sink. Nothing but frothy liquid and the two pink and beige capsules. He kept vomiting till there was nothing left in his stomach. Even then, he carried on, shivering as bile forced its way up his gullet and out his mouth. Eyes watering, he picked up the pills, turned on the tap with the heel of his hand, leaned over the sink, let the water clean the pills, swallowed them again. He put his mouth under the stream of water and sipped and spat, sipped and spat.

After a time, he reached into the medicine cabinet, found a fresh bandage. He needed more than that, but it would have to do for now. What he really needed was medical attention. But he knew what would happen if he went to the hospital not knowing how he'd lost his finger. They'd take him away, lock him up. And then he wouldn't be able to do what he'd planned.

Losing his finger wasn't going to kill him. The wound was cauterised. He had painkillers. The OXYs had started to kick in and the pain was bearable.

He even thought about having a shower but the idea made him feel sick again. As he shuffled past the bath, he noticed that Lorna had left the curtain pulled across. That wasn't like her, but he didn't mind, so he left it. While he took a leak, he wondered if there was any chance of salvaging their relationship. She was so different when she wasn't drinking. Sometimes he still felt that she loved him. She was gone, though. For now. She'd come back after he'd sorted out Watt.

Nothing had changed. Watt was still going to die. But for Watt to die, Glass needed an address.

Mad Will would know. But Glass didn't think Mad Will would tell him.

No point asking Mafia. He wouldn't rat on his brother, even if his brother made up evil shit about him. Could say there was equally no point asking Caesar. But there was a difference. Glass wasn't prepared to shoot Mad Will or Mafia to get the information. Caesar, on the other hand . . . well, Glass was almost wishing the fucker would refuse to speak. If anyone was responsible for fucking up Glass's life, it was Caesar.

Whatever happened, this time Nick Glass was going to see it through.

IN THE PRISON car park once again. Just like last night. Only this time, he took the gun out of the glove compartment. Held it while he made sure he really wanted to go through with it.

A whole day without any sign of Watt. Maybe he'd gone.

Nah, he'd be back. Of course he'd be back.

Glass got out of the car, gun shoved inside the waistband of his trousers and covered with his jacket. He walked towards the gatehouse feeling the gun rub against the base of his spine.

Crogan nodded at him once he stepped inside. 'Cold?'

'Yeah, bit chilly,' Glass said, looking at his gloves.

'You feeling okay?'

'Bit of a cold coming on.' Glass sniffed, wiped his nose with the back of his glove to make it look convincing. Fact was, he'd popped quite a few OXYs and felt great, no pain at all. Found some codeine in his stash, too, so he'd been topping up with those. Had the rest of the OXYs loose in his pocket for later. They'd been making him sleepy, though, so he'd had to compensate with a faceful of bennies. He knew it wasn't the best idea but he had to get through the night so he could do what had to be done. 'You alone?'

'Like I said.'

'So how do we do this?'

'Walk on through,' Crogan told him. 'Easy as that.'

Glass did. When he stepped through the metal detector, it beeped.

'Hang on a tick,' Crogan said.

Glass stopped in front of him.

'You got something there you shouldn't have?' Crogan stared at him.

Glass's stomach squeezed tight. What the fuck was Crogan up to?

'Going to have to search you, Officer Glass.'

Glass said, 'I fucking trusted you.'

'Got to be careful who you trust.'

'Fuck,' Glass said. 'Fuck.'

Crogan grinned. Then he burst out laughing.

'Jesus fucking Christ,' Glass said. 'Jesus fuck.' The fucker was messing with him. Glass felt anger like daggers digging into his shoulders. Wondered for a minute if the painkillers weren't working.

'Should have seen your face,' Crogan said. 'Priceless.'

Glass took a deep breath. Didn't help much. He took another breath. 'Don't fuck about like that,' he said. 'Jesus.'

'Go on,' Crogan said. 'Coast's clear. Just don't do anything stupid.'

Jesus fucking Christ. 'I won't.'

'All joking aside,' Crogan said, lowering his voice, 'if you land in the shite, I'm not going down with you. You get caught, then it's a mystery to us all how you smuggled a gun in, but you most definitely did not get it past me tonight. Maybe you brought it in soon after you first started? Probably you bribed a turnkey to let you through. Someone who's on the outside now. Got it?'

Quite a speech. 'Fine,' Glass said. He didn't need this. Really didn't need it. 'How do you know I have a gun?'

'You want to take something metal inside, it's either a shank or a gun.'

That was a fair point. 'So maybe it's a shank.'

'Wouldn't fancy your chances against Caesar with only a shank. Neither would you.'

'If it was a gun,' Glass said, 'would you be okay with that?'

'It's not going to be pointed at me, is it?' He was grinning again, no clue just how angry Glass was.

'It's not going to be pointed at anyone,' Glass said.

'You're not going to shoot Caesar? Now I'm disappointed.'

'It's just a threat.'

'Dodgy,' Crogan said. 'If you're not prepared to use it, it's a bit of an empty threat.'

Amazing how many people wanted to offer advice on what to do with a gun. 'I thought you didn't want me to do anything stupid,' Glass said.

'That's right,' Crogan said. 'Don't pull a gun on Caesar if you're not prepared to use it. You won't live long enough to tell me about it. You sure you're okay?'

AROUND ELEVEN GLASS calls Lorna.

'You woke me up,' she says. Yeah, she sounds sleepy. Or drunk. Her speech is sloppy.

'Just wanted to make sure you're okay.'

'Why shouldn't I be?'

'No reason,' he says. He thinks about telling her what he's going to do. But no good can come of her knowing. He hopes she'll understand later.

'So why fucking phone and wake me the fuck up?'

She has to ask that? His fucking wife wants to know why he's phoning her. Hoping she'll understand is futile.

'You know what, Lorna?' he says. 'It doesn't matter.'

He hangs up. Regrets it instantly, and toys with the idea of calling her back. Manages to hold off for a minute.

Then dials.

'Lorna, I'm sorry.'

'It's over,' she says. 'Fuck you, Nick. I've had enough. I'm packing my bags.'

When he's thought about her leaving him, he's never imagined it would be like this. He's always imagined she'd find out about the drugs. Maybe find the stash. Or the gun.

But to decide to leave him because he gets annoyed with her on the phone?

She doesn't mean it. She's pissed, that's all. Being melodramatic. She'll fall asleep again right away, forget it ever happened.

He almost dials again just to call her a bitch, tell her to leave, he doesn't care. But he does care, that's the problem. If it was just her, he's not so sure it wouldn't be for the better. But Caitlin? God, no.

Nothing to worry about, though. Just hangover talk. She won't leave him.

ACTUALLY, AT AROUND eleven when Glass called Lorna she didn't answer. Even when the phone was ringing, he imagined Lorna at home in the dark, deciding not to answer because she knew it was him. But, no, she was most likely still at her mum's.

He'd have called her mother's, but there was no point. He'd already called twice. Each time the old witch insisted Lorna wasn't there. Why she couldn't just say that Lorna didn't want to speak to him, he didn't know.

Since he woke up, he'd been praying he'd remember what had made her leave. It was possible he'd said something. Let slip that Watt had visited, maybe, and she'd freaked, taken Caitlin, got on the next train to Dunfermline. Back to mummy and daddy. And David.

He needed coffee. That'd sort him out. But he didn't want to make coffee. He couldn't face the prospect of finding another little present inside the container.

Fuck it, what was wrong with him? Did he really think he could kill somebody if he was scared of making a cup of coffee?

He strode over to the cupboard, dragged out the coffee, tried to flip the lid. Couldn't with his gloves on. He took off the left one, tried again.

No dead kitten tonight.

He spooned granules into his mug. Hands shaking so badly he almost missed. Poured in milk. Splashed some onto the counter. Picked up a damp cloth, same cloth that'd been used to clean up the sink area since he'd first started. Those were some filthy fuckers he had to work with.

After he'd mopped up the milk, he rinsed the cloth, smelled his fingers. They were sour. Left the tap running, held his hand under the water. Let the flow hit the index finger of his good hand.

The tip of his missing finger tingled.

And tingled.

And tingled.

He poured water into his mug. Stirred the coffee, watching the frothy top swirl. Stirred it again, the opposite way.

Picked up the mug.

Sipped.

Clamped his teeth round the edge of the mug.

Burned his lip.

Bit.

Burned.

Bit harder.

Yelled into the mug.

Liquid bubbled.

Let go.

Held it between his teeth.

Till it dropped.

It bounced off the carpeted floor, liquid splashing over his feet, the bottom of his trousers.

He sat down on the floor. Adjusted the gun in his waistband. Stared at the steam rising from the carpet. Smelled the coffee. Listened to the sound of running water.

Sat there while time passed and things happened in his head and he forgot them and then they happened again and he changed what happened because what he saw in his head wasn't right, couldn't be right, wasn't going to be right, hadn't been right. Time passed and he looked back on it and it was all wrong and twisted in on itself and knotted and he knew he had to unravel it and do what had to be done.

He took another couple of painkillers and some more speed to counter the drowsiness.

Twenty minutes later he got up. He had to peg in.

The gun dug into his spine every time he took a step. It was uncomfortable, but it didn't hurt.

He couldn't wait to whip it out, though. Shove it in Caesar's face. Realised he'd have to do it left-handed, so he stopped to practise. It felt odd the first few times, but then it sat in his hand and his finger found the trigger no problem.

He tucked the gun away again and finished pegging.

HORSE SAID, 'WHAT the fuck?'

Light spilled into the cell from the corridor, enough that Horse raised a hand over his eyes to block it out.

Glass showed him the gun. 'Move it,' he said.

Horse swung his legs out of his bed.

His cellmate, a spindly young drug-dealer, looked terrified.

'Keep your fucking mouth shut,' Glass told him.

He nodded.

Horse said, 'The fuck are you doing, Glass?'

'What I should have done a long time ago.'

Horse shook his head. Got to his feet.

He was wearing underpants, nothing else. But the way he was standing, comfortable with his body, you'd have thought he was wearing a fancy bespoke suit.

Glass hated the fucker's confidence. He told him.

Horse stared at him. 'The fuck you been taking?'

'I want that fucking recording of me.'

'I don't have it.'

'Course you do.'

'It's not here.'

'Where is it?'

Horse waited, looked at the gun, 'Why the fuck should I tell you?'

'Don't, then,' Glass said. 'Let's go wake up Caesar and ask him.'

Horse stared at him.

'Fucking move your fucking arse,' Glass said. 'You fucking hairy cunt.'

CAESAR'S FIRST WORDS were the same as Horse's. He said, 'What the fuck?'

Jasmine made do with squeaking noises.

Glass steered Horse in front of him.

'Shut up,' Glass said. 'The fucking pair of you, shut the fuck up.' He waved the gun at Caesar and Jasmine.

He was in control now. They had to see that.

Jasmine stopped squeaking, pulled her blanket around her.

Horse said, 'Look –'

'You fucking shut up,' Glass said. 'I fucking told you. I've had all the shit I'm going to take from you lot.'

'What's brought this on?' Caesar made to get out of his bed. 'Do a man a favour and this is the thanks you get.'

'Stay there,' Glass said.

'Or what?' Caesar said. 'You'll shoot?'

'Exactly,' Glass said.

'Ordinarily,' Caesar said, 'I'd be pissed off at being woken in the middle of the night. But on this occasion, I really don't mind.' He chuckled. 'You're a real fucking comedian, Nick.'

Prick, prick, prick. Fucking prick. 'This isn't a joke.'

'Oh, I think it is.'

'You think so?'

'I think so. What do you think, Horse?'

'I think so too.'

'Fucking pricks,' Glass said. 'I don't give a shit what you think. Either of you.' He looked at Jasmine. 'Any of you.'

'Bet that's not even a real gun,' Horse said.

Glass pointed it at him and pulled the trigger. Nothing. Felt awkward. Thought he hadn't pulled it hard enough. Then realised what the problem was.

'See?' Horse said. But now he didn't sound too confident.

Glass flicked the safety as Horse took a step towards him. Pulled the trigger again. In the confined space of the cell, the noise bounced back through his bones.

Horse collapsed onto the floor. And he did collapse. The kind of fall that had to hurt even if the bullet hadn't.

'I'll be fucked,' Caesar said.

Jasmine started squeaking again.

'You fucking shot him,' Caesar said. 'You really fucking shot him.'

'I'll shoot you too.'

'The fuck's wrong with you?'

Jasmine was screeching now. Really fucking painful ear-splitting horrendous noise she was making. Like a bag of cats somebody'd set alight.

And along the corridor, the shouting and banging had started from the other cells. They were awake. Heard gunfire. And the only thing they could do to let anyone know they were in danger was to start making a racket.

The officer at the gatehouse had probably heard something, too. It was quite a distance away, and the duty officer often had the radio on. But even if the sound had travelled, the response would take time. Time to decide what the noise was, what to do about it. Help would take time to arrive. That was the nature of help, especially in a place like this where nobody could go anywhere in a hurry. Glass would be okay for a while yet.

Anyway, he couldn't rush this. Had to be done properly. Couldn't concentrate with this racket, though.

'Shut up!' he yelled at Jasmine.

She screeched at him.

He pointed the gun at her and shot her too.

She shut up.

The relative silence was fucking beautiful.

'The fuck did you do that for?' Caesar said.

'If she'd shut the fuck up she'd still be alive.'

'You're a sick man.'

Had to hand it to Caesar. He was remarkably cool. Just had two people shot right in front of him and although he had to know he was next, he wasn't even breathing hard. Not that Glass could see.

Glass almost burst into tears, he was so impressed by Caesar. Thought about handing over the gun, telling him he deserved it.

Wished he was as fucking cool.

And, you know, dying was a way out. Problem solved. All problems solved. Well, they weren't solved, they became someone else's. But that was tempting too.

Glass didn't like too much responsibility. Caitlin was more than enough. But he didn't want to die just yet. That was too easy. 'Horse and Jasmine wanted to escape,' he said. 'There. They've fucking escaped.'

Caesar shook his head.

Glass supposed that meant something but he wasn't sure what.

'What do you want?' Caesar asked.

'That tape recording.'

Caesar nodded. 'It's gone. Smuggled out. Watt has it.'

'That's handy. I want to see him anyway. Where can I find him?'

Caesar looked up. 'I give you Watt, you'll kill me.'

'Maybe I'll kill you anyway.'

'You're fucked, Glass. You just killed two people.'

'Yeah, I'm fucked,' Glass said. 'My wife and kid left me.

Because of you. And Watt. So you're both fucked too. We're all fucked. Ask Horse and Jasmine.'

Caesar said, 'I gave you Fox.'

'Yeah, thanks. You set me up with your little note. Very nice of you.'

'You didn't think that was funny? Problem with you, Glass, you've no sense of humour.'

'You think? I'm having a laugh right now.'

'I can see that. You like killing. Feels good, doesn't it?'

'I didn't say that.'

'I think you'd like to cut off Horse's head, play football with it.'

Glass glanced down at Horse and noticed a movement out of the corner of his eye. When he looked up again Caesar was rushing at him, a flash of steel hurtling his way. A big fucking flash. A blade. Glass dropped to the floor, rolled, slid in some of Horse's blood. A clang as the blade struck something hard, something close to his body.

Glass twisted, got his hand up and fired.

Caesar looked at his arm. The bullet had ripped a hole in his bicep. He dropped the blade. It looked remarkably like Peeler's machete.

'Where did you get that?' Glass said.

Caesar was holding his arm, teeth bared, blood dripping through his fingers. 'Fuck you.'

'You couldn't have brought it in. Couldn't have got it through the metal detectors.'

'Fuck you, Crystal, you dopey cunt.'

'So how come?'

'Fuck you.'

'A con couldn't have...' Course a con couldn't have. Had to be an officer. But who? Only officer who was in the machine shop at the time was Glass. Until Fox arrived. Fox and Ross. 'Fox? Fox gives you a machete and you pay him back with a blanket party?'

'Fuck you.'

'No,' Glass said. 'Stop pissing me off.' He shot him in the knee. 'Fuck *you*.'

Caesar buckled. Yelled. Kept yelling.

'Was it Fox?'

Caesar roared. Pain or rage or both. Then: 'No.'

Then it had to be: 'Ross?' What a bitch.

'Fuck you.'

That was that.

Caesar was a constant moaning sound, the roaring gone.

There was banging from the peters all the way down the corridor now.

Glass had to hurry. He picked up the machete, tucked it under his arm. Big fucking bastard of a thing. How the hell had Caesar managed to hide that in his cell all this time? Could hardly have kept it concealed up his arse.

'Think it'd be funny if I cut your head off?'

Caesar said, 'You're fucking mental, you twat.'

Glass shot him in the stomach.

GLASS KNELT, LAID out Caesar's hand on the floor, palm down, fingers spread.

The racket the cons were making was ricocheting around in Glass's skull. Could hardly hear what he was doing, the sound making him dizzy.

He lined up the machete. Had to strike in the right place, as close to the knuckle as possible.

Difficult with his left hand.

Caesar wasn't dead yet – Glass saw his chest rise, fall. But he wasn't saying much, and his eyes were closed.

So, aye, okay.

Ignore the noise.

Here goes.

He swung the blade down as hard as he could. It cut through Caesar's index finger all right, and also half of his middle finger and the tip of the next one.

Caesar opened his eyes. His eyelids flickered. Then closed again.

Glass dropped the machete, picked up the finger. Squeezed blood out of it. Nice clean cut. Only question was whether it was going to fit.

He held it alongside his existing index finger. Looked a good match. Even in the dim light he could see that the skin colour wasn't ideal – Caesar's was much darker – but the length was good. First thing he'd have to do was trim the nail. Caesar's grooming left a lot to be desired.

Dirty fuck.

Dirty fucking fuck.

'Fuck *you*, you fucking twat.'

Glass took off his glove, moved Caesar's finger in place over the bandage on his own. Good. He put his glove back on, popped the finger in his pocket.

He'd sort that out later. More important things to deal with right now.

Had to find out where Watt lived.

He shook Caesar.

No joy.

Slapped his face.

No joy.

Grabbed his hand, squeezed the bleeding stumps of his fingers.

No joy.

Pressed the heel of his hand into the wound on his stomach.

No joy.

Smashed his fist into his wounded knee.

No joy.

Before he left the peter, Glass pumped a bullet into Caesar's head.

WHEN GLASS WALKED into their cell, Mafia and Darko were in their underpants. They were each holding a shoe, which they'd been using to bang on the walls along with the other cons.

Mafia said, 'The fuck's going on?'

'It's Glass,' Darko said. 'He's got a gun.'

'You the one who fired those shots?' Mafia asked. 'What have you done?'

'You have to tell me where to find Watt,' Glass said.

'Don't have to do fuck all,' Mafia said.

Glass paused. Fuck it, he was covered in blood. And everybody would know soon enough. 'I killed them,' he said. 'Horse and Caesar. And Jasmine.'

Darko said, 'Shit.'

'Yeah,' Glass said. 'Shit.'

Mafia said, 'Maybe you should leave it there, Nick.'

'I can't,' Glass said. 'Watt has a tape recording of me admitting I smuggled drugs for Caesar. And he's been coming round to my house, threatening my family. Now the boss he's so fucking fond of is dead. That's going to piss him off just a bit.'

'That's a fucker,' Mafia said. 'Caesar was probably the only thing keeping Watt in check.'

'You have to help me find him, Mafia. If you help me, I'll help you. I'll get you out.'

Mafia took off his glasses, looked towards him, eyes wiggling from side to side faster than Glass was used to seeing. 'He's my brother,' Mafia said. 'But the truth is, I should have dealt with him a long time ago. All I've done since coming in here is hide from the problem.'

'So you'll tell me where I can find him?'

'I'll do better than that. I'll take you there myself. If I'm going to snitch on him, I'd like to do it to his face.'

'You better get dressed, then,' Glass said.

WHEN MAFIA TAKES off his glasses, eyes wiggling, he says, 'He's my brother. I'm not going to give him up.'

'You have to,' Glass says.

'You going to shoot me too if I don't?'

'Fuck,' Glass says. '*Fuck*. I have to get out. I have to find him.'

'I'll come with you,' Darko says. 'But we need to go now.'

'Mafia?' Glass says.

'Go while you can.'

'You better get dressed, then,' Glass says to Darko.

'*WHICH IS IT?*' asked the prison shrink's voice in Glass's head.

'The first, of course. Mafia wouldn't let me down.'

'You sure?' Riddell asked.

Glass was sure.

For the plan to work, he had to hand over the gun so it would look like he was a hostage. It was a risk. But he had to put his trust in Mafia. There was no way he'd ever find Watt otherwise.

They'd been close, grown apart, made up. But whatever

Mafia thought of Glass right now, surely he wasn't stupid enough to kill a prison officer.

Glass offered the gun to him. 'Careful with that,' he said.

'No good to me,' Mafia said. 'I can't see well enough to hit a brick wall two feet in front of me.'

'Give it to me,' Darko said. 'If you're leaving, I'm coming too.'

'That's how Darko came along,' Glass said to Riddell. 'Even though we didn't want his company.'

No, Glass didn't know Darko that well, and after the incident with the kitten, maybe Darko wasn't as friendly as he'd once thought. Glass pondered the situation for as long as it took to realise he didn't have any option. He gave Darko the gun.

MAFIA HELD GLASS round the neck, Darko, gun in hand, to the side of them. They'd staggered down the stairs and through the deserted C-Hall, listening to the shouts and bangs coming from the cells as they passed. Now they were approaching the entry gate and had to look convincing for the cameras.

Darko gave Glass a good shake, making Glass reach for his key chain, find the key and open the gate. He fumbled it, cause he was using his left hand, but that just made it look more convincing, a bad case of the shakes.

He slid back the gate and they stepped into the corridor.

This was the spot where the corridors from the four halls converged. The corridor where they met led to the gatehouse. Glass had worried that somebody from the gatehouse might have come down to see what the noise was about. But that wasn't protocol. Protocol was to stay in the gatehouse and call for back-up. And then wait until back-up arrived.

With any luck, that would take a while. Everybody was

locked up, so there was no hurry. But even if back-up had already arrived, the three of them still had a good chance of walking out of there. Hostage situation like this, the cons armed with a gun, well, the authorities'd look pretty fucking bad if they let Darko shoot him. Three dead cons was bad enough. Three dead cons and a prison officer was a lot harder to explain to the press.

They moved along the corridor, and Glass saw the outline of a figure in uniform on the other side of the gate.

'Bollocks,' Darko whispered.

'It's okay,' Glass whispered back. 'We need him. We can't open the main gate from this side. Got to be somebody on the other side who does that.'

Darko said, 'Let's do it, then.' He grabbed Glass tighter. 'Fucker,' he shouted. 'Fucking screw.'

Mafia started swearing at him too.

Then Darko shouted to the officer, 'You better open up there or I'll shoot. Don't fucking think I won't.'

Glass was struggling to breathe. Darko's choke hold was full on. Bastard was putting on a hell of a performance. Glass's head was tilted back, but he peered down the corridor and made out the officer on duty.

It was Crogan.

By rights Crogan should have gone home when Glass started his shift. Glass hoped to Christ that Crogan wasn't thinking about playing the hero. Why the fuck had the fool stayed behind?

'Don't do it,' Glass said, playing his part.

'I'll fucking shoot him,' Darko said.

'Fuck off, you wee shite,' Crogan said.

'I just want you to open the gate and let us through.'

'Darko,' Crogan said, 'you know I can't open the gate.'

Glass felt something thump against him. A split second later he heard a loud roar and pain flared in his shoulder. He fell forward till an arm snatched him back up onto his feet.

His legs wouldn't hold him up, though.

Glass felt his other arm tugged and wrapped round a neck. Mafia's, he supposed.

'Fuck,' Mafia said. 'Fuck.'

'Next shot,' Darko shouted. 'I'll shoot him in the spine, Crogan. And I'll save the last bullet for his head. So open the fucking gate.'

Glass wanted to tell him that this was all unnecessary. Crogan had just been pretending to be stubborn. He'd have opened the gate no problem. Wasn't necessary for Darko to have shot him.

Jesus fucking Christ. Darko had shot him.

That wasn't part of the fucking plan.

CROGAN OPENED THE gate, stood back, hands in the air, palms exposed. 'You okay?' he asked Glass as they passed.

Glass tried to smile, but didn't have the strength. He was struggling to stay upright. Thought he might throw up.

'He needs a doctor,' Crogan said.

'Fuck what he needs,' Darko said. 'Go sit the fuck down behind your desk like a good screw. And don't move.'

Crogan raised his eyebrows but did as he was told.

Darko said, 'Are the cops outside?'

Yeah, Glass thought. Armed response unit. It'd be like the end of *Butch Cassidy and the Sundance Kid*, them running outside into a hail of bullets. Way to go. He was looking forward to it.

'No one's waiting,' Crogan said. 'Got a couple of officers on their way from B and D-Halls. That's it.'

'Expect us to believe that?' Darko said.

'Up to you,' Crogan said.

'Only two?'

Crogan said, 'All that were spare.'

'How come they're not here yet?'

'No urgency,' Crogan said. 'Just heard you fuckers making a noise in C-Hall and thought I'd better get some company. On the off-chance I might need it.' He glanced at Glass. 'What happened?'

'Jasmine's dead. And Horse.' Glass paused. 'And Caesar.'

'Christ,' Crogan said. 'Somebody deserves a medal.'

'Stop gassing,' Darko said. 'We need to take a look outside.'

They moved towards the window in a clumsy shuffle.

Darko peered through the bars. 'No sign of any cops.'

'I told you,' Crogan said.

Glass said, 'Which officers are coming?'

'McDee and Ross.' Crogan shrugged. 'Lazy pair of fucks at the best of times.'

Glass could hear the distant thumping from C-Hall, like toneless music from a nearby party.

'But you told them you needed help?' Darko said.

'Didn't know I needed any,' Crogan said. 'Just asked them to come over. In case.'

'That's good,' Darko said. 'I like your optimism.' He walked towards the gate, Glass pinned to him.

Heat had spread all over Glass's shoulder. Blood crawled down his back.

'Now, when they get here,' Darko said, 'we'll all keep calm and everything'll be fine. And keep the noise the fuck down, Glass.'

Glass realised he was moaning. He closed his mouth. It filled with saliva. He swallowed. Blinked hard. *More painkillers.*

Didn't know if he could keep quiet without them. 'OXYs,' he said. 'Pills. My pocket.'

'Get your hand away from there,' Darko said.

Glass let his hand drop to his side.

'Act like everything's normal,' Darko told Crogan, just as they heard footsteps in the corridor.

Then voices, one much higher than the other. Sounded like Ross and McDee had bumped into each other en route.

The voices got louder. Glass heard the clearly female voice of Ross saying, 'Crogan. Everything okay?'

'Seems to be. What kept you?'

'Took a look through the gate at C-Hall. No sign of Crystal. And they're making a real din. Reckon he's fucked up again.'

'Come on through,' Crogan said. 'If Glass doesn't check in, we'll get a key, go take a look.' He buzzed open the gate. 'How's Fox?'

'On the mend,' Ross said. 'But won't be back at work for a while yet. That's if he decides to come back.'

Ross and McDee walked into the reception area, looked up at Crogan.

Behind them, Darko said, 'Hands up.'

McDee turned. 'Fuck me,' he said. 'He's got a gun.'

'And he's not afraid to use it,' Darko said, giving Glass a shove.

Pain spiked in Glass's shoulder, skittered down his back. He cried out. Had a violent impulse to see what his shoulder looked like. Not that he could, but that didn't stop him wanting to. Couldn't be worse than his finger.

'He's bleeding,' McDee said.

'Thanks,' Darko said. 'You could you be Mafia's eyes. You've clearly got a talent for it.'

McDee's hands moved about like they had a mind of their own. He finally settled on clenching his fists, holding them tight to his chest and banging his knuckles together.

'Get your fucking hands up,' Darko said.

'Why'd you bring us here, Crogan?' Ross said. 'Fucking right into a trap, you wank.'

'They weren't here when I called you,' Crogan said. 'Couldn't do anything about it.'

'Tell that to the –'

'Quiet, *kuja*,' Darko said. '*Psi ti jebu mater.* In the arse. And for the last time, get your hands up.'

Ross shut up, raised her hands. McDee did the same.

Crogan said, 'Let me call an ambulance.'

'He told you to be quiet,' Mafia said.

'Put your fucking hands up,' Darko said.

They stood there staring at one another as the dull steady thump thump thump from C-Hall carried towards them. The cons would keep that up all night.

Darko said to Glass, 'You got your car keys?'

Glass said, 'Back . . .' Hard to breathe. '. . . pocket.'

'What do we do about them?' Darko waved the gun at the officers. 'The gate only opens from the other side. You know how to open it, Glass?'

Glass nodded. 'Button on the desk.'

'Okay, folks,' Darko said. 'Take your clothes off.'

Crogan, McDee and Ross stared at each other.

Mafia said to Glass, 'What are they doing?'

'Nothing,' Glass said.

Darko shouted at them: 'TAKE OFF YOUR FUCKING CLOTHES.'

One by one, they lowered their hands. McDee was the first to start to undo his jacket buttons. Then Crogan followed. Ross folded her arms.

Glass said, 'Do it, Ross. Do it or he'll shoot me.'

'Skinny wee fuck wouldn't dare,' Ross said.

'He already has.'

'That?' Turned her head to the side. 'It won't kill you.'

'It's no fucking joke.'

'He'll do it,' Crogan said.

'I don't give a fuck,' Ross said. 'I'm not taking my fucking clothes off.'

'You're such a cunt,' Darko said.

'You're a sleazy Slavic fuck.'

'Just fucking do what you're told,' Darko said.

Ross didn't move.

'We don't have time for this.' Darko aimed the gun in her direction and smiled.

She closed her eyes.

Darko fired.

McDee dropped to the floor.

'What happened?' Mafia said.

'Let's go,' Darko said.

'Did you hit her?' Mafia said.

'Let's go right fucking now.' Darko grabbed Glass's tie.

Glass said, 'How bad is it, Ross?'

She was bent over McDee. 'Fucker hit him in the chest. But he's still breathing.'

'Should've done what you were told,' Darko said. 'That'll keep you busy.' He tugged Glass's tie. 'Time to go. Right fucking now.'

'I can't,' Glass said.

'You'll do what you're told, too.'

'I'd like to,' Glass said. 'But I really don't think I can.' As if to prove his point, his legs buckled.

Darko and Mafia held him up. Been there before.

'You fucks,' Darko said. 'Don't fucking try anything till we're gone.' They shuffled across the room towards the outside door.

'Leave Glass,' Crogan said. 'He needs an ambulance as much as McDee.'

'Stop fucking telling me what to do,' Darko said. '*Drkadzijo.*'

They heaved Glass along. Got to the door. Found the handle, opened it.

A blast of wind hit Glass's face. Revived him a little. Not enough to hold himself up, though.

'Come on,' Mafia said.

A final look behind him and Darko said, 'After three.' He counted. Then they were moving again.

Something pressed against Glass's wound. He screamed. There was no let-up. Nobody seemed to care.

Mafia and Darko scampered across to the car park, Glass dragging his toes along the ground between them.

Tried to lift them. Tried to raise his knees. But that just increased the agony.

Must have passed out. Next he knew they'd come to a standstill. The pressure was off his shoulder, Mafia and Darko were breathing heavily, and Glass's face stung as if he'd been slapped.

'Which one's your car?' Darko was right in front of him, face in his face. Darko *had* slapped him. 'Your car?' he repeated.

Wasn't a lot to choose from. A dozen or so.

Glass wondered if he shouldn't just leave them to it. They'd find it eventually. They knew where his keys were. Could try the cars one after the other. That'd be fun. Staying awake was too much trouble.

But they wouldn't let him sleep.

His head snapped back as Darko slapped him again. Tasted blood this time. Felt a lump on the inside of his top lip. Raw round the edges.

'Car?' Darko said. 'Last fucking chance.'

Glass looked around, pointed it out.

'Easy, wasn't it?' Darko said.

Actually, it wasn't, but Glass didn't say so. His fingers and toes were tingling as if he had pins and needles. He was going to pass out again.

He was looking forward to it.

The voices came first. Before the pain. But when the pain hit, it deafened him to everything else.

Glass opened his eyes. Light pressed like thumbs into his eyeballs. A welcome relief from the craziness in his shoulder.

Took a moment, blinking, for his eyes to adjust.

Gradually, the bleary streak turned into a room. An unfamiliar one.

No recollection of how he'd got here. Mafia and Darko must have carried him inside.

Inside. Not there, no. They weren't in the Hilton.

They'd escaped.

Well, Darko and Mafia had escaped.

Given what Glass had done, maybe it was accurate to say that he'd escaped too. He'd killed Caesar. He'd killed Horse. He'd killed Jasmine. Holy shit, had he really done that? The memories seemed real enough.

He took a breath and looked around.

A couple of single beds, each with a cheap night table. A clock on the table telling him the time was 2:02. A desk against the far wall. A wooden chair. A more comfortable armchair that Darko was pacing up and down in front of.

Glass heard Mafia mention his name.

The curtains were drawn, the overhead light on. A TV, turned off, squatted in the corner. A kettle sat on a coffee table.

Who had a kettle in the bedroom, Glass wondered. Who had two single beds in the bedroom come to that?

Then it clicked: this was a hotel room. Of course. There was even a small bowl next to the kettle with sachets of coffee and tea.

Glass lay where he was, closed his eyes. He had a few painkillers left, in his trouser pocket. All he had to do was reach down. But he was too heavy. Maybe the pain would ease if he didn't move. Lying here, listening to the conversation, that was as much energy as he could summon.

'Doesn't matter,' Mafia said. 'You agree we need to get rid of Glass's car?'

'Yeah,' Darko said. 'Drive it somewhere and dump it.'

'They'll know we're nearby.'

'Not if we clear out of there straightaway.'

'We'll have to come back here for Glass. We can't take him with us in his state.'

'Can't babysit him either. He needs a hospital.'

'If he goes to a hospital,' Mafia said, 'then it's cheerio hostage.'

'A dead hostage ain't much good.'

'He won't die.'

'You sure?'

Silence for a bit.

Then Mafia said, 'We'll get somebody to patch him up. Take him with us.'

'Who? He needs a doctor.'

'I'll call someone.'

Glass heard Darko sigh. 'Even if we get him fixed up, he'll slow us down.'

'He'll be fine. Just a shoulder wound.'

'Might be infected.'

'We'll get it checked out.'

'Might *get* infected.'

'We'll fucking amputate.'

Pause.

Then Mafia said, 'This is what we get for you shooting him.'

Darko: 'Would you have done it?'

Silence again.

'So you should be fucking thanking me. Not complaining.'

Time dragged.

Mafia: 'We can't stay here.'

'I know.'

'I'll make that call, then. You better move the car. Take it as far away as you can.'

Another pause.

'Okay. But I'll come back,' Darko said.

'Don't bother. They'll be looking for us together. You'll be safer alone.'

'How are you going to cope?'

'I'll manage. Glass can be my eyes.'

'You trust him? I just shot the fucker.'

'Yeah, you did,' Mafia said. 'Better leave me the gun.'

'If you want. But it's a murder weapon. We should get rid of it.'

'No problem. I'll wipe it. Give it to Glass when I'm done with it.'

Glass sat up. No, he tried to sit up. Couldn't do much more than raise his head. Couldn't hold it there for long, though. He let it fall back against the pillow and groaned.

'Sleeping Beauty's awake,' Darko said.

'Wh—' Glass's lips were dry. He licked them. Mafia had gone. Must have slipped off to the toilet. 'Why are you still here?' he asked Darko. 'Go. Listen to Mafia. He's right.'

'You've been dreaming,' Darko said.

'I've been awake for a while,' Glass told him. 'You need to get moving. Take the car. Dump it. Don't come back. Of course Mafia can trust me.'

'Mafia?' Darko wanted to leave, Glass could tell.

And fuck it, it made sense.

'Can I give my wife a call?' Glass asked.

'You're a fucking hostage,' Darko said.

'Not a real one, though. So who's to know?'

Darko said, 'Are you totally thick?'

'Come on. She'll be worried. I just want her to know I'm okay.'

'Then the whole world will know I'm bluffing. No,' Darko said. 'I can't let you do that.'

Which was maybe just as well. Glass didn't want to get the reaction he'd got when he called earlier. No, of course he wouldn't. She wasn't that heartless. Why did he keep imagining the worst?

She'd threatened to go to her mother's. Packed her suitcase. And Caitlin's. He'd persuaded her to stay.

Yes, he'd persuaded her to stay. Hadn't he?

Shit, no. He *was* dreaming.

She'd gone. But maybe she *had* come back.

'Anyway,' Darko said to Glass. 'You're not okay. You need a doctor.'

Mafia stood in the doorway of the toilet. 'And some new clothes.'

Glass laughed. 'Fine time for a change of image.'

'Who's talking about your image?' Darko asked.

'Just being practical. The bloodstains don't look too clever.'

'I know what you meant,' Glass said. 'This is all wrong, you know. You should be enjoying this. You should be jumping up and down on the spot like a kid on his birthday.'

Mafia turned his head in Glass's direction. Waited.

'I have to explain?' Glass said. 'You're free.'

'Out of jail, maybe,' Darko said. 'But far from free. McDee's probably dead.' He paused. 'And they'll probably try to finger me for Caesar and his crew. I don't feel like celebrating just yet.'

'Hardly makes me feel like breaking into a song and dance routine, either,' Mafia said.

'Darko.' Glass closed his eyes briefly. 'Why did you shoot McDee?'

'Cause I couldn't kill Ross. I'm not going to shoot a woman.'

'That's it?'

'Had to shoot someone. Shooting you didn't work as well as I'd hoped.'

'Doesn't matter.' Mafia placed a restraining hand on Darko. 'Point is, they're dead and we have to handle the consequences.'

'Yeah,' Glass said, relaxing. 'You're right.'

'You should go, Darko,' Mafia told him. 'While you can. Staying together won't be good for our health.'

BEFORE HE LEAVES, Darko picks up the phone.

'Don't,' Glass says. 'You can't trust anyone.'

'You want to lie there and bleed?'

'No,' Glass says to Riddell. 'It wasn't Darko. Darko left. Mafia picked up the phone.'

'Quite sure about that?'

'Positive.'

'It wasn't you?'

'Who would I call? Anyway, they wouldn't even let me speak to Lorna.'

'Where was Lorna?'

'I don't know. But I'd have tracked her down.'

'And what would you have said?'

'That I was sorry.'

'For what?'

'I don't know. Whatever it was I did that made her leave.'

'Okay,' Riddell says. 'Carry on.'

After Darko left . . . where was he? Yeah, after Darko left, Mafia picked up the phone.

That made sense.

'Don't,' Glass said to Mafia. 'You can't trust anyone.'

'You want to lie there and bleed to death?'

'I'll be all right.'

'Not for much longer,' Mafia said. 'We did our best to stop the bleeding but we're no doctors.'

Glass looked at his arm. They'd cut the sleeve away, ripped up what looked like a hotel towel and folded it over his shoulder, tying the ends under his bicep. He was still wearing his gloves. Looked fucking silly. He pulled off the left one with his teeth, rummaged in his pocket and found some pills. Popped a couple more OXYs and a speed chaser.

Mafia dialled. While he waited for a reply, he mumbled to himself, swearing, idly waving the gun around with his other hand.

'Careful with that thing,' Glass said.

Mafia placed the gun on the desk. 'Come on,' he said. He hung up. Dialled again. He had to call three times before he got through. 'At fucking last,' he said. 'Same to you.' Pause. 'Doesn't matter what fucking time it is. I need your help.' Pause. 'It's me, Mafia.'

Glass listened as Mafia explained that they needed a doctor and a car. The guy on the other end must have kept trying to interrupt cause Mafia said, 'Will you fucking shut up and let me speak? I can't explain everything over the phone. Just do what I'm telling you. My friend's hurt. He can't travel till he sees a doctor.'

He gave the address of the hotel. Then said, 'No, you need to come over right now . . . Yeah, I know we can't take your car . . . Get someone else to nick one and bring it over to us. We don't need a driver, just a car, tell them. But get yourself over here in a hurry.'

He was being optimistic. Glass certainly couldn't drive. His arm was all stiff now. Not to mention his busted hand. And Mafia couldn't see. Between them they had the necessary working body parts, but individually they weren't up to much.

After Mafia hung up, Glass said, 'That was nice.'

'What was?'

'Calling me your friend.'

'I'm trying to save your arse here,' Mafia said. 'You think I'd call you a screw?'

Glass left it for a minute. Then he said, 'So is this just a case of you needing a hostage? Or would you want me alive anyway?'

'You're such a fucking kid.' Mafia didn't say anything else for a while. Contented himself with stroking the ribbed grip of the gun.

Glass didn't disturb him. He was right. Glass was a fucking kid.

So he'd had a sheltered upbringing. Grew up with his mum and big sister, Hazel. Never knew his dad. Occasional blokes, sure, but only one who lasted any length of time. He was okay, but they never really clicked, him and Glass.

Anyway, Glass met Lorna, first woman he ever fell for, when he was working a summer job in her dad's bakery, saving for university. Back then, before her dad lost the business, she was smart and scary and sexy and confident of what she was doing between the sheets. They'd only been going out for three months when she got pregnant.

'How?' he'd asked her.

'How do you think?'

'But you're on the pill or something,' he said. 'Aren't you?'

They'd never spoken about it. He'd just assumed.

'No,' she said.

'But,' he said, trying to get his head round what he was hearing, 'but you must have been taking some kind of precaution.'

'Why?' she said.

'Cause,' he said. 'Cause otherwise . . . you know, *this* was going to happen.'

'You think I don't want to be pregnant?'

'I – I don't . . . do you?'

'Yes. Absolutely. I love it. I want a family. Don't you? Isn't that the whole point of a relationship?'

He wasn't sure. Was it? He'd never thought beyond the sex. 'You could have asked.'

'I could have, yes.'

'It would have been polite.'

She laughed. 'It would have. I'm sorry. Would you have said yes?'

'I don't want to be a father,' he'd said. 'I'm too young.'

'You'll be a great dad,' she said. 'Anyway, too late for regrets.'

He left school, took a temporary job at the bakery till he found something better, moved out of his mum's and in with Lorna.

Hazel wasn't happy. Not that he'd left Mum on her own. No, Hazel had long gone herself. Met an American lawyer, got married, moved to Boston. Been trying to have a family ever since.

And here was her little brother impregnating his girlfriend at fifty yards. No, his sister wasn't happy. She threatened to visit to give him a talking to, but he told her to stay away.

In those days they'd got on well, him and Lorna, in their

little flat above the bakery. And he wouldn't have missed out on Caitlin for the world.

His mum died two years later. Pancreatic cancer. At least she got to see her granddaughter before she went. Hazel didn't appear for the funeral and Glass hadn't seen her since. She might as well not exist.

God, he wanted to be home right now with the only family he had left, curled up in bed, Lorna one side of him, Caitlin the other, sneaking into the bed and placing the soles of her cold little feet on his shins, complaining about his hairy legs.

But he was in a hotel room watching Mafia playing with his gun.

'Can you leave that alone?' Glass asked him. 'You're making me fucking nervous.'

Mafia sighed. Tapped his fingers on the desk.

Glass had to talk to him. Couldn't contain this. There were things he had to know. 'What's going on?' he said.

Mafia angled his head away from him. 'Got a doctor coming. Getting a car.'

'No,' Glass said. 'With us. Now. Am I a hostage? I don't know whether this is for real or not.'

Mafia said, 'Your arm hurt?'

'Not as bad, but yeah, I can feel it.'

'Then it's real. Pain is real. Maybe the only thing that is.'

'But you haven't changed, have you? You're still the person I knew inside?'

'We change all the time, all of us. We're different people from the people we were only seconds ago.'

'I don't think people change much.'

'Depends what happens to them.'

'You saying I *am* a hostage?'

Mafia didn't reply.

'You wouldn't shoot me. Back at the Hilton, you gave Darko the gun.'

'Being practical. Remember, I can't see.'

'But if you could, you wouldn't have used it.'

'We'd escaped from our cell. With a prison officer. Who knows what I'd have done if I'd had the gun.'

'What if I leave now?'

'You'll die, most likely.' Mafia looked over at him. 'I wouldn't need to shoot you.'

'Fuck it,' Glass said. 'I'm just trying to understand.' He breathed out. 'I don't understand why Darko shot me.'

'I'm sorry about that.'

'I don't want an apology. I'd just like an explanation.'

'No, I'm sorry you don't understand.' Mafia took off his glasses, rubbed his eyes, one after the other, with the heel of his hand. 'Seemed like the right thing to do. Show the fuckers we were serious.'

'And you didn't care about the cost?'

'What cost?'

'To me, Mafia. The fact that he could have killed me.'

He put his shades back on. 'He's not that bad a shot.'

'But I might die. Still. You just said so.'

'Only if you run. There's a doctor on his way. Stay here, you'll be fine.'

'That's not a lot of comfort.'

'You want comfort,' Mafia said, 'you're talking to the wrong person.'

They sat in silence, listening to the hum of the electricity.

Glass said, 'You're wrong.'

Mafia sighed. 'About what?'

'About comforting me. What you said before. It means a lot.'

Mafia said, 'You ever shut up?'

'I'm just saying. When you said I was your friend.'

'Glass,' Mafia said. 'I'm so fucking friendly I'll suck your cock if it'll stop you getting all fucking sentimental. And if you don't fucking shut up, I *will* put a bullet in you.'

Glass shut up.

He shut up for quite some time. In fact, they didn't speak again till Mad Will arrived.

WHEN THEY HEARD the car pull up, Glass raised his head, held it there as best he could. Half expected Mafia to go to the window, look out through a gap in the curtain. Then he remembered that Mafia couldn't see.

'Can you make it to the door okay?' Glass said.

'Jesus Christ,' Mafia said. 'I'm not fucking blind.' He picked up the gun, started to move in the direction of the door, paused after a couple of steps. 'Anything on the floor?' he asked.

'Path's clear.'

He made it to the door just as there was a knock on it. He fumbled for the handle, found it, opened the door a crack. 'Yeah?'

'Long time no see.'

'Tell me about it.' Mafia opened the door. 'How are things?'

And that's when Glass saw Mad Will and thought for a minute that his bullet wound was worse than he'd realised, that the blood loss and drugs were making him hallucinate. But, no, it wasn't just the familiar chubby face and big teeth: the voice sounded like Mad Will's too.

Glass let his head fall back onto the pillow, eased his neck muscles which were beginning to tire with the strain of keeping his head raised.

The fuck was Mad Will doing here?

'Ah, the patient.' Mad Will walked over to Glass, stubbed his roll-up out in an ashtray. 'We've got to stop meeting like this.'

Glass grunted.

'So what happened this time?'

Glass looked at Mafia. He was wiping his glasses on his sleeve, the pupils of his eyes darting around. 'An accident,' Glass said.

Mad Will said, 'We'll need to get you sitting up.'

'I've tried. Can't get the leverage.'

'Don't worry,' Mad Will said. 'I'll help.'

'Okay,' Glass said. 'But you can't put pressure on my shoulder.'

'Jesus,' Mad Will said. 'Who's the doctor?'

'I dunno,' Glass said. 'Are you really a doctor?'

'Well, yes,' Mad Will said. 'At least, I trained to be one.'

Just what Glass needed. A quack. 'You know what you're doing?'

'Take it easy,' Mad Will said. 'I'm the best unqualified doctor in Edinburgh. Didn't I take care of your finger?'

Mad Will knew about his finger. 'You did that?'

'I did what I could. But it was a mess after you'd finished with it. Any of those painkillers left?'

'A couple.'

'Lucky I brought some more, then. So let's see what you've done to yourself this time.'

And he did somehow manage to raise Glass into a sitting position.

Mad Will fluffed up the pillows from both beds and shoved them behind Glass's back. He removed the cloth from Glass's shoulder and inspected the wound. 'Gunshot,' he said, after a bit.

'No flies on you,' Glass said.

'Didn't I tell you no good would come from playing with guns?'

'I don't need a fucking lecture. How does it look?'

'Pretty clean,' Mad Will said. 'Punched right through the flesh. No great harm done. Not much for me to do other than clean it up, stitch you up and then we can sit back, enjoy a toke together.'

'Can't do,' Mafia said. 'Got to stay sharp. And then get moving.'

'You have to relax, man.'

'Fuck that,' Mafia said. 'I've been relaxing for years.'

'You need antibiotics, though,' Mad Will said to Glass. 'I already warned you, you're going to get an infection.'

'You did?'

'You don't remember?'

'Not a thing.'

'Trauma,' Mad Will said. 'That and the drugs. You were so out of your face I wouldn't have been surprised if you'd thought I'd done it.'

'Did you?'

'Very funny,' Mad Will said. 'You told me it was all your own work.'

Glass shook his head. 'It's a fucking blank.'

'You really need to go to hospital.'

'Can't.'

'No,' Mafia said. 'He's staying with me. The fuck are you pair talking about anyway?'

'Yeah, what happened?' Glass asked Mad Will.

Mad Will stared at him, eyes narrowed. 'If you don't know, how should I?'

'My finger, I mean. I don't remember.'

'I only know what you were rambling about yesterday.'

'What was that?'

'An accident. Another one.'

Yeah, an accident. Sounded possible.

'Chopping onions.'

Shit. Maybe not. 'Was Lorna there? At my house?'

'Didn't see her. You don't remember *any* of it?'

'Nothing. Why did I phone you? I didn't know you were a doctor.'

'You needed something for the pain.'

'Could have found something in my stash.'

'I'm pretty sure you tried.'

Glass nodded. 'Did you . . . did you cauterise the wound?'

'Shit, no. That's barbaric. You did that yourself.'

Glass winced at the thought. Glad he couldn't remember doing it. 'Did you find my finger? The part I cut off?'

'Said you'd got rid of it. Put it somewhere it couldn't do any harm.'

Glass wondered if he'd dropped it in the bin, thrown it outside, flushed it down the toilet. He had no idea.

'I tried to take you to the hospital,' Mad Will said. 'You weren't having it. Threatened to shoot me. So I just made you as comfortable as I could. Gave you some painkillers, and something to knock you out. Want me to take another look at it?'

'Thanks,' Glass said. 'And there's one more thing you could do.' He looked around, said to Mafia, 'Where's my jacket? There's something I need in the pocket.'

'Darko's got your wallet,' Mafia said. 'Had to use one of your cards at reception.'

'That's okay,' Glass said. 'I had something else in mind.'

AT FIRST GLASS'S arm ached under the tight new bandage and his finger throbbed in its new dressing but Mad Will told him to up the dosage on the pills if he needed to and Glass had done just that. Now there was only a stiffness and an itching. He didn't want to fall asleep, but he was all out of speed. He hoped the adrenaline from the night's events would help counter any soporific effects of the painkillers.

Mad Will had refused to sew Caesar's finger onto Glass's stump. He'd said too long had passed and then looked confused and asked Glass where he'd found the finger. And when Glass explained that it wasn't his finger, Mad Will just shook his head sadly.

Yeah, Glass knew it made no sense. But he was missing a part of himself and he wanted it back, even if it was dead and belonged to someone else.

'Whose finger is it?' Mad Will had asked.

'Doesn't matter,' Glass said. 'He doesn't need it.' But that made no difference to Mad Will. He wouldn't do the surgery.

'So what's the plan now?' Mad Will said.

'Someone's bringing transport, right?' Mafia said.

'Couldn't get anyone else this time of night,' Mad Will said. 'So the only car we've got is mine. How did you get here?'

'In my car,' Glass said.

'Where is it?'

'Darko's getting rid of it.'

'Mafia's cell mate?'

'Yeah,' Glass said, surprised at how little he cared. 'The guy who shot me.' He had to force himself to sound angry.

'So you did have a car?'

'Highly recognisable one,' Mafia said.

'With known plates,' Glass added.

'Could have swapped them,' Mad Will said. 'No problem at all. When's Darko expected back?'

'He's not,' Mafia said.

'Just you now, huh?' Mad Will rubbed the tip of his nose with his thumb. 'Sure you don't want to turn yourself in?'

Glass laughed. 'Mafia won't let me.'

'He won't?'

'Ask him.'

'Hmmm,' Mad Will said. 'Sure it isn't you who doesn't want to turn yourself in? What did you do?'

Glass's eyelids were heavy. The painkillers were knocking him out. 'I killed some people,' he said. 'I'm in trouble.'

'I thought you didn't remember anything.'

'I remember tonight. Wish I didn't.'

'You killed someone tonight?'

'Yeah,' Glass said.

'Shit,' Mad Will said. 'Let me get you out of this place. Somewhere they won't look for you. Cause if Darko's been caught, the police'll be here right away.'

'What have I been telling you?' Mafia said to Glass. 'We've got to get moving.'

'Your hangout?' Glass asked Mad Will.

'Precisely. It's safe. Nobody lives there. It's not that comfortable, but nobody's going to come looking for you. You can rest up for a while. Get some sleep before you move on. Or whatever.'

'Okay,' Glass said, and Mafia agreed.

'Just one thing,' Mad Will said. 'I'll need the gun.'

GLASS SAT UP front, the gun stashed in the glove compartment. He listened to the steady purr of the engine as Mad Will drove them along a twisty B-road away from the hotel. Glass closed his eyes. No point fighting it.

When he woke up, he remembered he'd been dreaming about Watt and Mafia as kids. They were playing together in a school gym, along with a bunch of other kids, all of them dressed in school uniforms.

Mad Will slowed down for a set of traffic lights. When they changed, Glass craned his neck, said to Mafia in the back, 'Were you and Watt once close?'

'Like brothers,' Mafia said.

Glass faced the front.

'What did you say?' Mad Will asked him.

Glass shook his head. 'Do you know where Watt lives?'

'Yeah.'

'Would you tell me?'

'Why? You want to go bleed on his floor?'

'I want to kill him.'

'Go to sleep,' Mad Will said. 'Maybe when you're better.'

The car was cruising again, the engine making a soothing sound. Glass leaned his head against the window. The vibrations in his skull felt comforting. He watched fence posts spring into life, then shoot past. Whuuump, whuuump, whuuump.

In the backseat of his mum's Volvo, as a kid, he used to pretend he was outside, running alongside the car. In his imagination, keeping up was never a problem. He liked running in the fields best. Soft underfoot, great smells, no risk of being run over, countless obstacles to hurdle. Cause not only was he a speed merchant, he could also jump enormous heights and vast distances.

If the weather was nice during the summer, his mum liked to drive to the country with him and his sister. Mum didn't like beaches, preferred grass to sand. She'd point the car in a different direction each time, drive till they found somewhere that looked nice and green.

They'd stop. Have a picnic. Only once did they have a problem. And it wasn't that they got asked to move by an irate farmer. None of that 'Get off my land' crap. Not once. But they did get asked to move by a handful of polo horses in a field on some poncey estate.

Glass had never been so scared in his life. He thought horses were friendly creatures. But he'd got up close to this bunch, who'd whinnied, and stamped as he approached. He didn't read the signs. He was only ten or so. Nice if he could say he felt brave, but that wouldn't be true cause he didn't know there was anything to be scared of. He just did what curious little boys do.

One of the horses, a chestnut, reared up on its hind legs. Then another did the same. And only then did the young Glass consider that he might be in danger. But, still, he stepped closer, maybe being brave now. Certainly determined. Determined to get near enough to stroke their noses and give them a handful of grass.

That's when the action kicked off.

Two of them turned their backs on him, one after the other, sudden movements like fleabitten dogs twisting to nibble their itchy backs.

They straightened up. Neighed. And kicked out.

One of their hooves narrowly missed his head. He'd have taken a serious wallop if it had made contact. He stood for a second, imagining his head caved in, and saw that another kick was about to come.

He forced his legs to move. Sprinted. Put some distance between him and those crazy beasts.

After a bit he looked over his shoulder.

The horses were charging after him. All of them. In a pack.

He shouted. Waved to his mum and Hazel, a couple of hundred yards away, sitting on a rug under the shade of a tree.

Mum looked up. Waved back.

Hazel looked as though she was laughing.

Glass shouted again. Kept running. Could hear the thud of hooves as the horses galloped across the grass. Getting louder. Catching up with him.

Closer and closer.

They were snorting. He could feel hot breath on the back of his neck.

And there, his mum, Hazel, both waving now. Hazel leaning over, asking his mum something. His mum ignoring her.

Glass's cheeks were hot with tears.

He tripped.

Hands smacked into the grass. Wrists wrenched with the impact.

He tried to scream.

Didn't have the breath.

He was going to die. Trampled to death. He knew it.

Hooves battered the earth behind him. Echoed in his bones.

Hands over his head. Braced himself for the crunch of his spine.

But the horses ran past him. Jumped over him. They didn't touch him.

They cantered to a stop and, shaking, he looked up at them from the ground.

He pushed himself to his feet.

Hazel was laughing so hard Glass could hear her from where he stood. Mum was scrabbling towards him.

'Go away,' Glass shouted at Hazel. 'Go away.' He ran towards his mum, still shouting.

When he reached her, she grabbed him round the waist and hugged him close. She panted in his ear.

Over her shoulder, Hazel was sitting on the grass, smiling. 'Go away,' he said, quietly.

His mum said, 'You want me to go?'

'No, her,' he said. '*Her.*'

'Oh, Nick,' his mum said. 'Is she laughing at you again?'

Glass nodded. 'Make her go away.'

His mum let go of him and turned. 'Hazel,' she said. 'You heard what Nick said. Now go away.' She paused, asked Glass, 'Has she gone?'

Glass watched as Hazel's eyes narrowed, and then she flickered and disappeared as if she'd never existed. 'Yeah,' he said. 'She's gone. Why was she laughing at me, Mum?'

But his mum didn't know. Hazel was always a mystery to her.

Glass had survived without injury, and Hazel had appeared again after a few months and said she was sorry, but he'd never liked horses after that.

Always felt safe in the car, though, on those trips with his mum and sister.

Yeah, he'd imagine he was outside in the field, horses chasing after him, snorting crazily, but he was perfectly safe. He'd pound through the grass, swish through fields of rapeseed, dance his way through turnips put out for sheep to graze on. He'd hurdle fences, leap over ponds.

Nothing could harm him out there. That world was no more real than memories. Around him, out in the field, Glass saw the city lights surrounding them. There was a soothing feel to all this. Maybe it was the painkillers giving him a sense of wellbeing. The stump of his finger pulsed.

He'd killed three people.

He'd been shot.

He'd cut off his own finger.

Lorna had left him.

He'd be okay. He just needed to sleep.

THURSDAY

Glass shook his head. Bad idea. Felt like a bird inside his skull was trying to peck its way out.

He was aware of water dripping down his face. He couldn't see anything and then a beam of light struck the backs of his eyes and he cried out.

'Are you with us, Nick?'

Glass tried to raise his hand to shield his eyes. Something stopped him, though. His hand bent backwards but his wrist wouldn't budge. He felt something dig into his skin above the glove.

Shit. *Shit.*

Tried his other hand. Same. He tugged harder. Both hands. No give.

He couldn't see, the light dazzling him. He ducked his head.

'Am I blinding you?'

Glass looked down, and saw through aching, bleary eyes that he was in a chair, wrists strapped to the arms.

Jesus fucking Christ.

He tried to move his feet. Fuck it. His ankles were tied too.

Glass blinked water out of his eyes. Licked his lips.

Fucking fuck fuck.

The light moved away and he followed the beam.

Saw pizza boxes tucked down the side of a camera tripod and realised they were in Mad Will's bedroom. Only it was different from how Glass remembered it from the porno shoot. The bed had gone. And it looked from the reflection of the torchlight on the floor that someone had put down a plastic sheet.

Some additional light was spilling through the curtainless window, splashing the dark of the room with a pale grey.

He looked up. Made out Watt in a shirt, sleeves rolled up, torch in one hand, gun in the other. Behind Watt, about ten feet away, was another chair. Glass thought he saw someone slumped in it.

'Mafia?' Glass yelled.

'He's not going to help you.' Watt bent down in front of Glass, shone the torch at him.

Glass dragged his gaze away. Saw a half-empty bucket of water by his feet. A coil of rope.

'Let me ask you something, Nick,' Watt said. 'Did you kill Caesar?'

Jesus fuck. He knew. Mafia must have told him. *Fuck.*

Glass pulled against the ropes binding his wrists. No give at all. Just set his shoulder on fire again. Must've been out long enough for the painkillers to have worn off.

'That looks like a guilty reaction,' Watt said. 'Or is it just fear?'

Then Glass realised that Mafia couldn't have told him. If he had, Watt wouldn't need to ask. Glass yelled: 'Fuck you, you piece of shit.'

'Not so loud,' Watt said. 'The neighbours might hear.' He laughed at his own joke. They both knew there weren't any neighbours.

Glass strained again. The ropes dug into his skin.

'You're going to tell me the truth, Nick.' Watt shone the torch on his own face. 'See how serious I am?' He paused, no trace of a smile. 'The truth. Or you die.'

Glass felt as if the bones in his ribcage were contracting with each breath. They were going to crush his heart. He needed something to calm himself. More painkillers. No chance he'd get to them. 'I swear I'll kill you,' Glass said, hoping to release some of the pressure inside him.

'Oh, right.' Watt angled the torch back at him. 'And how will you do that?'

Glass planted his feet on the floor, tensed. He didn't plan it. Just seemed the right thing to do. He lurched forward and up. Hoping to get lucky, smash his head under the bastard's chin.

Watt saw it coming and swerved.

Glass lost his balance, crashed onto his side. He lay there gasping, staring up at Watt, pain searing through his shoulder. Not a lot of give under the plastic sheet. He'd kick-started the pain in his finger too.

Watt booted him in the mouth.

Blood spurted from Glass's lip, burst onto his tongue. He spat.

Watt's foot moved again. Glass squeezed his eyes shut, but the second kick didn't come. When Glass opened his eyes again, he saw that Watt had stepped over him. He was round the side, one hand on the back of the chair, the other grabbing a fistful of Glass's shirt.

Watt eased the chair onto its back. 'I heard someone cut Caesar,' he said. 'Mutilated him.'

Glass said, his voice unsteady, 'I wouldn't know.'

'Chopped off his fingers.'

'Well,' Glass said. He swallowed. 'Is that right?'

'Why would someone do that?'

'Maybe they just wanted one.' What was he saying?

Watt nodded. 'They just wanted one. That's fine. It's okay to take one if you just want one, is it?'

'Caesar didn't need it.'

'The fuck are you talking about?'

'He didn't need it. If he was dead.'

'But *you* did?'

'I didn't say I took it,' Glass said.

'So what's this?' Watt held something under the torch.

Glass squinted. Watt had found Caesar's severed finger. 'That's mine,' Glass said.

'I don't think so.'

'Take my glove off.'

'Don't be stupid.'

'Take it off.'

There must have been something in Glass's voice, because Watt leaned over and touched the index finger of the glove. Then he grabbed hold of it and pulled. The glove slid off.

'See?' Glass said.

'Well, well,' Watt said. 'Full of surprises. That must have stung. Who did it?'

'I don't remember,' Glass said. 'But I think it was me.'

'Was that before you killed Caesar or after?'

Glass said nothing.

'You don't want to talk. I tell you, though, I'm glad we had this little chat. Now I know that if I want a finger, you think it's okay to take one.'

'I didn't say that.' Glass balled his fists, tucking his fingers out of sight. Pain shot through the stump, made him gasp.

'You did. Anyway, relax,' Watt said. 'Did I say I'd take *yours?*'

What was the sick fuck planning? Cutting off one of Mafia's?

'Take mine,' Glass said.

'You're a bit short.'

'Take mine,' Glass said. 'Please.'

'Let me get this right,' Watt said. 'You're begging me to cut off one of your fingers?'

Glass was silent for a second, then whispered: 'Yes.'

'Well, how can I refuse?' Watt asked. 'Lucky I brought my knife with me. Hang on.' He disappeared into the shadows, returned seconds later, looming over Glass with the light shining on a steak knife. 'Think it's sharp enough?'

GLASS SCREAMED BECAUSE he remembered the pain from the first time.

He remembered being here before. Not when he bought the gun from Mad Will. Not later during one of the drug pick-ups. No, he remembered being here in this room, tied to this chair. No, maybe it wasn't here. He remembered being at home.

Yes, Watt barged into the bedroom. Barged into the bedroom, right. He had a knife. Watt held Glass down, held him down, yes, flattened his finger against the floor, that's right, yes.

Brought the blade down.

There was a smell too. A sour smell. Can't forget that smell.

When the remembered pain got more than he could endure, Riddell said, 'It's good to remember.'

'It's agony.'

'It's your agony.'

Glass said, *'This isn't the worst part.'*

'It's all in the past.'

That's not true. I'm here now.'

'Who's there with you?'

'Me, Mafia, Watt.'

'Are you sure?'

'Concentrate,' Watt said. 'Does it hurt? Does it hurt? Does it? Did it hurt Caesar?'

Glass didn't answer.

'Answer me, you fucker, or I'll do it.'

HE CAME ROUND again to another bucket of water, light shining in his eyes.

His finger throbbed deep in the bone. The memory hadn't faded.

Watt must have set the chair upright cause Glass could feel a solid surface beneath his feet.

He looked down at his finger. Watt had ripped off the bandage before he hammered the handle of the knife down on the stump. It was bleeding again. Glass gagged. His mouth filled with sick. The acid bit into his cut lip. He spat, aimed for Watt's shoe, but missed.

Watt moved the beam away from Glass and Glass saw that he had the gun in his hand now, the knife gone.

Glass tried to see if Mafia was okay but he couldn't make out a thing. He wouldn't put it past Watt to do something to his brother while he was unconscious. 'Do what you want to me,' Glass said. 'Just don't hurt Mafia.'

'What does he have to do with it?'

'Nothing,' Glass said. 'I swear it wasn't him.'

'You really have a thing about him, don't you? What are you, queer after all? Surprised you have a kid.'

Glass didn't want him talking about Caitlin.

'Lovely little girl,' Watt said.

Stop it.

'I'm very fond of her.'

'You fucking paedo,' Glass yelled. 'Fucking beast. Fucking stoat bastard.'

'Don't call me that, Nick, it's not nice.'

'You think Caesar would be proud of you? You think? He'd fucking gut you, you nonce cunt.'

'Look,' Watt said. 'I may be many things, but I'm no paedo. I do like Lorna, though, in that special way. Might have some fun with her later if you don't mind. Or even if you do. Particularly if you do.'

Glass said, 'They're not a part of this. For God's sake, leave them alone.'

'You're a lucky man.' The soles of Watt's shoes scuffed the plastic sheet as he walked up and down. 'You should treasure them.'

'I'm begging you,' Glass said. 'Please.'

'I'm a reasonable kind of guy,' Watt carried on. 'But I'm wondering if you are. Now let's look at this rationally.' He paced another couple of steps away from Glass, turned to face him. 'Someone shot Caesar to death. With this gun. Which is yours, so Mad Will told me before he fucked off home to his bed. Course, I recognise it myself and don't need that fucker's help. Will tries to be friends with everybody, and that's no way for a man to live. I don't think he'd have told me about you if I hadn't heard myself, you know. So don't take it to heart. He only brought you here because he knew what I'd do to him if he didn't. Anyway, this person who killed Caesar with your gun, they killed Horse and Jasmine too. But I'll be honest, I didn't much give a shit about those two. Caesar, though, he was like kin to me.' He paused. 'Unlike my actual blood brother. Anyway, if you could just convince me that you weren't responsible for Caesar's murder, then we can all get on with our lives. But if you did kill Caesar, then you'll have to get what you deserve.' He ducked down till he was at eye level with Glass, turned the torch off. His voice came out of the darkness right next to Glass's ear. 'Did you kill Caesar, Nick?'

Glass's heart thumped so hard he felt his shoulders lift. He said nothing. The silence stretched and his heartbeat grew faster and louder.

Finally Watt straightened up, switched the torch back on. 'I'm sure you wouldn't want any harm to come to your family.'

'They're innocent.' Glass clenched his teeth to deal with the pain. Imagined knocking back a mouthful of painkillers. But that made it worse. He said, 'They have nothing to do with this. Me and Caesar, we were involved in all this shit. It's our fault.'

'Caesar's fault? You saying he deserved to die?'

'Fucking right he did,' Glass said.

Watt's eyes narrowed. 'You shot him?'

'I didn't say that.'

'Near as fucking damnit.'

Glass shook his head.

'So it was Darko, then?'

It'd be so easy to lay all the blame on Darko. 'I didn't say that either.'

'It was one of you.' Watt stared at him. 'I know that much.'

'How do you know?'

'Someone told me.'

And Glass knew who that someone was. The machete in Caesar's peter had given it away. Maybe Watt would admit what Caesar wouldn't. 'Ross,' Glass said. Not a question.

'Very good,' Watt said.

A drop of water trickled down Glass's chin. 'What do you have on her?'

'Nothing,' Watt said. 'She was Caesar's business partner.'

'Jesus.' Glass didn't understand that kind of greed. 'She knew I was involved?'

'Yep. Wasn't all that happy about it, though. Thought you'd lose it and snitch. Like Fox.'

'Fox was a snitch?' Glass said.

'That was his plan. He found out about Ross. Threatened to blab.'

'Jesus,' Glass said again. So that was the real reason Caesar arranged the blanket party.

'So,' Watt said, 'this is fun. But you still haven't answered my question. Last chance. Which one of you killed Caesar?'

'Okay,' Glass said. 'Darko killed Caesar.'

'Oh, my,' Watt said. 'This is sweet. You think I can't tell when someone's shitting me?'

'It's true,' Glass said. 'You have to believe it.'

Watt licked his lower lip, sucked it into his mouth, spat it back out. 'I don't think so,' he said. 'If it was true, you'd have told me right away. There'd be no reason for you to protect Darko.'

'I didn't want you to kill him.'

'Crap. You didn't want me to kill him because he's innocent. If he was guilty, you wouldn't have thought twice about giving him up to save yourself.'

'No,' Glass said. 'It's not like that. You've got it wrong.'

'Hold this.' Watt placed the torch in Glass's lap so the light was directed at him. Then he bent down, picked up the coil of rope off the floor. 'Who do you love most in the world?' He measured a piece of rope. 'Mafia?' He cut the rope. 'Nah, I don't think so. It's purely sexual with him, isn't it? Maybe you love yourself most.' He looped the rope, formed a second loop, crossed one loop over the other. 'But if you do, cutting your own finger off's a pretty strange way of showing it.' He moved behind Glass, feet scraping on the plastic sheet, and yanked his head back. 'Lorna?' He looped the knot around Glass's exposed neck. The rope fibres tickled Glass's skin. 'Caitlin?' Watt tightened it.

'Leave them alone.'

Watt pulled the ends of the rope and Glass's head snapped back. He started to choke. Watt kept the rope taut. 'I'd advise you,' he said, 'to sit very still. I'm going to tie this off on the chair legs. Once I've done that, there'll be just enough slack for you to keep your head level without strangling yourself.'

'You don't need to do this,' Glass said.

'You'll just sit there and not try to escape till I get back, will you?'

'It was me,' Glass said. 'I killed Caesar. I admit it.'

Silence.

Then he felt a sharp tug on his hair and the pressure on his throat eased.

'I'd like to kill you,' Watt said. 'But that would be too easy on you.'

'Do what you have to do,' Glass said, breathing fast. 'But do it to me.'

'Cut a few more fingers off? Some toes? Your nose? Your balls? I could do that. All of it. Maybe I will. But first I have to go see Lorna and Caitlin.'

'Don't,' Glass said. 'I'm begging you, don't.'

'Enough talk,' Watt said. 'Save your breath.' He let go of Glass and crouched down again.

The rope tightened. 'Please,' Glass said.

'Nearly there.'

The rope dug into Glass's throat, constricted his swallowing. 'Too tight,' he said, his voice sounding different, nasal, a pressure building up behind his nose.

'It's a clove hitch,' Watt said. 'With this little beauty, the more you wriggle, the more it'll tighten. Wriggle enough and you'll choke yourself to death.'

'I'm not moving.'

'If I were you,' Watt said, 'I'd think long and hard about that.'

'HE'S BLUFFING,' GLASS said into the dark room once Watt had gone.

Glass wished Mafia was awake. He needed reassurance. After the momentary relief of seeing the back of his torturer, the realisation of what Watt had threatened took over.

Lorna and Caitlin weren't at home, Glass reminded himself.

They were safe. Watt couldn't touch them. They weren't at home. They were at Lorna's mother's. Yep, that's where they were.

'Glad that fucker's gone.'

'Mafia?' Glass said. He was alive. 'You all right?' There was a pause and Glass wondered if Mafia had lost consciousness again.

'I've been better,' Mafia said, finally. 'My head aches. I'm tied to this chair and I've got a noose round my neck. I can't move.'

Glass knew how he felt. 'You been awake long?'

'Few minutes. Thought I'd keep quiet till I worked out what was going on.'

'We have to get out of here,' Glass said. He leaned forward. Immediately the rope tightened round his neck. The pressure behind his nose increased. He could feel it in his cheekbones. He could hear it in his ears. It beat in his shoulder, in his finger.

Maybe he should keep struggling, let himself choke. Maybe Watt was right. It was all he deserved.

The rope dug into his throat. His eyes started to throb. He got scared, let his head go back. The knot didn't slacken. He tried to shrug it loose, but the effort was no good. He'd have to sit here till Watt returned, throat squeezed, hoping he didn't faint.

'I can't move either,' he said, his voice odd. 'We're not going anywhere.'

'Well, maybe we can try to get someone's attention,' Mafia said. 'Maybe someone's around.'

'Maybe,' Glass said. Maybe. It was possible. Just as it was possible that Lorna had changed her mind and come home. That she'd be at home right now. Her and Caitlin. Unaware that Watt was on his way over.

'I'll have a go, then.' Mafia paused and Glass imagined him

filling his lungs. Then he shouted: 'Help.' And again: 'He –'. The shout was cut off. 'Jesus,' he said, gasping.

'Keep your head steady,' Glass said, adjusting to the new sound of his own voice. The pressure in his head was harder to get used to. 'Don't lean forward when you yell.' He took a breath and shouted, 'Help.'

The noose round his neck muted the cry. He pretended it wasn't there. Tried again. Loud enough for someone close by to hear.

Mafia joined in.

Together they cried into the darkness.

Then stopped, catching their breath.

Glass felt light-headed. The pulse in his temples beat hard and fast. He waited, hoping he'd hear a reply. Maybe there was a squatter in one of the flats in the building.

But he heard nothing except the thump of his heart.

It was possible that Lorna had changed her mind, yes. More likely, though, the police had been in touch with Lorna's mother and when Lorna heard Glass had been taken hostage, she'd decided to come right on home so she could be there for him when he was released. That wasn't just possible, that was probable.

He yelled again. 'Heeeeelp.'

And again, Mafia joined in.

Started off loud, hearty, enthusiastic. Quickly turned into a series of doleful wails. They kept it up till they were out of breath.

Glass listened to the blood rushing in his ears. If he hadn't been tied to the seat, he'd have fallen off it.

They were alone. No one was coming to rescue them. All this, it was pathetic.

Glass couldn't make out Mafia's face, but he knew how he'd look. Defeated. Glass felt the same. 'Is there nothing you can think of?' he asked. But he was really speaking to himself. He needed to feel angry again. The way he felt in Caesar's peter. He had to take the pressure in his head and use it. 'I need to get out of this chair. I need to –'

'You'll die trying,' Mafia said. 'Just calm down.'

'I can do it. First thing is to free my wrists.'

'My brother knows how to tie someone up,' Mafia said.

If the police had been in touch with Lorna, though, they'd have someone at home with her. Wouldn't they? Would they leave her in the house on her own?

'Oh, Jesus,' Glass said. 'He won't hurt them. Tell me he won't hurt them.'

Mafia said nothing.

'It's a bluff,' Glass said. 'Please God tell me it's a bluff.'

IT FELT AS if twenty minutes had passed.

Glass had tried shouting for help again. He'd ripped his throat raw. And he'd made several attempts to free his arms. All he'd succeeded in doing was half-strangling himself and causing new levels of pain in his shoulder and finger.

His head pounded like his heart was where his brain should be.

But he tried once again, fighting against the rope as it cut into his throat, his muscles on fire as he tried to lever his hands off the arms of the chair.

The painkillers had worn off completely.

Watt would be arriving at Glass's house about now. Glass couldn't give up.

He opened his mouth and yelled, even though he knew there was nobody but Mafia to hear him.

EXHAUSTED, MUSCLES ACHING, his fringe soaked in sweat, his throat swollen, his shoulder on fire, blade-like pulse in his finger, a balloon expanding in his head, Glass said to Mafia, his voice a croak, 'Tell me why you were in jail.'

Mafia said nothing.

'Don't blank me,' Glass said. 'Please.'

'You don't want to know.'

Glass laughed as best he could. Sounded like a wheeze. 'Not only do I want to know, I think I deserve to know. What did you do?'

'Now's not the time.'

'Now's the only fucking time. Just tell me. I'm a big boy. I can handle it.'

'I'm not sure —'

'Mafia, I may never have another chance.'

Mafia said, softly, 'Okay.'

BACK WHEN MAFIA was running with Caesar, so Mafia told Glass, Watt wanted to be part of the action. Mafia wouldn't let him. Watt was bright, could have made something of himself. But he liked getting off his face too much. Managed to stay away from smack, more or less, but he'd take everything else that was on offer. And with Caesar around, there was always plenty on offer. Mafia wanted Watt to stay away from him.

Watt had other ideas. Thought he was a big boy, old enough to decide for himself what he wanted to do, what drugs he could take, what company he would keep. He resented Mafia giving him orders.

He married young, had a little girl soon afterwards.

Like me, Glass thought.

'Just like you,' Riddell agreed. *'Quite a coincidence, don't you think?* *Carry on.'*

'Carry on,' Glass told Mafia.

Well, things weren't working out between Watt and his wife. Watt was getting fucked up too often for her liking. He told her he could stop any time he wanted. Who knows, it might have been true. Problem was, he didn't want to. Denied the drugs were having any negative effect on him. But Mafia could see he was losing it. Showing signs of his head getting messed up. You know, sleeplessness, paranoia, aggression, memory loss, talking to himself, hallucinations. Both Mafia and his wife wanted him to see someone about it. He refused.

Things built up. He got worse. Reached a point where he got a gun from Mad Will. Later, Watt told Mafia that Mad Will had been reluctant to give it to him, but Watt had convinced him he just wanted the gun for protection. He'd pissed off quite a few people along the way. Which was true enough: it wasn't all paranoia.

But the gun was the turning point for his wife. She said she didn't recognise him any more. He wasn't the man she'd married. She coped with their failing marriage by drinking. More than once she'd threatened to leave him, but one night she packed a suitcase for herself and their daughter, said she'd had enough, finally, and they were going to her mother's, and that's when Watt flipped.

That evening Mafia had been out with him all night, knew he'd taken a shitpile of something earlier, in the gents, gone home with him to make sure he was okay. Mafia'd been drinking himself, so he crawled onto Watt's couch, sank into it and fell asleep.

Watt went upstairs to bed.

When he flicks on the light, she stirs. He looks over to the suitcase, open on the floor, neatly packed.

She rolls over, alert. Probably only pretending to be asleep. Isn't that late, clubs only just come out.

'Are we going on holiday?' he says. 'I can't just now. Got a lot on.'

'You have nothing on,' she says. 'Spending what little money you earn taking drugs with Caesar and Horse and that blind brother of yours.'

Straight in with the criticisms. 'He's not blind. And he doesn't take drugs.'

'Good for him,' she says. 'Maybe you could learn something from him.'

'Keep your voice down.'

'You think he'll hear us all the way across town?'

'He's downstairs. On the settee.'

'Something else to look forward to in the morning. I should just get up and go now.'

'Go where? What's going on?' He has no idea. He's given up trying to figure her out. He's the one with the problem but it doesn't take a genius to see that her behaviour is irrational at the best of times. If you love somebody, it doesn't matter what they're like, though, does it?

'I didn't want to leave a note.'

'I don't follow.'

She grabs a fistful of hair at the nape of her neck and tightens her fingers round it. Her voice is flat. 'We're leaving.'

'I can't, I told you.'

She tugs her hair, and as she does so, her head rises. 'No, we're leaving you.*'*

Then he understands. At least, he understands what she's saying. But he doesn't understand why. 'You can't. I can't cope on my own.'

'Typical,' she says. She lets go of her hair, thumps her fist down on the bedclothes.

'What?'

'Your selfishness. You can't cope, so I have to cope for you.'

'No, just help me. I'll sort myself out. I promise.'

'I'm not the person to help you. I can't do it.' She lowers her gaze. 'It's not safe any more.'

'What do you mean, it's not safe?' he says. 'I'm here. I'm keeping us safe.'

'You?' she says. 'You're a mess.'

That isn't true. He'd never been as together as he is right now. He's fucking invulnerable. He pulls out the gun. 'I've got this,' he says. 'Help keep the three of us safe.'

'I told you to get rid of that,' she yells.

'Shhh,' he says. Then, louder, as the shrill sound continues: 'Be quiet! Shut up, for Christ's sake.'

She's quiet only while she fills her lungs. Then she screams, 'Get rid of it.'

'There's no need for this shit,' he shouts back at her. 'Pack it in.'

No joy.

She screams, crazy faced, mouth wide open, cheeks jiggling.

His ears suck her screams out of the air. Each scream breaks into pieces. Tiny needles of sound dart into his eardrums and lodge there, quivering.

He yells, 'You'll wake up —'

'Don't argue, Daddy, ple —!'

He turns, sees the bullet rip through his daughter's chest. Then the explosion.

She stands for a second, tumbler of milk in her hands, then sinks to the floor.

The screaming stops.

It's over, just like that.

'Jesus,' Glass said. 'I almost feel like I was there.'

Watt gazes down at the gun in his hand. Can't make the connection between it and his daughter. What appears to have happened can't have happened. He can't have pulled the trigger. And even if he has, the *safety should be on. It should be. His ears ring from the sound of the shot, from the sound of his wife's screaming, making the needles in his eardrums vibrate.*

Maybe if he doesn't move, this will all go away. Maybe if he stays still, never moves again. Never blinks, never takes a breath. Maybe.

Yes, if time stops. He can make it stop. He will make it stop.

'What the fuck have you done?' his wife yells at him.

He shakes his head. He doesn't know. He isn't sure. He can't put it into words.

But she can.

'You killed her,' she says. 'You killed my baby.'

'No.'

'You murdering bastard. You killed our daughter. YOU KILLED HER.'

'I can't have,' he says. 'No. It's a mistake.'

'She's dead.'

'How?'

'You bought a fucking gun,' she says, crouched over her daughter, picking her up, cradling her.

He looks at the gun again. It's huge.

'You're going to pay for this.' Her eyes are mad. 'I'll make sure of it.' Tears pump out of her eyes, roll down her face. 'I fucking hate you. I've never hated anyone like I hate you right now.' She strokes her daughter's face. 'If you don't get out of my sight, I can't be responsible for what I'll do to you.' She kisses her daughter's shiny smooth brow. 'My baby,' she says.

'She can't be gone,' Watt says.

His wife lowers their child to the ground, jumps to her feet. 'Get out of here, you piece of shit,' she says. 'Get the fuck out. Or God help me . . .'

'I want to hold her.'

'Get out!' she screeches. 'I'll fucking kill you.' She charges at him, fists flying. She hits him on the chin. Snatches at the gun.

He jerks his hand out the way.

Her expression freezes, and she wilts, a small red hole in her forehead.

What seems like seconds later, Watt hears the explosion and the needles in his ears sing so loudly he feels he's drowning in the sound.

'I'm struggling to believe that,' Glass said, after a while. 'One accidental shot, maybe. But two's a stretch.'

'Well, that's my best guess,' Mafia said. 'I've no way of knowing if it's true.'

'What do you mean?'

'By the time I got upstairs, Watt was huddled in a corner. Couldn't get a word out of him.'

'So he told you this later?'

'Not exactly. We didn't have a lot of time for talking.'

'Then how do you know it happened like that?'

'It's the way I pieced it together.'

'Jesus. You're just guessing?'

Mafia paused. 'The minute I stepped through the bedroom door, there was only one scenario that made any sense.'

'You're just guessing,' Glass repeated, not a question this time.

'The fact Watt couldn't tell me what happened makes no difference. It went down like I said.'

Glass didn't argue. Mafia'd carried this with him for a long time and if that's how he coped with what happened, there wasn't much Glass could say that'd make a difference. But it didn't sound right to Glass. 'So what did you do?'

Couldn't get any sense out of Watt, and Mafia knew it looked bad. It looked worse than bad. And Watt couldn't go to prison, no way he could do the time. His head was in enough of a mess already. They'd probably send him to Carstairs or somewhere, lock him up with the psychos. Since Watt was his little brother, Mafia decided to do what he could to protect him.

The only way to keep Watt out of jail was to frame someone else. Even then, the police might spot the cover up. Unless the scapegoat confessed.

Mafia eased the gun out of his brother's fingers. He aimed at the wall and pulled the trigger a couple of times. That got his prints on the gun, and gunpowder residue on his skin and clothes. He dabbed the cuff of his shirt gently in the blood oozing from his sister-in-law's head. He couldn't make out much more than a general red smear, but it would have to do. He couldn't bring himself to do the same to his niece.

He'd done enough, though. He was confident no one would doubt he was the one who'd pulled the trigger.

He dragged Watt out of the house, managed to stumble to the car, told him to drive. Watt wouldn't, just sat there staring, not saying a word. Mafia dragged him back out and told him to go, just walk away, go find Caesar. He hated himself for throwing his brother into Caesar's arms, but he couldn't think of anyone else who'd lie for him.

Watt wasn't speaking, but Mafia had to hope he was listening. On no account, he said, was Watt to tell Caesar the truth about what had happened. Caesar didn't need to know. Tell Caesar that Mafia was to blame. Mafia had taken advantage of the fact that Watt was out of his face, comatose on the couch. Mafia'd paid his sister-in-law a bad-intentioned bedroom visit. Things got out of hand. Provoked an accident.

Still no response from Watt. Mafia couldn't even see his brother's eyes to tell if there was anything going on in there. He had to trust that Watt was hearing him. That he understood. That he had absorbed the lie.

Watt needed Caesar to give him an alibi. Did Watt understand?

But Mafia was pretty sure by now that he was just talking

to himself, clearing matters in his head. Watt wasn't taking in a word.

Mafia went back in the house, felt his way over to the phone and called the police. Then he called Caesar. Told him the story he'd just made up for Watt.

Caesar said, 'You do this to Watt and then you call me? What kind of a cunt are you?'

'Watt's here too. He needs an alibi.'

'For what you've done to his wife and child?'

'He's in a bad way. Won't talk. Wandering around outside. I need you to look after him while I'm in prison.'

'You won't get that far,' Caesar told him and hung up.

Maybe the police would arrive before Caesar.

Mafia went outside to see how Watt was coping, but he'd gone.

'I always knew you were innocent,' Glass said, trying to absorb what Mafia had told him. 'Did it play out like you planned?'

'Pretty much. The police arrived. Accepted my confession. I was at the scene, had blood on me, even had the murder weapon. No reason for them to doubt me.'

There was a silence in the room that lasted too long.

'What happened to Watt?' Glass asked, eventually.

'Caesar found him a few streets away, sitting on a wall.' Mafia cleared his throat. 'The police just assumed his reaction was due to grief. And then Caesar took him under his wing. Became his new family. That's how they got so close.'

'I can see why Caesar would hate you. But how come you hated him?'

'I dunno. He was the only person I could turn to. Even though I knew Caesar's idea of looking after Watt was to involve him in drug dealing and porn. I hated him for forcing me to make that choice.'

'But you used to work with Caesar. Weren't you involved in those things too?'

'Now and then,' Mafia said. 'But I always wanted better for Watt. Caesar didn't. Caesar got him hooked on cheap thrills. Destroyed his ambitions. Turned him into the kind of crazed junkie who'd endanger his family by waving a loaded gun around. And once the damage was done, Caesar tried to turn him against me.'

'Can you blame him? Caesar thought you'd murdered Watt's family.'

Mafia paused. 'I don't think he did,' he said.

'Watt told him the truth?'

'I imagine Caesar worked it out for himself. I'm not the kind of guy who'd force myself on a woman. Caesar knew that. And I might be as blind as a bat but I wouldn't shoot someone. Not by accident, anyway. Caesar knew that, too. But he liked to pretend he didn't. Fitted with the way he wanted me to be.'

'But why didn't Watt say anything? He knew what you sacrificed for him.'

'Well, that's just it.' Mafia paused. 'I'm not sure about that. I don't think Watt remembers anything about that night. He needed help. Psychiatric help. Maybe the kind he'd have got if he went to prison, I don't know. Maybe he should have done. Maybe I was wrong. On the outside, he couldn't get any help without admitting what he'd done. And without help, he couldn't handle what had happened.'

'Not many people could.'

'So he believed the story I told him. Blanked out the real events. Made up an alternative version from the lines I fed him. The story Caesar repeated and reinforced. The story the courts believed. It all made my version of events real. We've hardly spoken since that night. I never knew what was going on in his head. I suspected. But I never knew for sure until tonight.'

Glass took a moment to make sure he'd understood. 'He genuinely believes you killed his wife and kid?'

'Yeah, I think he does.'

'That's too fucked up.' Glass blinked back tears.

'It's fucked up that I should be here, tied to a chair, while he's . . .'

'You did your best.'

'I can't help thinking that all of this could have been avoided.'

'Yeah, maybe. If we'd all been born different people.'

'I can't protect him any more. I can't.'

'You're right,' Glass said.

'He needs to stand on his own two feet. Face the consequences of his actions.'

'Yes.'

'It's time for me to let go.'

'Please.'

'There's only one way I can do that.'

Glass wondered what he meant. But soon Glass heard choking, spluttering, wheezing. And he knew exactly what Mafia meant.

He called Mafia's name. Loudly at first. Then more quietly. Over and over. Until the choking stopped and he was left whispering his friend's name.

The silence that followed clamped Glass's head in its cold hands. Pressed its chilled lips to his brow. Breathed icy air onto his cheek. 'Don't let me die for nothing,' it said in Mafia's voice. 'There's still hope.'

There was hope. In fact, Mafia's story had given Glass the hope he needed. If Watt believed Mafia had killed his family, then Watt wouldn't think of himself as a killer. So maybe when faced with the reality of the situation, he'd find he couldn't do it.

Threatening to pull the trigger was easy. Doing it was a lot harder.

Glass had to believe that. If he didn't, he didn't think he could live with the agony in his head. Mafia was dead, so it wasn't him who said, 'Lorna's at her mother's.' He didn't believe it. The pain in Glass's head wasn't just from the pressure from the rope round his neck. 'She's not at home.' *Yes, she is.* It was something else. Felt as if his brain was made of glass and it was all broken up in there now. 'She's not alone in the house with my babygirl.' *Stop lying.* Like he needed something to fix it. He wanted to knit the pieces together again. Stop the silence from reaching inside him, invading the gaps in his mind. It was him, Glass, speaking aloud. 'The police will be there. A policewoman.' *No, she'll be alone. Just her and Caitlin.* His chest moved up and down too quickly. 'Watt won't hurt them.' *Yes, he will.* And there was a crashing in his ears.

He could only just make out Riddell saying, 'Good try. Getting closer all the time. It won't hurt for much longer.'

GLASS'S STOMACH JOLTED when he heard the front door close. Footsteps stamped down the corridor and in a cocaine heartbeat, the door opened and a torchlight snapped on.

Glass narrowed his eyes to slits, peered through them, trying to tell by sight alone what had happened. Glass imagined he'd be able to read the truth in the fucker's eyes. But when Watt looked at him, Glass couldn't hold his gaze long enough to find out. He realised that he didn't want to know. He didn't want to know if Lorna'd come back home. It was okay, not knowing. As long as he didn't know, he'd be fine.

Watt was sucking at his lip, like it was bleeding. He spat it out with a pop. He moved nearer. Pointed the torch at his face. 'Look at me.'

Glass had been wrong. He couldn't tell a thing from Watt's expression. The way the beam hit his face, he could be dazed or angry, happy or terrified. His eyes revealed nothing, not even Glass's tiny reflection.

'I called the police,' Watt said, his voice flat. He touched Glass's cheek, then pulled his hand away again. 'It wasn't me.'

'What wasn't?' Glass stared at him. 'What wasn't you?'

'I thought the place was empty.'

Glass said, quickly, 'Yes, Lorna was at her mother's.'

'No,' Watt said. 'She was at home. I found her.'

Oh, Christ. 'What did you do to her?'

'Nothing.'

'Let me go. Let me out of here.'

'It wasn't me.'

'Stop saying that.'

'Someone else . . .'

'No. Don't.'

'Someone else got there first.'

'I don't believe you. I won't believe you. What the fuck are you saying?'

'Don't blame yourself.'

Glass shouted, 'They're alive.' His voice quietened, a tremble in it when he said, 'You didn't touch them. They're alive. In bed. Asleep.'

He closed his eyes and heard Watt say, 'Sound asleep.'

'Both of them?'

'Both of them.'

Watt was lying.

Glass shivered. He breathed in hard. 'Kill me if you want,' he said. 'But just tell me the truth. What did you just do?'

'I swear I'm not lying to you. I didn't lay a finger on them.' He nodded. 'But they're dead.' He paused. 'They're both dead.'

'No,' Glass yelled, flinging himself forward, the rope tightening round his neck. 'No,' he screamed again, but his voice had gone and it came out as a croak. He pushed harder, trying to get at Watt, his temples buzzing, not caring he was strangling himself.

Watt took a step back.

Glass jerked against the rope, hard, squeezed out another pitiful yell. The rope wrapped tight around his windpipe. His face filled with blood, felt like his eyes were going to pop. He sucked in, but there was nothing. He wasn't breathing. He gasped at nothing.

Watt darted behind him, scrabbled about underneath the chair.

Glass knew what he was doing and wondered why. He hoped the fucker failed, even if it meant Glass died in the process.

Fuck him.

Glass was ready for this.

His ears roared.

And then he felt the knot round his neck give a little. A trickle of air slid down his throat.

A breath. Then another.

Then he heard Watt shift behind him, and before long the rope slackened till there was scarcely any pressure.

Glass gulped in air.

Watt walked round in front of him, knife in hand. He lifted the noose over Glass's head, threw the rope away.

Glass took another deep breath. 'You should have let me go.'

'I am.' Watt hacked at the ropes tying Glass's left arm to the chair.

'What are you doing?'

'What does it look like?'

Saving him from strangling himself so Watt could have some more fun was one thing. But this? Glass couldn't think through it. Couldn't find an answer. The last piece of rope split and Glass's arm broke free. He clenched and unclenched his fist, pumping the blood back into his hand.

'Here,' Watt said, and offered Glass the gun.

Like before. At home. In the bedroom. So that was his game. More of the psychological torture. As if telling him Lorna and Caitlin were dead wasn't enough.

'You think I'll fall for that again?' Glass said.

Watt said, 'Fall for what?'

'You want to laugh at me, you want to make fun of me, go ahead. But I'm not playing.'

'You think it's empty?' Watt drew the gun, moved to the side, aimed in Mafia's direction and fired a bullet at him.

Did he know Mafia was already dead? Or was he really that callous?

'No trick,' Watt said, once again offering Glass the gun. 'Go on,' he said. 'You need to take it. You have to trust me. Believe what I'm telling you.'

Slowly, Glass reached out, expecting Watt to pull the gun away. But he didn't. He let go and Glass took hold of the gun.

'I didn't kill them,' Watt said. 'Shoot me if I'm lying.'

Could be that that was the last bullet Watt had just fired. But it could also be that he was completely crazy.

Glass pointed the gun at Watt. 'You sure you don't want to torture me a bit longer?'

'I don't need to,' Watt said.

GLASS FREED HIS other arm, then made clumsy work of untying his legs. He got to his feet, stamped some life into them.

He swallowed half a dozen painkillers.

Watt lay still, slumped on the floor. Glass had struck him a fierce blow with the butt of the gun, but he could wake up at any moment.

Glass tucked the gun in the back of his waistband, bent over Watt, dug in his pockets, found his car keys and a cassette tape.

Only two things on Glass's mind. Get out of here. Get home.

HE FOUND WATT'S car no trouble at all. He was shaking too badly to drive, but there was no choice. He climbed inside, shivered in the seat.

The engine started. The radio came on. Late night jazz. A lonely piano played a series of aching chords over a tired bass, while a drumbeat fluttered and spat.

He drove off. Slowly. Thinking of Mafia. Felt like he was abandoning him. Knew there was no logic to the thought. Mafia was gone. Strangled and shot. All Glass was abandoning was a body.

The piano punched out a sequence of crazy chords, the bass plucking a rapid melody that stood alone, fighting the piano. Underneath, the drums brushed and tapped, tapped and brushed. Then all three instruments broke off to play a fast sequence of syncopated notes, ending with a crash in the lower registers backed by a cymbal roll and a rapid heartbeat stamped out on the bass drum.

Glass heard everything and it was too much. He switched off the radio.

The headlights bore holes in the darkness. Tall buildings rose in front of him, came closer. He veered away and turned onto the main road.

In the distance, taillights retreated. He followed them, heading for home.

The silence was worse than the radio.

He turned it back on. The music was dissonant and grating, pulled at his insides, unravelling him, whisking his brain.

A repeated high note on the piano merged into a thin spear and the point slid into his finger, made him cry out.

He smacked his knuckles into the driver's window.

The road moved from side to side.

He clicked the radio off again. Quiet was better. He could live in the quiet. But there was no longer any quiet. The noise of the engine separated into sharp slices that rammed themselves into his ears.

He dug the tape out of his pocket. Slid it into the cassette player. That fucking pop song. 'Ebeneezer Goode'. He ejected the tape, tried the other side. More shite.

Too much to have hoped that the tape was the one Horse had made. Didn't matter though. Didn't make any difference now.

He wound down the window, tossed the tape out.

He wiped his nose with his hand. Wiped his mouth. Wiped his eyes.

He didn't have far to go.

It was just over there. Over that way. Home was close.

LIGHTS IN THE garden. Cars, other vehicles. Bustle. People. Too much to take in.

He pulled up twenty feet away, jumped out of the car. Broke into a run.

A man in uniform shouted. Glass ignored him, carried on running, ran right past him.

'Hey,' the guy said, chasing after him.

Glass bumped into someone. Bumped into someone else. Sent him sprawling.

'Stop him!'

A hand on his shoulder. The good one. Firm grip. Something ripped. Not firm enough.

Fuck that.

Then another hand grabbed him.

He pulled the gun out of his waistband.

Shouts and cries.

'It's him,' someone said.

He ignored them. Ignored them all. Walked into the house, gun drawn, made his way through a hushed cordon of cops and upstairs.

The landing and bathroom were crammed with people in white suits.

'Get out,' he shouted.

They looked at one another.

'Get the fuck out.' He raised the gun.

They left in a scurry, squeezing past him, hands held aloft.

He looked around. The bathroom door stood open. He stepped towards it.

The shower curtain was pulled all the way back.

Lorna was lying in the bath in her nightdress. Caitlin was on top of her, face pressed into her mum's neck, a purple blanket tucked round them.

'Thank Christ you're okay,' he said. He dropped to his knees on the floor. 'Thank Christ.'

Lorna stared at him.

'What?'

She said nothing.

'Talk to me,' he said. 'Please talk to me.' He looked at Caitlin. 'Caitlin, babygirl. Say something.'

'Drop the weapon,' Lorna said. Her voice sounded deep.

Glass didn't mind how it sounded. 'Of course,' he said and placed the gun on the floor.

'Kick it over here.' Her voice came from behind him.

He shoved it with the side of his foot and it slid along the bathroom floor towards Lorna's voice. 'Don't worry, Caitlin,' he said. 'It'll be okay. I can tell you a story if you like.'

'Shut the fuck up.' A man with Lorna's new voice walked into the bathroom. He was dressed in a uniform and holding a gun. Another man crouched behind him. 'Get on the floor,' the first man said. 'Face down.'

Glass did as he was told. No sooner was his cheek touching cold tile than he felt something dig into his back.

'What I don't understand,' Lorna said, 'is why the fuck you came back.'

'I couldn't leave you,' he said.

'Fuckhead,' she said, and something exploded in his skull.

PART THREE
Cognitive Dissonance

TUESDAY, 16 February 1993

'Run that past me again, would you?'

'Again?' Glass looked at Riddell. Scotland was a small place. Riddell was everywhere. He'd been at the Hilton. Now he was here. In fact, he'd always been here. This was his base and he'd only visited the Hilton on Mondays. Here he had a proper office with a carpet and window (barred, admittedly) and bookcases lining the wall.

Apparently this was the perfect spot to ask Glass to go over the story again and again. Day after day after day.

Glass was tired of it.

'Just the end. From where you arrive home.'

Pressure built in Glass's head, like it always did, as if he was being choked. He felt that rope round his neck again. 'I can't.'

'But you just did.'

That was true. He'd never got that far before. But he couldn't go back.

'Try again.'

'No.'

'What happens when you try?'

'You know. It's like trying to reverse a car into a wall.' He'd described it like that before.

'Give it a shot. Maybe you've dislodged a few bricks and that wall will come tumbling down.'

Glass doubted it, but he concentrated, pictured a wall in his head and took a sledgehammer to it. Light appeared through chinks in the mortar, but when he struck the wall again, the hammer bounced off the bricks and he felt sick. The harder he struck the bricks, the sicker he felt. He shook his head, turned away, glanced round the office, hoping he might find the answer in the room's familiarity.

But the room told him nothing. It was just an office. Neat, tidy. 'Shadows in the dark?' Riddell asked him.

Glass had explained it that way once or twice too. He couldn't be bothered explaining about the wall.

'There's something there but you don't know how to turn on the light?'

And he'd explained it like that too. Different images for different days. It all amounted to the same thing. There was something he couldn't see and trying to see it made him physically ill.

Riddell fiddled with his pencil, pushed a sheet of paper around on the desk. 'But this is good, Nick,' he said. 'You've managed to piece events together from the start to the end. Twice is maybe pushing it.'

The nausea came back again and Glass swallowed. 'The drugs,' he said. The medication switched him on and off. Sometimes so fast he could feel himself flickering. Sometimes he buzzed as he flickered. 'I'm better. I don't need them.'

'We cut down your dosage,' Riddell said. 'I'm going to cut it further.'

A sharp pain bore through Glass's right temple. He wanted to be angry, knew he should be. He didn't want to do drugs; they were dangerous. But he couldn't summon up the energy. 'Take me off them.'

Riddell adjusted his specs.

Glass said, his head throbbing, 'I'd remember better if I could think straight. I know I would. They don't help any more.' He got to his feet. 'I don't want drugs. You know the damage they can do to you. People get up to mental shit when they're on drugs.'

'Sit down,' Riddell said. 'Sit down, please, Nick. This is prescribed medicine, you know that. Not illegal drugs you buy on the street to get high. I'm a doctor.'

'You're a *shrink*.'

'Okay. And how does that make you feel?'

Glass didn't laugh like he was supposed to. Or at least he thought he was supposed to. A layer of fuzz had covered Glass's brain. It happened like that. One second he was fine, the next he could hardly remember a thing. Made concentration almost impossible. He had a book in his room, *Pilgrim . . . Pilgrim on the Hill*, that was it. He must have started it fifty times and never got beyond page ten.

'I've forgotten the question,' he said.

'Take a seat, Nick.'

He was still standing? So he was. He put his hand on the back of the chair, moved it, sat down. He said nothing. Saying nothing seemed like a good tactic.

Riddell turned his pencil upside down and scratched the back of his hand with the eraser. 'Do you mind if we go over something you were talking about before?'

'Can't we move on?' Glass had had his fill of this. He'd thought enough about the past. He'd been here for three months and every day for the past couple of weeks they'd talked about the bloody past. What was wrong with the present? The past was over. Nothing anybody could do to change it. Why did it matter if he recalled exactly what happened or not?

'Remember how you were when you first arrived?'

Yeah, he remembered that. The blow to the head had knocked him out. Apparently they'd been worried about internal bleeding. But he came to, no problem, just groggy and confused. Until he remembered what he'd seen in the bath.

Then he'd gone berserk. Tore up the hospital room. Broke everything that would snap and shatter. Ripped everything that would tear. Including his own wounds. Once that was done, he smashed his head off the wall hard enough to make it bleed. Rocked him backwards and he fell on his arse but it didn't knock him out. Maybe the bone in his skull had hardened since the whack in the bathroom with the policeman's gun. He'd scrambled back up and was aiming for a second attempt when a couple of male nurses rushed into the room and pinned him to the floor.

He didn't resist.

But, still, they moved him here, a secure psychiatric hospital. A prison, like the Hilton. But unlike the Hilton, this wasn't a modern building. It was Victorian. Dark and cold and gloomy. Full of ghosts. He could see them and hear them and sometimes he could feel them.

Riddell had asked him a question. He'd forgotten what it was, though.

Sometimes he saw . . . shit, he couldn't remember their names. His wife. His daughter. How pathetic was he now? He saw their faces. Lorna? *Yes.* Caitlin? *Yes.* Flames lit inside his skull, burned his brain clean. Fuck, it hurt and it felt good, felt *deserved.* He saw them lying in the bath. Lorna's voice. No, not hers.

'She sounded different,' he said aloud.

'Who?'

'Maybe it was the smack on the head. Maybe I'm remembering it wrong.'

'Who, Nick? Who sounded different?'

'She sounded like a man.'

'Ah, Lorna.' Riddell spread his fingers.

Glass put his hand to his head. Ran his hand over his scalp. No lumps, no stitches. Didn't even hurt when he pressed down. He was getting used to the change. He had hair again now too.

'I'd like you to answer some more questions,' Riddell said. 'Would you mind?'

Glass shrugged. Every day, the same routine.

It went like this. Alarm goes. He gets up. He has a wash. He gets dressed. He waits. Nurse brings his breakfast. He takes his pills. Waits. Nurse comes to take him for exercise round the yard. Then back to his cell. He waits. Different nurse brings him his lunch. He takes his pills. Waits. Nurse takes him to see Riddell. He talks about what happened. Riddell asks questions. Back to his cell. He waits. Another nurse brings him his dinner. He takes his pills. Waits. He watches TV with the zombies. He used to be a zombie. He doesn't really remember, but he's been told. It couldn't have been so bad. Sometimes he wishes he was still a zombie. He talks to the few who can talk. Nurse takes him back to his cell. Takes his pills. Reads a few pages of his book.

Sleeps. Dreams. Wakes up. Sleeps. Dreams. Wakes up. Stays awake.

In the morning the alarm screams and it starts all over again.

It was his life, and he was coping with it.

'Back at the Hilton that night,' Riddell was saying. He paused and Glass nodded at him to continue. 'Why did you take Caesar's finger?'

That was easy. All of this was perfectly clear in Glass's mind now. His brain was sizzling, all that fuzz burned off. That's how it happened. Sometimes he'd feel like his head was so heavy with shit that he was about to faint and then almost instantly he'd be fine again, all the crap burned away.

'I'd lost mine.' Glass was aware that what he was about to say sounded crazy. He said it anyway. 'I thought somebody might be able to sew his one in its place.'

'That's not possible. You know that.'

'Of course. But at the time, I wasn't thinking too clearly. I just remember thinking that he was responsible for me losing my finger. Seemed right that I should take his.'

'Do you still think he was responsible?'

'Depends what you mean,' Glass said. 'I think I cut it off myself.'

'Do you have any idea why?'

'I don't remember.' Glass closed his eyes, puffed his cheeks.

'Don't make yourself sick again,' Riddell said.

Yes, once, he'd spewed. He looked at Riddell, sucked air into his lungs. 'I want to remember.'

'I know.' Riddell glanced away. 'Let's change the subject till you feel better.' He clasped his hands together. 'Tell me about Jasmine and Horse and Caesar.'

Glass paused. He'd shot them, but he hated saying it out loud. Shooting somebody, even if he deserved it, wasn't something you wanted to talk about. Still, Glass had never denied what he'd done.

No point crying about it. Glass had had his fill of self-pity.

He was a murderer. No getting away from it. He went crazy. This was why he was in a psychiatric hospital. And they wanted to know why. Couldn't blame them.

He wouldn't mind knowing himself.

He blamed the drugs. They were nothing to what he was on now, though. He felt like a pair of dogs had dug their teeth into his shins and were shaking him. Just because he wasn't moving didn't mean it wasn't happening. He could feel it, just like the creatures were there, under the desk, chomping at him. He stretched his legs out, kicked the beasts away. Then he composed himself and said, 'I shot those fuckers.'

Riddell leaned back. 'What about Mafia? Did you shoot him too?'

Now that was a question Riddell had never asked before. Normally he just listened, nodded, asked a question that helped Glass move the story along. Not that it had ever moved quite so far. But this? This was new.

Come to think of it, the last couple of days Riddell had been asking all sorts of weird shit.

Glass tucked his legs back in, away from the dogs' teeth. Stared at Riddell until Riddell sat forward again, that milky smell clinging to him. Glass said, 'That was Watt. Why would *I* shoot Mafia?'

'Mafia strangled himself and then Watt shot him.'

'That's right.'

'I'm confused. I'm not sure why Mafia killed himself.'

'Because he knew that as long as he was alive, he'd protect Watt.'

'I see. And why did Watt shoot him?'

'I don't know. Why don't you ask him?'

'Good answer.' Riddell inched forward. 'If Mafia killed himself, then his body would've been in the flat, right?'

Glass nodded.

'And the police would've found it?' Riddell said.

'I suppose, yeah.'

'They found Watt. Unconscious where you left him.'

'He was still out?'

'Don't believe the books you read. Knock somebody out, they stay that way for a long time.'

'Wish to fuck I'd killed him.' Glass sometimes dreamed that when Watt handed him the gun, he pulled the trigger. In the dream, Lorna would be tugging at his arm, trying to wrestle the gun out of his hand. 'Is there a date yet for the trial?'

'No,' Riddell said. 'We'll talk about that another time.'

'Will I be allowed to go?'

'Not now, Nick.'

'Just answer me that one question. It's important.' Riddell had no idea how important. But Glass had to be there. He wanted to hear Watt explain himself.

'Yes,' Riddell said. 'You'll be at the trial. Can I carry on?'

'Sorry, yes.'

Riddell said, 'So the police found Watt. Curled up on the floor. Like you'd expect.' He paused. 'But there was no sign of Mafia.'

That made no sense. This was definitely going in a new direction. 'What are you saying?'

'What do you think I'm saying?'

Glass thought about it. 'You're saying Mafia got up and walked?'

'Am I?'

'I don't know. Are you?'

'That's not very likely, Nick. Dead people tend to stay where they are.' Riddell twiddled his pencil again, tapped it on the desk, tapped it on his chin. He'd grown his beard. There was a streak of grey in it that snagged the light. 'So if we're agreed that he didn't get up and walk, where did he go?'

Took a moment before Glass realised the question wasn't rhetorical. 'How am I supposed to know? I wasn't there. I'd left long before the police arrived.'

'Have a think, anyway. See if you can give me an answer, however far-fetched. Take your time.'

Glass tried, couldn't concentrate. Saw Caitlin's face, heard her voice, she was crying: 'Where's Mo?' She'd lost her teddy. Then, an image from a different occasion, her face white and shocked, and the words: 'Don't argue.' A metal spike slammed into Glass's brain, as fast and solid as a bullet.

Ignore it. Concentrate.

Mafia's body. Riddell wanted to know where it had gone. Dead bodies didn't just get up and walk, so he said. He was right, of course. Even when Glass was a zombie, he couldn't remember getting up and walking.

He swallowed a mouthful of saliva and said the first thing that came into his head. 'Aliens must have abducted him.'

Riddell smiled. 'Any ideas that are maybe a little less far-fetched than that?'

That was far-fetched? Well, maybe it was. What, then? Hmmm. 'Somebody must have moved him.' Zipped straight into his head. The spike had snatched the thought out of the air, a lightning rod for ideas that would otherwise have struck elsewhere, a chair leg, wastepaper basket, umbrella.

Riddell nodded. 'Who'd move a dead body?'

'Mad Will?'

'You think Mad Will came back, got rid of Mafia, and left Watt lying there for the police to find?'

'Maybe he ran out of time.'

'Are you absolutely sure?'

'Well, no, I've no idea. I'm just giving you my best guess.' Glass stretched his legs out again, asked, politely, 'Can you explain it?'

'No,' Riddell said. 'I meant, are you absolutely sure about what happened to Mafia?'

'Why wouldn't I be? I didn't get hit on the head till afterwards.' Glass wiped sweat off his eyebrow. 'Look, Mafia choked himself to death. And I saw that cunt Watt put a bullet in him.' He held out his left hand, clenched his fist. 'I can see the gun like it's here right now in my hand.' He straightened two fingers, formed the shape of a gun. Pointed it at Riddell.

'You going to shoot me with that?' Riddell asked.

Glass spread his fingers, let his hand fall down by his side. His brain flickered. Stayed on, a question stretched across the inside of his head, wrapped around the spike, touching both sides of his skull, curved at one end, a dot at the other. He tried to grab it but it crumbled to dust in his fingers and a wind rose and blew it away. Flickering. He was flickering.

'I have one more question,' Riddell said. 'The day you woke up and found your finger missing and Lorna and Caitlin gone, why did it never occur to you that Watt had kidnapped them?'

'I don't know,' Glass said. 'It just didn't.'

'Don't you think that's odd?'

'No.'

'But Watt had made threats.'

'I didn't think it was odd.'

'Maybe you knew —'

'I didn't fucking think it was odd,' Glass said. 'Get me off these fucking drugs.'

'Maybe we should call it a day.'

'Please.' Glass ran his hand over his scalp, let his fingers wrap round the tip of the spike sticking out of his skull. 'They're screwing with my head.'

'Okay,' Riddell said. 'We'll reduce your dosage a little each day. You'll be off them before you know it.'

'I just want to feel normal for a change.'

'Of course.' Riddell nodded. 'I'll get someone to take you back to your room.'

THAT NIGHT, GLASS woke up so suddenly and completely that he wasn't even sure he'd been asleep. But his room was darker than before and all he could see now were blobs of colour, mainly greens and oranges.

His eyes were wet. His cheeks were wet, too.

He heard voices. He sat up, listened to them. They came closer, stopped outside his room.

Then the door opened and the light clicked on. He blinked several times, peered through narrowed slits at half a dozen white-clad figures.

He didn't want them here. This was *his* room.

'Get out,' he shouted, his voice as bright as their clothes.

They looked at one another.

'Get the fuck out.'

They made a decision, moved towards him. He saw the flash of a needle.

He dug under his pillow. His fingers touched something solid. *Quick. Before they get too near.* He clasped the grip in his fist, pulled the gun out, aimed it at the ceiling. Give them one last chance. 'I'm warning you.'

They froze. Not sure he'd use it.

He pointed the gun at them, eyes wide now, absorbing the light. 'Don't fucking doubt me.'

They backed up a couple of steps, looking at one another. One turned, then they all turned, left in a scurry.

Glass breathed in the still air. Tucked the gun back under the pillow. They wouldn't be back any time soon.

They'd left the light on. He knew when he'd woken up in the dark that this wasn't home. He couldn't get familiar with this room no matter how long he was here. It wasn't his. He was just visiting.

This wasn't his bed.

He didn't want to stay in it any longer. He didn't want to stay in this room.

It wasn't his room. They could have it.

He should leave. Let them take over.

He should call them back.

Why didn't he? What was stopping him?

He couldn't remember.

He levered his legs out of the bed.

On the floor, by his feet, an open suitcase. Jeans, blouses, a hairdryer, all neatly packed.

The spike slammed into his skull again. It hurt to turn his head, but he forced his neck around, tendons groaning.

Lorna was sitting a couple of feet to the side of the suitcase, propped against the leg of the bed. Opposite, Caitlin was slumped against the wall, milk from her tumbler spilled on the floor, turned sour.

He stood up. Took a few steps. With each one the spike bored deeper. He dropped to his knees.

Lorna stared at him. He saw Watt in her eyes.

'What did he do?' he asked her.

'It wasn't Watt,' she said.

He looked at Caitlin. 'Caitlin, babygirl.' He kissed her cheek. Her skin felt hard.

'This is what he did?' he asked her.

'No,' Lorna screamed. 'He never touched us.'

In the space between Lorna and Caitlin.

Glass grabbed the spike with both hands, yanked it out of his head. Threw it at the wall. It bounced off, twanged onto the floor, clattered. He stayed there, on his knees, until he felt his heels ache.

Then he got to his feet, climbed back into bed. He took the gun out from under the pillow and stuck it in his mouth.

Thumb inside the trigger guard. He pulled the trigger.

No pain.

Death was just like life.

No difference at all.

THURSDAY

'When do we get to watch TV?' Glass asked Riddell. They were thirty minutes into the session, going over the same old ground. Only today, there was a TV and video recorder on a stand against the wall.

'Let's try something first.' Riddell fanned out the sheets of paper on his desk. Absent-mindedly touched his photo frame. A different one from the one he'd had at the Hilton. This one was wooden and had a family portrait in it. Glass had caught a glimpse of it a couple of times. Riddell, his wife, two girls. 'Let's imagine that only one prisoner took you hostage.'

'You serious?'

'Never more so.'

'You all set on demonstrating that you're as crazy as the rest of us?'

'Humour me. Just one prisoner. Okay?'

'Okay. But there were two of them.'

'Just imagine that Mafia decided to stay in his cell.'

'Why would he do that?'

'Remember what you said when I asked you why Mafia killed himself?'

'Not exactly.'

Riddell looked at his notes. 'You said that as long as Mafia was alive, he'd protect his brother.'

'Yeah,' Glass said. 'That sounds about right.'

'So if that's how Mafia felt, don't you think it's strange that he'd have offered to lead you right to Watt?'

'He said he had unfinished business. Stuff he should have sorted out with Watt a long time ago.'

'And he did that by killing himself?'

'I don't know,' Glass said. 'Things didn't exactly go according to plan.'

Riddell opened his desk drawer. Took out a jiffy bag. He drew a videotape out of the bag and waved it in front of Glass like a fan. 'Know what this is?'

'A tape,' Glass said. 'Porn?'

'It's a copy of the security tape from the Hilton. From the night you were taken hostage.' The shrink placed it on the desk. Pushed it across to Glass. 'You want to see it?'

'You think I want to watch myself get shot?'

'I don't imagine so.' Riddell picked up the tape. 'But it's curious. I think you'll find it interesting.' He walked over to the TV stand, switched on the TV, slid the tape into the video machine. Pressed a few buttons.

And there it was. A grainy black-and-white picture. Glass recognised the Hilton. The corridor leading to the main gate. Saw himself. Staggering along, a gun on him.

'What's missing?' Riddell asked.

Glass watched. 'Jesus.'

'Or should I say, *who* is missing?'

Glass kept staring at the screen. Couldn't believe what he was seeing.

On the TV, there he was. And there, next to him, was Darko. But where was Mafia?

'Stop it,' Glass said. 'Stop the fucking thing. You're messing with my head now.'

Riddell pressed the pause button, freeze-framed Darko and Glass, arms around each other. It was just seconds before Darko would shoot Glass in the shoulder.

Glass said, 'I'm not lying. Mafia was there.'

'Here's the thing, Nick. It's not that I don't believe you. Or should I say it's not that I don't believe you think you're telling the truth. I completely believe you think Mafia was there.' He nodded at the TV. 'But the evidence suggests otherwise. Darko took you hostage. He was alone. Just you and him. Look at the screen.'

'No, the tape's been doctored.' Glass lifted his right foot off the floor, rotated his ankle, placed his foot back down again. He did the same with his other foot. Right foot again. He could do this all day. Someone had erased Mafia from the tape. That's all there was to it. No big deal.

'Nick?'

'Yeah?'

'It's not just the tape. There were eyewitnesses . . .'

Glass put both heels on the floor. 'They're liars.'

'Not just them. Darko told the same story.'

'He's been caught?'

'Yes,' Riddell said. 'But let's get back to the —'

'Why didn't you tell me?'

'I didn't think you were ready to discuss this.'

'But you do now?'

Riddell frowned. 'I think so. I hope so.'

'Well, let me talk to him. I'll get him to tell you the truth.'

'I don't think that's the answer.'

Why was Riddell insisting on playing these stupid games?

'You feed me this pile of crazy drivel with your fucking so-called evidence on doctored videos and . . . and you won't let me show you how wrong you are?' The spike sank deeper into Glass's brain. He wiped his forehead. Felt his armpits prickle.

'Like I said, Darko was caught,' Riddell said. 'Quite some time ago.'

Glass could see the spike, wedged there, and recognised it. The cons had made it in the machine shop, thrown it at him. They hadn't missed this time.

He didn't like the idea that he could see inside his own head.

'About five days after he escaped,' Riddell said. 'With you. Just you. Just the pair of you.'

'Stop saying that. The fuck do you hope to gain by lying like this?'

'I'm trying to help you, Nick.' He pointed the remote at the TV, turned it off. 'Mafia never left his cell that night.'

'You can help me if you stop talking shite.' Glass winced as the spike throbbed.

'Are you okay?'

'I am. But just now and then . . .' He shrugged. 'I'm fine.'

Riddell stared at him for a while, then pursed his lips, walked back to his seat. 'Let's move on. To the hotel room. Darko said he had to leave you there. He thought you might die if he dragged you any further with him.'

That was sort of true. Glass put his hand to his shoulder, remembering. No pain there now. He'd healed fast. He lowered his hand, felt its heat through the leg of his trousers. 'He did leave me, but I wasn't alone. Mafia was there too.'

'Nick, I think it best we do this now.'

'Do what?'

'There's someone here to see you.'

Glass bent down, pressed his face into his hands, breathed, pushing his fingers into his eyeballs. He ignored the steady pounding of the spike's heart in his head.

'He's just outside.'

Glass massaged his forehead with his fingertips, looking up at Riddell through the gap between his hands. 'Darko's a con. Lying's second nature to him. He left me in that hotel room with Mafia, I'm telling you. God's honest truth.' He sat back, folded his arms. 'I swear it.'

Inside Glass's head, the spike vibrated. He shivered. He couldn't figure out Riddell at all. He sounded genuine, like he really believed what he was saying. But he had to be lying, or playing a game. Trying to provoke a reaction, *testing the subject*. Maybe Riddell had doctored the video himself. Glass wasn't so easily fooled, even if he was drugged stupid. 'What about that murdering fuck, Watt? He saw Mafia all right.'

'No, he didn't.'

'He shot him!'

'Watt says he fired the gun in the flat, yes. But not at anyone. There was no one there but you.'

Fuck off. Fuck off, fuck off. 'Mad Will, then. He saw Mafia in the hotel room. Drove us to the flat.'

Riddell shook his head. 'Mad Will said you were alone all the time. Delirious. Talking to yourself.'

'No.' Glass rubbed his temples with the heels of his hands.

'You were full of drugs. All those painkillers. And speed. Blood loss. Shock. Been that way for a while. Since cutting your finger off.'

'They're lying,' Glass said. 'All of them.'

'Then perhaps you'll believe the truth when you hear it from your visitor's lips.' Riddell got to his feet, placed his hand on Glass's shoulder as he passed him.

Glass didn't move, didn't turn round. Stared straight ahead.

He heard the door open. Whispered voices. Footsteps behind him, closing on him. Then a hand once more on his shoulder.

And then a voice he never thought he'd hear again. 'Nick,' Mafia said. 'How've you been?'

GLASS STARED AT the dead man. 'You're a ghost,' he whispered.

'Christ, no,' Mafia told him. 'Flesh and blood.'

'If he was a ghost,' Riddell said, 'do you think I would see him?'

'But you can't be here,' Glass said to Mafia. 'You died.'

'So I hear,' Mafia said. 'Strangled myself, I believe.'

'Yeah.' Glass lowered his head, stared into his lap. 'I don't understand. I saw you.'

'Like you see your sister?' Riddell asked.

Hazel? What the fuck was he bringing up Hazel for? 'Hazel's . . . she's different.'

'Yes,' Riddell said. 'Why did you tell me about her?'

'You wanted to know what happened.'

'That story about the picnic. The horses. Her laughing at your fear. Why mention it, Nick?'

'That's what I was thinking about at the time. Anyway, what does my sister have to do with any of this? I haven't seen her in years. She couldn't even make it to my mum's funeral. Can we not talk about her? Mafia −'

'You were in a car,' Riddell said. 'Thinking about your sister.'

Glass squeezed his hands together.

'What triggered that?' Riddell asked.

'How should I know?'

'Imagining Mafia was in the car with you, maybe?'

Glass said, 'He *was* there.' He looked at Mafia again. 'Tell him. You were there.'

Mafia shook his head.

'In the flat,' Glass said, 'you told me all about how you took the blame for Watt. You don't remember that?'

'What did I take the blame for?'

'For Watt killing his wife and kid.'

'He's never been married.'

Now wasn't the time to be pedantic. 'His girlfriend, then.'

'Watt's got no kid.'

'Watt killed them,' Glass said, his chest tight. 'By accident.'

'I don't know where you got that idea.'

'You told me. In the flat.'

'This is the first time I've been out of the Hilton since I got sentenced.'

'But you didn't kill anybody. You're innocent.'

'I'm no more innocent than I'm dead.' Mafia sighed. 'Nick, I killed two people.'

'No,' Glass said. 'You covered for him. Watt told me his wife and kid were dead.'

'He didn't,' Riddell said. 'That's just what you heard. According to my notes, Watt said, "Beautiful daughter. Lovely wife. Perfect family. Where's mine? and you asked, "Your wife and kid? Did something happen to them?"'

'You think you know everything,' Watt said.

'No, I don't —'

'Shhh. Just listen. Do you know why Mafia's in prison?'

'For murder.'

'And do you know who he murdered?'

'Mafia would never do that. No way.'

'Ask him.'

Riddell said, 'Watt never said who Mafia killed. You made an assumption.'

'Why are you doing this to me?'

'It's his job,' Mafia said.

'So who *did* you kill?' Glass asked, sure Mafia wouldn't answer.

'My parents,' Mafia said without hesitation. 'They were going to kick me out of their house. My home. I'd grown up there. Never lived anywhere else. But Mum and Dad told me they were fed up with me bringing my friends home. They kept nagging at me about the noise, and about a couple of times when some stuff went missing. Videos and that. After I'd had a wee party. But that was petty shite. I couldn't cope on my own. Eyesight's worse than I let on. I got upset. Each day they got on my back about when I was going to move out. And each day I got more upset. Finally they went to see a lawyer, to see if they could evict me. From my own fucking house. I hated them for that. Making it public how much they despised me.' He paused. 'So one night I strangled them.'

'Just like that?'

'Wasn't a whim, you know. Didn't happen overnight. It'd been building up for months.'

'But you killed them because they wanted you to move out?'

'I killed them because they rejected me.'

Glass swallowed. God help him, but he could almost understand. 'Why did you never tell me?'

'Killing your folks isn't the sort of thing you brag about,' Mafia said.

'Do you . . . do you regret it?'

'What'd be the point of that? They rejected me. I rejected them.'

If Mafia could kill his parents and feel no remorse, then Glass didn't know him at all. Mafia had come back from the dead a different person. 'How come nobody at the Hilton would speak about it?'

'Respect.'

'For you?'

'A bit,' Mafia said. 'But mainly for Caesar. He shattered a guy's legs for talking about it.'

'Why did it matter to Caesar?'

'My parents were his uncle and aunt. Me and Caesar are cousins.'

'Jesus,' Glass said. 'How come he didn't have you killed?'

'Dunno. I think he would've done if Watt hadn't asked him not to.'

Watt had saved Mafia's life? 'Why would he do that?'

'He's my brother,' Mafia said.

'I know, but being family didn't stop you doing what you did.'

'I'm not sentimental.'

'And Watt is? That fucker?'

Mafia didn't reply.

'Why tell me all this now?' Glass asked.

'Riddell begged me to. Said it would help you. I hope it does.'

'I thought you weren't sentimental.'

Mafia stood there for a moment, then said, 'I should go now.'

A couple of weeks later and Glass was off the worst of the drugs. He was so much better that Riddell thought he was well enough to go to group therapy. It was held in a room off the kitchen where Glass smelled meat cooking.

A middle-aged woman was looking at him as if she wanted to say something. He'd seen her before. Or someone like her. Maybe her daughter.

'What is it?' he asked her.

'My knickers,' she said, in a quiet voice. 'They're falling down.' She turned to the rest of the room. A circle of seated bodies, their pain dulled enough that they could cope.

He counted them. Seven. Plus the three nurses standing. And Glass and this woman. Twelve.

'Everybody,' she said, loudly this time. 'My knickers are falling down.'

She was wearing jeans. Glass thought it unlikely she was telling the truth about her knickers.

'Don't worry,' a tall bald guy in a T-shirt said. 'We'll not look.'

'But you must, Jason,' she said.

Glass looked at the guy's arms. One was massively scarred down the inside forearm. Maybe he'd taken a machete to it, like Peeler, stood there with his veins in his hand.

'I must have an audience. What's the use of me performing in adult films if I don't have an audience?'

'Annie,' Riddell said. 'I'd like you to stop that now, please. You'll get everybody over-excited.'

'That's the idea.' She held out her wrists. 'Would you like to tie me up?'

'I don't think so.'

'I'm excited,' another guy said, fists clenching and

unclenching, mouth jerking into a series of split-second smiles. 'I'll do it.'

'How about you, Nick?' she asked Glass. 'Or would you rather I tied you up instead?'

'Do I know you?'

'Oh,' she said. 'I thought you were better. Isn't he better?'

'Annie,' Riddell said, 'that's not polite.'

'Why is this slut here?' Glass said.

'Nick, that's not polite either.'

'I've every right to be here,' Annie said.

'Fuck you,' Glass said.

'Well, fuck you too,' Annie said. 'How does it feel to kill your wife and kid?'

Glass stared at her. She was on a bed, tied up, Watt slamming his body against hers. At Mad Will's flat, making that porno film. Was it her? Was it someone who just looked like her?

Riddell touched Glass's elbow. 'Let's go to my office.'

'You're a bastard,' she shouted at Glass as a nurse tried to calm her down. 'You killed them.'

'I never,' Glass said. 'I never did that.'

Nobody said anything. Everyone was staring at him.

'I never did what she said,' he muttered. 'It was Watt.' He looked at Riddell. 'There's going to be a trial.' He whispered, 'I'm going to be there.'

'MUST HAVE COST a packet,' Glass said. Riddell had a fancy new computer on his desk.

'Not really. It's just a 386, 50-meg hard disk. Don't need anything too slick.'

'Right,' Glass said, the jargon lost on him.

Riddell looked at his computer screen. 'About Annie,' he said.

'Why did she say that about me?'

Riddell took a dustcloth out of his drawer and wiped the screen.

'Eh?' Glass said. 'Did you tell her that? This another game?' Funny thing, Glass wasn't angry. He was more disappointed than anything else. 'Or maybe it's that she's mad. They're all mad, or they wouldn't be here. That's a fact. You can't argue with that.'

Riddell ran his hand over his face. He looked up at Glass. 'Do you think *I'm* mad?'

Glass stared at him. 'No, course not. Why would I think that?'

'I thought you trusted me. I thought we'd established that I'm not here to screw you over. I'm here to help you.'

Glass glanced away, then back at him.

'So, do you trust me?' Riddell asked. 'It's important that you do.'

'I suppose so. Apart from the games.'

'So you don't really think I told her ...'

'I don't know,' Glass mumbled.

'Nick,' Riddell said. 'This isn't easy. But we do need to move on.'

Glass crossed his legs, folded his arms.

Riddell looked straight at him, held his gaze. 'I need you to remember.'

Glass uncrossed his legs, sat back in his seat. 'I've told you what I remember.'

'We need to go further back. We need to know what happened when you cut your finger off.'

'I don't know what happened.'

Riddell was struggling to get something out, his cheeks

literally bulging. Finally, he said, with a puff, 'You can't hide from this for ever.'

A reflex: 'I can.'

'Is that right?' Riddell turned sharply towards him. 'Is that what you want?'

'I don't know,' Glass said. 'What am I hiding from?'

'You finished night shift. You drove home. What happened when you got there?'

Glass didn't remember. How many times did he need to tell him? 'Why does it matter?'

'What happened?'

'Watt shot my family. I couldn't help them. Don't you think I've gone over this enough?'

'You couldn't help them because you were tied to a chair in an abandoned flat in Niddrie.'

'Yeah.'

'You sure?'

'You saying I made that up? I imagined that too?'

'No, Watt confirms it.'

Thank Christ.

'But there is a problem, Nick. A big problem. So big that Watt won't be on trial. Not for murder, anyway.'

Glass felt as if someone had shoved a fist down his throat and was stirring his stomach with their fingers. 'What's happened?'

'The post mortem reports on Lorna and Caitlin tell a different story from the one you'd like us to believe.'

Glass shoved his hand to his mouth and gnawed his knuckles.

'Nick,' Riddell said, 'please don't do that.'

Glass groaned, let his hand drop. He breathed. Breathed, breathed, breathed.

'Take your time,' Riddell said.

Post mortem reports. Different story. You'd like us to believe.

Glass sat for a while until he felt he could speak. 'Tell me.'

'Lorna never went to her mother's.'

'Where did she go?'

'Nowhere.'

'She had to have gone somewhere.'

'No. Nick, she was at home all the time.'

'She wasn't. Don't be ridiculous. I know she wasn't –'

'She was in the bath, Nick. Her and Caitlin. By the time Watt found them, they'd already been dead for over twenty-four hours.'

Glass bit his knuckle till he tasted blood.

'They weren't shot in the bath,' Riddell said.

'Stop.'

'It happened in your bedroom. Someone carried them into the bathroom. Laid them in the bath.'

'Stop!'

'Draped a blanket over them. Pulled the shower curtain all the way round.'

'Stop. Please stop.'

'Any idea who that might have been?'

HE LAY AWAKE all night thinking about it.

After a couple of hours, he imagined what Riddell wanted to hear.

Glass picks up Lorna, carries her through to the bathroom, tries to lay her down gently, the back of her head cracking off the bath anyway, making him cry, red tears dripping into his palms.

Back in the bedroom, he picks up his babygirl, clutches her to his chest. The smell of milk and blood, and the salt taste in his mouth. He takes her to lie with her mother. Lowers her head into the crook of her mother's neck.

He drapes a blanket over them to keep them warm. Slides the shower curtain across to let them sleep.

He closes the suitcase, slides it under the bed.

Runs hot water, soaks up the stains, the water turning crimson.

Heats a meat cleaver over the cooker's gas flame. He cuts off the finger that squeezed the trigger. Blood gushes into the sink. The smell of meat cooking as he presses the blade against the wound.

Before he faints, he phones Mad Will.

Glass's imagination was a powerful one. He almost convinced himself.

By morning, he felt as though someone had sucked out his insides through his belly button.

He washed his face in cold water. As he rubbed a towel over his skin, he caught his reflection in the mirror.

He lowered the towel.

At first he thought the mirror in his room had distorted the image. But everything behind him was clear.

What Glass saw was a mockery of who he was. The short hair. Those shadows under his eyes. And the fat he was carrying. He looked like a fucking chipmunk.

He saw everything clearly.

He walked back to his bed, removed the gun from under his pillow and returned to the bathroom.

He shot the mirror. The glass shattered. His reflection lay in thousands of pieces. That was better. It was how he saw himself.

WEDNESDAY

The next day, in his office, after the small talk, Riddell said, 'You've thought about it?'

'Yes,' Glass told him.

'And what do you think?'

'Watt killed Lorna. He killed Caitlin. He killed my family.'

He heard Riddell breathe. Not where he wanted to go, clearly. Glass felt detached. At the moment, he couldn't see a future for himself, couldn't imagine one. The present was all there was, and it was as if it belonged to somebody else.

Riddell slumped back in his seat. 'Nick, the weapon that killed Lorna and Caitlin was in your hand.'

'Doesn't mean anything.'

'You can't ignore the evidence.'

'I'm not,' Glass said. 'Watt could have got the gun anytime. He got it before. He could have got it again. He could have killed them when I was at work. Made it look like I was responsible.'

Riddell drew his lips into his mouth, then said, 'Why would he go back to your house once he had you tied up at the flat?'

'How do you know he did? Maybe he just wanted to scare me. Maybe he just stepped out into the corridor and stayed there for an hour or so.'

'And listened to you and Mafia talking about him killing the wife and kid he never had?'

'I might have imagined that. But it's what I remember.'

'The story Mafia told you. Where do you think that came from?'

'I suppose I made it up.'

'You ever wondered why you made up a story about a guy who killed his wife and kid and then had someone cover up the whole episode for him? In fact, this guy not only has someone cover up for him but he can't even remember he's done it. You see a parallel?'

'No,' Glass said. '*You* see a parallel.'

TUESDAY, 16 March

A table. It was okay for Glass to eat in company now. The cutlery was all plastic, though, just in case.

Voices bubbled in his veins. One in particular, a stream of gibberish – 'I-don't-know-why-nobody-believes-me-I-didn't-touch-the-clock-it-touched-me-don't-you-get-it?'

'Shut up.' Glass dropped his fork onto his plate. Splashed a little gravy.

'Nick,' a nurse said, 'stay calm.'

'Well, get him to stop that.'

'It's what he does,' Jason said, scratching the underside of his arm, reddening the scars. 'It's all he does. Just sits wherever he's put and spouts crap till they take him away again. You not noticed?'

'Haven't had the chance.'

'Needs heavier sedation. But they've tried it and he reacts badly. Poops himself.' Jason tapped Glass on the elbow. 'Can I ask you something?'

'Depends.'

'What happened your finger?'

'What happened to my finger?' Glass repeated. 'I wish I knew.' He looked at Jason, saw a blur. He wiped his eyes, wiped his cheeks. He smiled. 'I'm in the wrong place,' he said. 'We're all in the wrong place.'

'Amen to that.'

'I don't know who I am any more, Jason.'

Jason leaned in. 'Here's the thing,' he said. 'Nobody does. Not you, not me, not this lot of nutjobs we're saddled with, not any of that bunch in charge either. You are who you think you are. You are what you remember.'

'You sure about that?'

'If you're not, then what the fuck are you?'

'What if you don't remember anything?'

'Ah,' Jason said, 'then you're in trouble.'

THURSDAY, 18 March

He was sitting next to Annie watching TV when she turned and said, '*You opened your bedroom door. Lorna's sprawled on top of the bed in her nightdress, snoring. There's an empty gin bottle on her bedside table. You walked round the suitcase, on the floor, open, packed. She must have done it last night.*'

Yes.

He shakes Lorna. '*Going on holiday?*'

She wakes up, instantly alert. '*I'm taking Caitlin to my mother's.*'

'*You can't do that!*'

'*Don't fucking shout at me.*'

'*I'm not fucking shouting.* THIS IS ME FUCKING SHOUTING.'

She grabs a fistful of hair at the nape of her neck and tightens her fingers round it. Her voice is flat. '*We're leaving now. I'll get Caitlin up. We'll get dressed and go.*'

'*You can't. I can't cope on my own.*'

'*Typical,*' *she says. She lets go of her hair, thumps her fist down on the bedclothes.*

'*What?*'

'*Your selfishness. You can't cope, so I have to cope for you.*'

'*I've been through a lot, for Christ's sake. I need your support.*'

'*I'm not the person to help you. Look at me. I'm a fucking mess, too.*' *She lowers her gaze.* '*We're not good for each other. You've driven me to this, Nick.*'

'*Me?*' *He presses the heels of his hands to his temples.* '*You're blaming me?*'

'*Take some responsibility, for once. Look, being around you, it's not safe. Not safe for you, for me, for Caitlin.*'

'*What's brought this on? Is it Watt?*'

'*I found your drugs stash. Without his help.*'

Glass knows his expression changes before he can stop it.

'Don't tell me you didn't expect this,' she says. 'I've not noticed your behaviour?'

'I've stopped.'

'So why's there a pile of drugs in the tea chest in the garage?'

He could lie, tell her they're not his, but then he'd have to admit to smuggling them into the Hilton. 'Look, it's safe, now,' he says. 'Watt's going to be dead soon.'

'What makes you think that?'

'I'm going to kill him.'

'And that'll solve all our problems?'

'Yes. I'm going to do it.'

She laughs. 'You're a fucking punch bag,' she says. 'You'd never kill anybody.'

'Don't be so sure.'

'You're so full of shit. How're you going to kill him?'

Glass pulls out the gun.

'I told you to get rid of that,' she yells. 'I told you to fucking get rid of it.'

And the yelling grew louder and more shrill and Caitlin appeared and there was a gunshot and the tumbler fell to the ground, bounced gently, rolled in a tight arc, came to a stop.

And later, Lorna yelling at him, asking what he'd done, telling him he was a murdering bastard, he'd killed their babygirl, and a struggle as she tried to get the gun from him, and him shoving her away and . . . and . . .

He gives her the gun. 'Do it,' he says and closes his eyes.

He sees nothing other than images of the tumbler as it rolls in a reverse arc, bounces gently, rises into the air and into the hand of his daughter.

This time when he hears the gunshot he expects darkness.

But nothing changes. He stands there with his eyes closed, waiting.

When he finally opens his eyes, he sees Lorna on the floor, neat red hole in her forehead.

'She hated you so much she shot herself,' Annie said.

With her mouth shut, Lorna whispers in his ear, tells him what to do, makes sense of everything, allows Glass to carry on living. 'Remembering is too painful,' she says. 'But you need pain to forget.'

'That's how it happened,' Annie said.

Glass grabbed Annie's hand, tried to bite off her finger. Clamped his jaws together so hard his teeth hurt. But he couldn't get through the bone.

ONCE HE WAS back on his medication, Glass remembered nothing at all for a long time.

Every two weeks, Nick Glass had an injection that wiped him out for a couple of days, and on the third day, he started to feel normal again. Today was the third day. Sun streamed into his room, sliced across the bed. He liked to sleep with the curtains open. His scars itched otherwise.

He looked at his watch: 8.20. These days, they let him sleep on. Pointless waking him up when he was climbing out of the hole. He hoped they hadn't forgotten that today was different.

He pulled back the covers, rotated his arm, rolling the stiffness out of his shoulder. Swung his legs out of bed, dug his toes into the carpet. He'd been moved into a much nicer place these days. He'd behaved himself for the last five years. Only had his privileges revoked once during that time. For breaking a mirror. He fucking hated mirrors. Most of the time he managed to avoid looking at himself, but that time he'd caught sight of his own smirk and smashed his fist into the glass.

Now he had no mirror. He liked it that way. Best solution for everybody.

He picked up Riddell's photo frame off the dresser. Well, it turned out it wasn't Riddell's, just an old pewter frame that had sat on the desk in the office at the Hilton for as long as anyone could remember. But when Glass asked Riddell what he was going to do with it after he'd left, Riddell had said he'd see what he could do. A few days later, he presented it to Glass as a gift. Glass hadn't seen the old bastard for a long time. Riddell was out in the community now. Gave up the job when he'd decided he'd had enough of being sued by prisoners. All that time on their hands, lawyers at their beck and call, the inmates had nothing better to do. They never won – not against Riddell – but the process was draining and Riddell finally couldn't take any more.

Glass was sorry to see him go. Riddell had come to know him better than anyone.

Riddell's photo frame – he'd continued to think of it as Riddell's – now housed a shot of Lorna and Caitlin. They'd just bought Glass's babygirl a new dress, floral pattern, yellow and red, and shiny black shoes with buckles. For her fourth birthday the following weekend. She'd insisted on wearing her new outfit home. She was showing it off to the camera, ankles crossed, shy but happy, clutching her mother's hand.

He cried again. He cried a lot. He'd turned into Lorna's old man, crying at the stupidest thing. Sometimes Glass wasn't sure why he cried, didn't even feel sad, but this morning was different. He knew exactly why he was crying.

He replaced the photo, then took his clothes off and climbed onto the windowsill. Closed his eyes. Imagined he could smell warm bread rising from the bakery below. Imagined Lorna standing next to him. He stood there with her for five minutes, then opened his eyes and stared at the high wooden fence twenty feet away.

He jumped down, walked into the en-suite, where he washed his face, brushed his teeth. Then he dressed in the smart black clothes he'd laid out last night. He didn't want anyone to take his picture, though. The story would reach the newspapers soon.

He sat by the window and waited for his door to open.

One step at a time. He still wasn't well, but he knew now that he could get better. Maybe one day they'd let him out for good. He didn't dare hope. Hope was the surest way to destroy a man. He knew that by now.

He waited.

It was a while ago that Mafia had asked to see him. A month ago. No, maybe a couple of weeks. Or maybe just before his last injection. It was hard to pinpoint the exact time. Anyway, whenever it was, Glass was far from delighted at the idea of seeing Mafia again. Didn't know what Mafia wanted and Mafia wouldn't tell him over the phone. All he'd say was that he was out on parole and everything was good with him, he'd even made up with Watt. But there was something important Glass had to know. Told Glass he'd bring Watt along with him, that his brother had to be the one to explain.

Glass eventually agreed to see them after Mafia kept stressing how important it was.

In the visitors' room, Glass realised that he'd never seen Watt and Mafia together before. They didn't look like brothers.

'I don't want to dirty Mad Will's good name,' Watt had said. He looked almost as Glass remembered. A little more pinched around the eyes.

'But you're going to.' Mafia hadn't been as lucky as his brother. He looked his age, even with his shades on. Sat hunched over too, like his head was too heavy to hold up. Once he'd looked cool, but now he just looked like an old guy trying to look cool. 'Get on with it.'

Watt shrugged. 'Mad Will's dead,' he said to Glass. 'Shot himself.' Watt demonstrated with his hand, head tilted back, fingers pointed under his chin.

Mad Will had driven Glass right into Watt's hands all those years ago, but Glass still felt his eyes well up. He could cry about anything. Once he lost a shirt button and didn't stop crying for a fortnight. 'Why are you telling me?' he said. 'Why aren't you in prison, you murdering fuck?'

'Just about to explain that,' Mafia said.

Watt looked at Mafia and Mafia punched him on the arm. 'Spill,' Mafia said, 'or I'll do it.'

'Mad Will didn't leave a suicide note, but he left a confession of sorts.' Watt paused. 'I saw him the night he died. And he told me something.'

'Which my brother kept to himself,' Mafia said. 'Until a couple of nights ago. Fucking arsehole.'

'I didn't believe him,' Watt said.

'You didn't want to believe him.'

'That's right.'

'Much easier to blame Nick here.'

'Yeah, I know. I'm not disagreeing. But it nagged away at me. After all, Mad Will shot himself so he must have been seriously fucked up. I had to tell somebody.'

'That's what he wanted.'

'I don't know. I don't think he wanted to make it public. I think he just wanted to confess.'

'He could have seen a priest for that. He didn't. He saw you. He knew you'd tell someone.'

As he listened to them talk, the spike sunk into Glass's head again. It'd been a long time since he'd felt it. He'd forgotten how cold it was. 'What did he tell you?'

Watt rubbed his forefinger across his forehead and back again. 'He said it was him. He said he'd done it.'

Glass's vision blackened for a second. 'Done what?'

'Murdered them.'

Mafia said, 'Lorna and Caitlin.'

'He did?' Glass didn't know what to say. He didn't believe it. The spike twisted in his head and the pain paralysed his brain. In his chest, his heart grew until it filled his insides, crushed his lungs so he couldn't breathe.

'My brother's fault,' Mafia said.

Glass managed to say, 'How?'

''Cause I'd kept telling him what a nice piece Lorna was,' Watt said. 'Apparently.' He scratched his head. 'So he went round to your house to see for himself. Early morning, while you were still at work.'

'You're just making this up. Deflecting the blame.' Glass's eyes watered. He felt saliva gather at the corners of his mouth. 'How did he get in?'

'Knocked at the door? I don't know. He didn't tell me all the details.'

Glass wiped his face with his hand. 'Lorna wouldn't have let him in.'

'She wouldn't have let *me* in,' Watt said. 'But she didn't know Mad Will.'

'I still don't think she would've.'

'Why don't you want to believe the truth?' Mafia said.

Glass shook his head. He didn't know he didn't want to believe. 'I'm just saying.'

'We're telling you what happened, Nick.'

'I've had all the time in the world to go through every conceivable possibility of what might have happened,' Glass said. 'Not a lot to do here but think.'

'Yeah,' Mafia said. 'I know what it's like.'

'I've thought of everything. But never Mad Will. Never Lorna opening the door to him.'

'Use your imagination,' Watt said. 'We know you have one. Maybe she was expecting a parcel or something. Thought he was the postman.'

'He was wearing a uniform?'

'No, but he could've pretended he was delivering something. Or maybe he was asking for directions. Or said his car had broken down.'

'Well, we don't know how he got in,' Mafia said. 'Other than that he didn't break in. And he's not around to ask.' He turned to Watt. 'So carry on.'

'I don't believe you,' Glass said. 'But carry on.'

Watt looked at him. 'What do you remember about getting home from the Hilton that morning?'

'More or less a complete blank. I think I remember pulling up outside the house. But I might have imagined even that.'

'Mad Will told me he was . . . tidying up when he heard your car. He grabbed his bag. Went downstairs. Waited for you to open the front door.'

'His doctor's bag,' Mafia said. 'With all his drugs and shit in it.'

'Then once you stepped into the hallway, he grabbed you from behind and injected you with a massive dose of some kind of sedative.'

'Tidying up what?' Glass asked.

'What?'

'You said he was "tidying up".'

'Right. Well, he was packing a suitcase. Trying to make it look as though Lorna was going to leave you.'

'Why would he want to do that?'

'Motivation. Things took a bad, bad turn. You interrupted him. You had patsy written on your forehead. He was thinking on his feet. So, like I was saying, he grabs you, injects you . . .'

Glass feels the needle pop out of his neck. He takes a few steps but the drug acts quickly and he stumbles. Mad Will slips an arm around him and helps him into the kitchen. Sits him down in a chair, lets him slump over the table. Glass's tongue feels as numb as his brain. He tries to sit up, but gravity drags him back down. Resting his head in the crook of his arm, his breath sticky on the table, he watches Mad Will as he turns on a ring on the cooker, grabs the meat cleaver, heats the blade.

Mad Will steps over to the table, lifts Glass to his feet, hauls him across the room, bends him over the work surface. Straightens Glass's arm, index finger flat on the chopping board next to the sink, his other fingers curled out of the way.

'What're you doing?' Glass says. He knows.

Mad Will slams the cleaver down. Before the agony hits, Mad Will grabs Glass's wrist, presses the flat of the blade against the bleeding wound.

Glass hears a sizzle and passes out.

When he wakes up, he's on the landing, passing the bathroom, pain pulsing down from his finger into the rest of his hand. The bathroom door's open, blood streaked along the bath.

Where did the blood come from? Is he bleeding? He was in the kitchen with Mad Will. What's Mad Will doing here? 'Lorna?' he cries.

'Don't worry,' Mad Will tells him. 'It's not real. You're in shock. I'll give you something to help you forget.'

In the bedroom, Glass sees the suitcase.

'Going,' Glass says, 'to her mother's. Lorna and Caitlin. To her mother's.'

'If you like,' Mad Will says. 'That's right.'

'My finger,' Glass says.

'You cut it off,' Mad Will tells him. 'Flushed it down the toilet.'

The carpet's red underfoot.

'Mess,' Glass says.

'I'll give this a bit of a clean after we get you into bed.'

Glass's foot hits a tumbler that's fallen there. It's green and it rolls and spins and the spinning won't stop.

In the visiting room, Glass looked up from the floor where Watt and Mafia were crouched over him.

'You fainted,' Mafia said.

'I remember,' Glass told him. 'I remember.'

And now, in his room, he waited for the door to open.

He'd never be released. He'd murdered three people and they still thought he was crazy. But today he was going to visit the graves of his wife and daughter. Finally, he could say goodbye.

The door opened at nine thirty. The nurse balanced the breakfast tray in one hand, jiggled his keys with the other. 'Morning, Nick. Hope you're hungry.'

Glass clasped his hands together. 'When do we leave?'

'Leave where?'

'Leave here. For the cemetery.'

'Ah.' The nurse placed the tray on the desk. 'You been talking to your friends again?'

'Watt's not my friend.'

'I'm sorry.'

'Mafia is, though. They both said Mad Will did it.'

'Is that right?'

'It wasn't me.' He was crying again. 'They told me. In the visiting room.'

'That's good. Don't know how you can eat cornflakes dry like that.'

'Milk makes me sick.'

'Well, eat up. You'll feel better.'

'I'll feel better after I see Lorna and Caitlin's graves.'

'Nick . . . I don't think so.'

'It's not today?' Glass asked. 'Mafia said it was today.'

'No,' the nurse said, 'he's mistaken.'

'Then tomorrow? I think I'll see them tomorrow. Yes, it must be tomorrow.' He shoved a spoonful of cereal into his mouth. Crunched it. Tomorrow. He'd waited this long. He could wait another day.

When the new patient arrived, Glass thought she looked familiar. But it wasn't till she was left alone in a chair that he managed to make eye contact. He felt light, as if a balloon had squeezed out of his stomach and into his chest and expanded into his shoulders. Could it really be her? Glass looked again at the woman in the chair, doubting himself all over again. After all he'd been through, he had to be careful.

He shuffled over to the seated figure. 'That really you?' he whispered.

'Nick?'

Glass reached around Hazel and hugged her.

'Careful,' she said. 'They might be watching.'

'Bet on it.' Glass stepped back. 'Fooling the fuckers is a full-time job.' He whispered, 'I thought you were dead.'

'I had to go away.' She squeezed his hand and he noticed she was wearing black gloves. 'It's not that I wanted to make you seem crazy.'

'What about Mum's funeral?' Hard to keep the anger out of his voice.

'Last person you needed there was me.'

'But Mum needed you.'

'She was dead, Nick. She needed nobody. I never thought you'd really go crazy, though.'

'Did I?'

'That's how it looks.'

'I don't know any more. Sometimes I think I am. Sometimes I think it's everybody else.'

'Maybe it's a bit of both.' She held his hand. Studied the stump of his missing finger. 'What happened to Lorna and Caitlin, that's enough to drive anybody over the edge.'

Glass pulled his hand away. 'Mad Will killed them.'

'I know,' she said, nodding.

'You didn't think it was me?'

'Never.'

Glass placed his hand on her shoulder.

'I have something for you.' She reached into her pocket, removed a coffin-shaped jewellery box about five inches long.

Glass took it. Opened it. Registered no surprise at what was inside. 'Yours?'

'Yeah.' She held her right hand out, showed him the dangling index finger of the glove. 'Figured I owed you. For not being there.'

'Thanks.' Glass slipped the box into his pocket. He bent over and kissed her head. Then he walked over to one of the nurses. 'Can I have some sellotape?'

'Why do you want sellotape?'

'Got a couple of things I need to piece together.'

'I'll bring some to your room later,' the nurse said.

'Appreciate it.' Glass turned, stopped, stared at the empty seat where Hazel had been sitting. He put his hand in his pocket, rubbed his thumb over the jewellery box.

GLASS WAS ABOUT to get into bed when there was a knock at the door and the nurse walked in. 'You still want that sellotape?' she said.

Ah, yes. He'd forgotten. It seemed a long time ago. Years ago. At first he couldn't remember why he'd wanted it, but then it came back to him. He wasn't so sure he wanted Hazel's finger, though. Maybe it was better to have no finger at all.

Wasn't such a hardship functioning without a part of yourself. Not when you got used to it. He'd give Hazel's finger back to her the next time he saw her.

'No,' he said to the nurse. 'I'm fine just as I am.'

Acknowledgements

For their contribution and support during the writing of
this book, a huge thanks goes to the following: Tom Laird,
whose anecdotes of life as a prison officer have been used
and mercilessly abused; Ray Banks, my invaluable first
(and second, and third) reader; Stacia Decker, my ridiculously talented and industrious editor; Stan, my agent, for his
un-wavering faith and his marvellous strategising pants;
Alison Rae, for that all-important final spit and polish;
Kate Horsley, Daniel Kern, Simon Hynd, Donna Moore
and Stuart MacBride for those early reads; all the good
folks at Polygon and HMH for their continued support;
and, of course, my wife and my best friend, Donna, whose
selflessness knows no bounds.